Contents

The Patient at Peacocks Hall   1

Part One   3

Part Two   47

Safer than Love   97

Part One   99

Part Two   135

Part Three   173

Join the Margery Allingham Community   203

A Note on the Author   205

The Patient at Peacocks Hall

Part One

'I never did think her *eyes* were a patch on yours, Miss Ann. Take a good look. You can see them. They're as plain as anything. Now let me get you a hand mirror.'

Rhoda planted the folded newspaper with the photograph in it squarely in front of me, supporting it against my after-lunch coffee cup. She was forthright and innocently excited in every one of her two hundred pounds, and she tore open an old wound as surely as if, with her plump, well-meaning fingers, she had found the cicatrix and ripped it from my flesh.

It was so unexpected. I had had such a busy morning and was so full of other people's troubles that my own life was utterly forgotten. She took me completely off guard and got right through at a stroke, without my being aware.

'No, thank you,' I said politely, hoping I had not turned white from the sudden frightening pain, for I knew her so well that my armour slips into place by reflex action, and I knew she would be watching me anxiously to see if my recovery was complete. (Rhoda is the kind of woman who digs up the mint outside her kitchen door two days after she has planted it, to find out if it has started to grow.) 'I've seen my eyes this morning, bloodshot again. What do you think it is? Alcohol?'

She was nearly sidetracked. The buttons on her white overall

3

strained as she took a breath and peered at me.

'Nonsense, they're lovely, just like your poor mother's, only a different blue and not so round.'

'How true,' I agreed. 'Like her, I've got two of them.'

'Now you're trying to be funny like your father. I never laughed when he wanted me to and I shan't at you. You have got nice eyes and you're getting quite good-looking altogether now you've finished working yourself to death at the hospital and settled down as half a country doctor. You've lost that puggy look you had. I was mentioning it to Mr Dawson when he came with the veg.'

'That was interesting for him,' I murmured, remembering that gaunt, asthmatic greengrocer. 'I'm not half a doctor, by the way. I've been qualified for some years.'

'Four and a half,' she said. 'But you're an assistant to Dr Ludlow, poor old gentleman, aren't you? You don't do it all yourself.' Her kind unlovely face wore its most characteristic expression, part suspicion, part belligerence, and nearly all affection. 'Aren't you going to read the bit about *her*? Or perhaps you don't want to?'

I ignored the emphasis. Rhoda did not mean it, or at least not much. She was sixteen when she came to work for my mother three weeks after I was born, and now that there is only myself of the family left, and I have my own little cottage at the far end of Dr Ludlow's estate, she has continued to work for me. She does it just as faithfully and a good deal more chattily than ever she did in that busy doctor's home in Southersham.

My father, who delighted in her and called her 'Rhododendron'. used to say that she was the only woman in the world who knew everything about him and understood absolutely nothing, but I think he did her less than justice. She understands, a little, not quite enough.

It was very pleasant in my room – or it had been before she brought the newspaper. The cottage has only one downstairs room other than the kitchen and it is a big one. It is furnished with the nicest bits from home and is long and low, with french windows giving on to a small mossy yard, and it looks on to the broad tree-islanded meadow which marks the end of the built-up area on this side of the little town of Mapleford.

I love it, and I was happy and peaceful and content before she spoke. Now, since she was watching me, I had to read the paragraph about Francia Forde.

I did not linger over the photograph. Let me be honest and say at once that I have never really studied any of the reproductions of that lovely Botticelli face with its halo of pale hair. I never saw any of the four films she starred in and I never let myself envisage her as a real woman, lest I should fall into that most self-punishing sin of all and hate her till I burned myself to ash. I had no idea if she was tall or short, shrill or husky, witty or a fool. As far as I was concerned, Francia Forde had never existed, nor John Linnett either.

Anyhow, that was my story and I was sticking to it, pretty well. I had my own way to make and I was enjoying it. At twenty-eight I was the chief assistant to an old man who had a practice twice too big for him. My experience was growing every hour. I liked my patients and their troubles were mine. I could still rejoice when they were born and feel a genuine pang when, despite my best efforts, they died. Love was now just another natural malady suffered or enjoyed by other people. I had experienced it, I knew about it, it was over.

At the moment my real passion was whooping-cough. The paragraph could hardly, therefore, be expected to hold much interest for me, and I was surprised to find how difficult it was to read. I have no intention of reproducing it. I couldn't if I tried. The words danced before me and their sense didn't seem worth discovering. But it was something about the 'beautiful Francia Forde whom everyone had loved so much in *Shadow Lady*' having taken leave of the studios for a while to become the 'Moonlight Girl' in an enormous press advertising campaign which Moonlight Soap and Beauty Products Ltd were about to launch on a breathless world – and there was a mention of television.

To me it simply meant that I was going to be reminded of her in every magazine or newspaper I opened, and that even the air would not be free of her. Movies I could and did avoid, but now she was going to be everywhere.

Rhoda had stamped off with the plates, so I did not have to watch my face. I put the folded paper down and sat looking across the table at the rock flowers and the meadows beyond.

The past is a terrifying thing. One finds one cheats so. John was four years older than I. We were the children of friends. Our fathers were doctors in the same town, and from our babyhood they had set their hearts first on our taking up medicine and then on our marrying. At that moment I could have sworn that it had all been a silly mistake of the old people's and that we never could have loved each other, and yet in the next instant I was remembering the night I first noticed John had grown so breathtakingly good-looking. It was the night before he was off to war as a fully fledged major in the RAMC and I was still in my first year at hospital. We had walked in the Linnetts' walled garden, and the ilex trees had whispered above us and the sweet earth had breathed on us with a new tenderness.

Without wanting to in the least, as I sat there with Francia Forde's smile flashing up at me from the page, I remembered the feel of his fingers on my shoulder and the hard, unexpectedly importunate touch of his mouth on mine. I could understand still and even recapture all the crazy magic of that moment when we realized that the one really important thing in all the world was that we were ourselves and no one else, and that together we were complete and invincible.

All that was quite vivid. I could remember the plans we made and how none of them seemed at all grandiose or impossible. Even the children's clinic, which was to grow into a hospital and a research station, was more real to me than – say – the puzzled misery of the last time he came home on leave just after V.E. Day.

By that time terrible things had happened. Old Dr and Mrs Linnett were both gone. They had stepped into a crowded train after a flying visit to London, only to be taken out in the screaming darkness in the midst of a raid two stations down the line. They were both dead, killed by machine-gun bullets, the surprised expression still on their kind old faces. My own father, too, was fuming in a bed in his own hospital as the cruelty of his last illness slowly consumed him.

I don't think John and I quarrelled on that last leave. We knew each other too well. We were still friends, still in love. We made plans for our wedding, which was to take place as soon as I had finished at St James's. But there was a change in him. He had become nervy and preoccupied, as if the strain of war had begun to tell. At least, I think I put it down to the war. Women were just beginning to suspect that the experience might have had some sort of strange effect upon their menfolk about that time.

I know his looks had become remarkable. He had always been considered handsome in Southersham, but now there was something outstanding about him. He had his father's dark red hair and wide-shouldered height, his good head and wide smile, and he had Mrs Linnett's short straight nose, thick creamy skin, and the narrow dancing eyes that were more attractive in a man even than in her. There was no doubt about it. Old friends, let alone strangers, looked hard at him twice and, if they happened to be young and female, were inclined to blush for no good reason at all. To do him justice – and it was terribly hard for me to do him justice at that distance – he had not seemed to be aware of any change.

I could remember all that, but later, that long lonely period in the winter of '45 when I had no letters, the time which semed to go on for years – as I sat thinking that afternoon it had no reality for me. I had forgotten it. The psycho people have a theory that one only remembers the things one desires to, secretly. I cannot believe that, for every line of the Southersham *Observer's* bombshell that spring was as clear to me as if I had had the fuzzy small-town print before me, and if there was ever anything I should want to forget it must have been that. The owner and editor of that paper was my father's only local enemy. Daddy always said he had a 'corseted soul'. and certainly the way he presented that extract from the film company's publicity sheet was typical of him. He conveyed he did not approve of it but he got every word of it in.

Miss Phillimore sent the paper to me in London and I got it on a day that was pure poetry, green and gold, and blue skies. No one but she could have written, This may surprise you dear,' in that spidery 1890 hand. The editor had quoted a few paragraphs written in the out-of-this-world style some of those writers achieve. I could recite them still, though I had only read them once.

FAIRYLIKE FRANCIA FORDE
CAPTURES GLAMOUR HERO FROM ARMY

Medicine Relinquishes Its Handsomest Man. Runaway Wedding
Ere Film Goes on Floor. Francia Forde, Bullion's new and scintillat-
ing starlet, who is to portray the daughter (Yetta) in the new Dolores
Duse epic *Chains*, has married John Linnett, Director Waldo's latest
discovery. Linnett, who has been granted indefinite leave from the
army to play opposite his bride, will take the part of Yetta's tempes-
tuous lover.

And so on and so on. There was a final line or so written in the
same vein:

The Rumour Bird whispers to us that there is a certain little lady
doctor in Linnett's home town who is going to feel badly over this
development, but cheer up, Miss Medico, you can't keep a star on
the ground – not when it's hitched to Francia's wagon.

The Southersham *Observer* finished the piece with a reference to
'an engagement notice printed in these columns not long ago', and
a snappy hark-back to the tragedy of Dr and Mrs Linnett's death in
the raid.

I remembered that all right. Although I was heart-free and cured
and wedded to whooping-cough, I remembered every paralysing
word of it. Incredibly enough, that was all there was to remember.
That was all I ever heard. I had no letter, no message, not even
gossip through friends. It was as though John had died. He had
turned his back on his home, his ideals, and everything he had ever
lived for. It was so unlike him that for months I could not believe it.

When *Chains* appeared, Francia was in it but not John. She made
her first hit in that film in which Dolores Duse, the veteran French
actress, was so moving, and in her next film she was a star. Since
then she had gone from strength to strength. But John had vanished. If he was still married to her, he kept in the background. He
never wrote and he never came back to Southersham.

Well, there it was, that was my story, and if I had not forgotten
quite as completely as I had thought, I had at least got over it. That
afternoon I honestly believe that the only thing I still felt I could not
forgive John for was the waste, the wicked betrayal of his career.

That was something a million times more important than I could ever be, and yet …

Old Dr Percy Ludlow saved me from myself just then. I glanced up to see him trotting across the meadow and I got up to open the glass doors to meet him. Anyone less like the popular conception of a doctor I have yet to see. He is a tough, slightly horsy little man with a face like red sandstone and a gay, colourful style of dress he can't have changed since he was a boy. Local people whisper to me that he is eighty, which is absurd. He looks sixty and still rides to hounds whenever he gets a chance.

Percy has not been quite the same since he was 'nationalized', as he is pleased to refer to his position under the new National Health scheme, and of course the change has been a sensational one from his point of view. After a lifetime of behaving like some benevolent and beloved Robin Hood, soaking his rich patients to pay for his poor ones, and preserving a religious impartiality in his treatment of disease wherever he found it, he awoke one July morning to discover himself a paid government clerk as well as an unpaid general practitioner. In fact, instead of having the one master in his sacred calling, he found he had two, and the second (who held the purse strings) was a vast, impersonal, remarkably uninformed machine with a predilection for having its million and one queries answered in triplicate. He says he's going to die of writer's cramp, but I think it is more likely to be apoplexy!

I suppose, in my more serious moments, I ought not to approve of him. He is obstinate and old-fashioned, hopelessly conventional and a snob. And yet, when science has let me down and a diagnosis is beyond me, when I've thought of everything and worked out everything and am still in the dark, he will shuffle up to the bedside, pull down an eyelid, sniff, and fish up out of some experience-taught subconscious an answer which is pure guesswork but which happens to be right.

Just then, as he came dancing in, I saw to my surprise that he was angry. His rather light brown suit was buttoned tightly round his compact body, and his vivid blue eye glared at me belligerently from his red face. He paused just inside the room and began to play with the coins in his trousers pockets.

'I suppose you're very pleased with yourself, Dr Fowler.'

That 'Doctor' was a danger signal, and I spoke cautiously.

'Not more than usual. What have I done now?'

He thrust his chin out at me. 'Overconscientious, that's what's wrong with women in the professions. No thought of consequences. Lose a packet of aspirin and rush off to the police,'

'Oh,' I murmured, enlightened. 'The Dormital.'

'Dormital!' He repeated the word as though he had never heard of it, as perhaps he hadn't. 'What is it? One of these rubbishy phenobarbituric derivatives, I suppose. Where did you get it? Some darned silly firm send it to you as a sample?'

Since he had clearly been talking to Brush, our local Inspector, to whom I had reported everything, this was not too clever of him. Had he been a little less angry I might have pointed that out. As it was, I nodded.

'It's new. They've increased the solubility and –'

'Have they?' He could not have been more disgusted. 'Never dream of using that sort of filth myself.'

I knew he was reputed never to prescribe anything save senna or old port and I nearly laughed.

'I'm sorry,' I murmured, 'but it is a poison, and I think someone must really have taken it out of my bag when I was on my round, so I reported it.'

At first I thought he was going to explode, but he thought better of it, and I could see him making up his mind how he was going to manage me. Presently he disarmed me with a smile.

'I like a girl who stands up for herself,' he announced. 'You get that from your mother, no doubt.'

This time a grin did escape me. I had always suspected it was my mother's rather famous country family who had got me the job when Percy was checking my background. He shook his head at me then and asked me for the list of calls I had made on the day of the loss, and when I fetched it he went over each entry, calling everyone by his first name, which wasn't really surprising, perhaps, since he'd brought most of them into the world.

'Lizzie Luffkin,' he read aloud, putting a square fore-finger on the page. 'Yes, I heard you'd been there. She's a strange old lady,

Ann, rather a dangerous old lady. Makes up what she can't learn. Pity you called. Left the car in the road, I suppose? Unlocked?'

'I'm afraid so.'

'Don't blame you. Never locked a car in my life. Told Brush so. No, there's no one doubtful on this list, Ann. You couldn't have taken it with you.' He eyed me with a curious expression which was half shrewd and half obstinate. 'Make up your mind to that. You don't know Mapleford as I do. We're old-fashioned down here. Maybe we're even a little bit narrow. Am I making myself clear?'

'Not frightfully,' I said helplessly, and he sighed.

'You're young, my dear. The people down here are not, and I'm not speaking of years. Brush and I have been discussing the matter, and he agrees with me it would be very unwise to broadcast the loss. We don't want a lot of chatter in Mapleford about – well, to put it bluntly, about drugs.'

I gaped at him. To me all drugs are drugs, so to speak, dangerous or otherwise. I thought he was going to shake me.

'Veronal!' he exclaimed, making it sound like an improper word. 'Veronal, Ann. All your fancy barbituric fiddle-me-faddles are only veronal, and we've heard quite enough about *that* in our time.' He lowered his voice, although we were alone. 'The old Duke's sister died of it, poor wretched woman. She was an addict.'

Perhaps I was not as impressed as I ought to have been. I knew the Dukes of St Pancras, whose gothic towers overshadowed the little town, still dominated Mapleford minds, but the 'young Duke', as he was called, had seemed on the elderly side to me.

'But *when* was all this?' I demanded.

Percy Ludlow met my eyes solemnly. 'Only thirty years ago,' he said without a tremor. 'No time at all in a place like this. I remember it as if it was last week. So do most other people. So you see, once we start muttering about lost or stolen veronal there'll be no end of talk. I know the people down here. Half of them have got nothing to do except chatter about their neighbours. You take my word for it, young woman, you'll have every maiden lady on your register suspected of taking narcotics if you're not very careful.'

It was a jolt to me. Although my intelligence told me he must be crazy, I knew in my heart that he was right. It was his famous trick of correct diagnosis all over again. I might be right in theory, but he knew the people of his funny little town.

'I'm terribly sorry,' I began, and he grinned at me.

'I hate scandal,' he remarked. 'In fact I'm terrified of it. I'll get you out of anything in Mapleford except scandal. Then I wouldn't lift a finger.' He shot one of his bright birdlike stares at me. 'What's your new friend at Peacocks like?'

That took me by surprise. It showed me, too, what I ought to have known about the size and efficiency of Mapleford's espionage system. I had been down to Peacocks Hall exactly five times since old Mrs Montgomery had let the house to Peter Gastineau in February. This man was one of my very few private patients – that is to say, one of those who, although they paid the compulsory weekly premium under the new scheme, elected to pay their doctor as well. That alone made him something of a rarity. I explained at once.

'Well, he's arthritic,' I said, 'and he had quite a "heart". He spent some time in a prison camp, and not one of the better ones either, by the look of him. He has a man and his wife looking after him.'

Ludlow grunted. 'All foreigners, I suppose?'

'Gastineau is naturalized, but I imagine he's French or Belgian born. The servants aren't English either.'

'I see.' He seemed gloomy. 'I don't like foreigners. Pure prejudice, of course, but they all seem sly to me … all except the Americans and the Scots, and they've got other faults no doubt. What did Alice Montgomery want to let her house for?'

'She's gone to London for the spring.'

'Oh.' That cheered him. 'I didn't realize he hadn't come to stay.' He paused in his meanderings up and down the room and raised his eyebrows. 'Very lucky to let that old house for such a short time this weather. Why does a foreigner want to come down here in the cold? Darned damp hole to take his arthritis to, I should have thought. Well, I shouldn't see any more of him than you need, you know.'

He went off to the french windows, but before he left glanced round.

'You're a bit too pretty with that black hair and blue eyes, and

12

your figure's too good,' he said seriously. 'These old gals round here, they suspect that.'

(So it was Miss Luffkin, was it? Her little house was very near Peacocks. I might have known.)

'Those are faults I'll recover from with the years,' I said aloud.

'Eh? Oh yes, I suppose you will.' The notion did not appear to comfort him particularly. 'Goo'bye, my dear. Not another word about that other matter, mind. Leave that entirely to me.'

He went dancing off across the meadow like a gnome, and as I watched him Rhoda came up behind me.

'I couldn't help hearing and it reminded me,' she said brazenly. 'This cottage is too small for secrets. That Mr Gastineau rang up twice this morning. He's quite well but he wants to see you very urgently. Wouldn't leave a message.'

I could feel her curiosity bristling like a hedgehog.

'He's well over forty and he's one of the ugliest men I've ever set eyes on,' I observed.

'Is he?' To my surprise she sounded quite relieved. As a rule any faint promise of romance sets her up for a week. I deduced that an arthritic foreigner was not acceptable, but as if she had been read-ing my mind she said suddenly: 'I've been remembering Mr John, you see.'

So had I, of course. There are times when I find old Rhoda very nearly unbearable.

It was ten past five when I left the Cottage Hospital on the other side of town and surgery was at six, but as I neared the lane which leads past Miss Luffkin's cottage to Peacocks Hall I thought I could just fit in a call on Mr Gastineau. I was not going there because he attracted me irresistibly. He didn't. To my mind there was little that was entrancing about that battered and racked shell of a human being, but there was something there that I recognized and thought I could sympathize with, and the interesting thing about it was that I couldn't give it a name. He and I shared a frame of mind, or I thought we did. There was something about his attitude towards life which struck a responsive chord in me. I could not define it. I had no idea what it was. It was an undercurrent, emotional and rather frightening, and it made me curious. I did not even like him, but I certainly wanted to know more about him.

Miss Luffkin was pruning the ramblers which grow over her hedge. As far as I know she never does anything else. Whenever I pass, be it winter or summer or merely the right time of year for pruning, there she is, secateurs in hand, snipping and brushing and tying and bending, while her quick eyes turn this way and that and her green gardening bonnet is never still.

I waved nonchalantly and sped by. I guessed she would stare after me and probably glance at her watch, so that later, when I came back, she could look at it again. It couldn't be helped.

Peacocks is one of those sprawling Elizabethan houses that seem to be nestling into the earth for warmth. As I pulled up, the front door creaked open and Gastineau himself appeared. He was delighted but also embarrassed to see me, I thought, and he came stiffly forward to open the car door.

'This is so kind that I am ashamed,' he said in his clipped, over-precise English as he led me into the house. 'I did not mean to drag you all the way out here. I merely have a little favour to ask, and I seem to be making all the trouble in the world.'

He glanced at me out of the corners of his dull black eyes and I thought again how extraordinarily ugly he was. He was a tall man who was bent into a short one and his skin was sallow and stretched over his bones. Worst of all, he gave one the impression that there had once been something vital and attractive about his looks, but that he was a ghost of himself and his deepset eyes were without light.

I did not sit down. 'What can I do?' I inquired briefly. 'Surgery at six, and I've got to get back.'

He grimaced. 'Children with spots and old ladies with pains. An extraordinary life for such a pretty woman. But you like it, don't you?'

'I love it,' I admitted, 'and I'm afraid I never find it even distasteful.'

'I see you don't. You are more than clever, you are kind. That is more rare,' he said gravely. 'That is why I have turned to you. Doctor, I have to have an ambulance.'

It was so unexpected that I laughed and was sorry for it at once, he looked so worried.

'I realize I am being ridiculous,' he said slowly. 'I am – as they say – in a flat spin. A most awkward and difficult thing has happened and I have to do something about it. It is the widow of a very old friend and compatriot of mine. I have just heard that she is alone and ill in London. I fear she may be' – he hesitated and watched my face as he chose a word – 'difficult, also.'

'Nerves?' I suggested. That was the usual story.

'It may be more than that.'

'Alcoholism?'

He threw out his stiff hands. 'I do not know. It is possible, anything is possible. All I can tell you is that I have to go to fetch her with an ambulance and to bring her here.'

I felt my eyebrows go up. I was beginning to learn that there is absolutely no depth of human folly to which the most unlikely patient will suddenly descend, but I was still green enough to venture a protest.

'It sounds a very tall order,' I began cautiously.

'Does it? It is all I can do.' He spoke with a queer obstinacy. 'I promised Maurice as he died that if there was ever anything I could do for Louise, I would. Now the moment has come and I must have her here.'

'It's a great responsibility.'

He turned on me. 'Please don't think I do not know. I have thought it out from every angle. For a week I have been deciding, but I know in my heart that I must bring her home. Radek and Grethe will look after her, and you, if you please, will come to see her and advise me. Then I shall know I have done what I could.'

He watched me to see if I was impressed, and I was, of course. I was glad to see him taking so much interest in a fellow human being. I had not thought there was so much kindness or duty left in him. I only hoped he knew what he was in for.

'I can order an ambulance for you,' I said gently. 'It only seems odd that her present doctor does not arrange it.'

'Ah, I was afraid you would notice that.' He smiled at me awkwardly. 'She has quarrelled with him, of course. There is nobody to look after her except the landlady, who says I must arrive with the ambulance. You will come with me, won't you, Doctor? You go to London on Saturdays.'

There I put my foot down. I was gentle, I hope, but firm. I could just see Percy's face if the 'foreigner' and I went gallivanting off to London in the local bone-wagon. Besides, he was asking too much. My Saturday trips to the capital were the week's one escape from Mapleford, and I felt my sanity depended on them. I was mildly surprised that he knew so much about my habits.

I could not dissuade him. 'But you could see her in London before she leaves.' He pleaded as though his life depended upon it, urgent as a child, his eyes two dusky holes in his head.

I weakened. I knew it was silly, but I did, and I turned to the open bureau in the corner to find a scrap of paper to write the address on. He nearly wept with gratitude as he dictated it to me.

I am certain I should never have noticed the scrap of blue tissue protruding from one of the tiny drawers which lined the desk if I had not heard his sudden intake of breath and looked up just as he leaned past me to thrust the thing out of sight. As it was, I hardly saw it at all. I caught a glimpse of something which looked vaguely familiar and then there was nothing there save his twisted and stiffened hand, which was shaking violently.

When I glanced up at him in astonishment he was trying to laugh, but his eyes were anxious, I thought.

'It is a pigsty of a desk. That is what you are thinking, aren't you? Let me see what you have written. Yes, that's right. The name is Louise Maurice, the address 14 Barton Square, West 2.'

I was still rather surprised. I had plenty of patients who might have thrown a fit if I had lighted on an unpaid gas bill or an overdue demand for rates. Mapleford was full of them. But I did not think Gastineau was quite the type. I was fairly certain he had been genuinely alarmed, and I wished I had seen the blue slip more closely. It had suggested something so familiar that I just could not place it.

My puzzled expression seemed to delight Peter Gastineau. He became quite lighthearted, suddenly, and insisted on seeing me to the car.

'I think I am a most brilliant judge of character,' he remarked unexpectedly as we shook hands in the drive. 'You are kind but you are also very practical, aren't you, and you have a great sense of what is expedient.'

'I should be a menace as a doctor if I hadn't,' I said lightly and climbed into the car.

'And you are not forgiving?' He had to raise his voice, since my foot was on the starter, and the effect was to make the question sound anxious and important. At the same moment I saw the clock on my dashboard and let in the clutch.

'I have a heart of flint,' I shouted over my shoulder as I shot away. It was only as I was waving to Miss Luffkin, who, as I had expected, was waiting in the dusk to see me go by, that it occurred to me that it was a most extraordinary remark for him to have made.

Percy was not on duty that night, and when I got back there was a crowd at the surgery. The waiting-room was packed and I cursed socialized medicine. To my mind its weakness was elementary, and I felt somebody might have foreseen it. Since everyone was forced to pay a whacking great weekly premium for medical insurance, nearly everybody, not unexpectedly, thought they might as well get something out of it, and, as far as Mapleford was concerned, the three who stood between nearly everybody and the said something-out-of-it were Percy and his two assistants, who had not been exactly idle before.

Percy hired us a secretary, paying her out of the private fortune his wife left him, but she, poor girl, could not sign our names for us or weigh up the merits of a claim, so the stream of importunates demanding free chits to the dentist, free wigs, postal votes, corsets, milk, orange juice, vitamin tablets, pensions, invalid chairs, beds, water-cushions, taxi rides to hospital, crutches, bandages, artificial limbs, and a thousand and one likely or unlikely requirements dogged us wherever we went. As Percy said, it was almost a relief to find someone who just had a pain.

To make matters more difficult, the more ignorant (and less sick) among the crowds had lost their old respect for our calling, and treated us as if we were officials trying to cheat them out of their rights. However, I was not so dead against it all – except at surgery time – as was Percy. I thought I should probably learn some way of coping with it in the end, and meanwhile I strove to keep my mind clear and to remember at all costs that I was a doctor first and a form-filler second.

That night I worked until I was in a lather. The secretary was close on angry by the time I had finished, and was taking a couple of minutes to listen to poor old Mr Grigson's interminable tale of the strange noises his chest made in the night. He is a retired sea captain, full of years and dignity, and he had walked up to the surgery with his bronchitis because 'since he was not paying' me any more he did not like to drag me out to his cottage. I wished everyone was as thoughtful, but hoped it had not killed him. In my gratitude and guilt I listened far too long until the recital was ended abruptly by the telephone.

I fully expected the call to be from Rhoda, fuming over a spoiled meal, but I had been too sanguine. The message, uttered in a child's squeaky voice, was brief but explicit. Mrs McFall had 'begun'. I took down my coat. Once Mrs McFall 'began' it was time for all men of good will to get out the boats, man the defences, batten down the hatches, and call out the fire brigade, and the fault was not hers, poor fecund lady, but her husband's. Mrs McFall had a fine baby every year, and had been doing so with the beautiful regularity of sunrise or the autumnal equinox for as far back as anyone remembered. But Mike McFall, her lorry-driving husband, had never got himself used to the phenomenon. Each essay into fatherhood came upon him as a new and terrible experience only to be endured with the help of alcohol in such vast quantities that the man was a raving lunatic throughout the whole affair.

Nurse Tooley ministered to the people in that area. She was a woman after my own heart. Her courage made me ashamed of my own and her endurance had to be observed to be credited. But even she felt Mrs McFall's ever recurrent crises were two-woman jobs. I had promised her that if I was above ground the next time Mrs McFall 'began' I would be there.

'You deliver the child, Doctor,' she said, 'and I'll control himself.'

So I had to go.

It was dawn by the time we had finished. As the first cock crew the youngest McFall let out his first furious bellow at the world he had hardly inherited, poor chicken, and soon after a stalwart neighbour and her son agreed to take over the parents.

Nurse and I crept out into the grey light, and because she was if anything more weary than I we loaded her bicycle on to the car and I drove her home. Despite the hour, nothing would content her save that I step in for a cup of tea. Her round red face was full of anxiety.

'Sure I've got a little word I'd like to be saying to you, Doctor.'

I am easy, of course. Sometimes I hope it is not just weakness of character. I staggered in. The cottage was tiny and neat as a doll's house, and as Nurse Tooley scurried about putting out china I sat in the best chair and felt my eyelids grow sticky with sleep. There was something rather special about this woman, I thought idly as I watched her square energetic form, solid and strong as a cob pony. She was deft and shrewd and loyal, and the idea shot into my mind that when John and I got our children's clinic we should need her. In an instant I had remembered and the furious colour rushed into my face. It was the kind of idiotic trick my subconscious was always liable to play on me whenever I got over-tired.

Nurse handed me a steaming cup and sat down beside me.

'You're done up. You look flushed,' she observed with concern. 'I ought not to have kept you out of your bed but I did want to speak to you. You're in trouble with the police, I hear.'

I blinked at her. 'I sent Sergeant Archer home with a chip on his shoulder after that accident on Castle Hill last week, if that's what you mean,' I said. 'He infuriated me. Fancy trying to get me to estimate if the dead driver had been drunk, there and then in the roadway! Especially as his hip flask had burst all over him.'

She shook her kind old head at my indignation.

'It's excited he was,' she said. 'But he's a bad enemy, Doctor, and you don't want enemies in the force, though God knows it's not my place to be mentioning it to you. No, I was wanting to inquire about this dangerous drug.'

That woke me up. I could just see what was happening now that Percy had decided to shut the stable door well after the horses had been stolen. I did my best to explain whilst keeping the irritation in my voice to a minimum.

'Dormital. Yes, I wrote it in my book as soon as Inspector Brush mentioned it to me.' Her Irish brogue was warm and deeply apologetic. 'He told me to keep it under my hat but to keep my eyes open for it just the same. You'll not have had it stolen, Doctor, not in Mapleford, for it's not at all useful. If it had been a nice sizeable packet of cascara, now, I wouldn't have trusted some of them. No, you've let it slip out of the car and someone has upped and slung it over the hedge. Could you tell me what it was like at all, for if it's found the chances are I shall be having it brought to me?'

I had described my loss carefully to the Inspector and I had no need to visualize it again.

'Why, yes, I can,' I said. 'It was a white carton with some blue round the edges – a narrow band, I think. There was printing on the outside, just the usual details and guarantees. The carton had been opened and it held a two-ounce capsule bottle with the seal unbroken. Oh yes, and there was the ordinary literature inside, a flimsy, tightly printed blue paper …'

My voice dried suddenly as I heard my own words. A *blue* paper, tightly printed!

'What's the matter, Doctor?'

'Oh, nothing. Nothing of importance.' I managed to sound normal and to say good-bye and to get myself back into the car, but as I sped home through the half-awake streets it went through my mind like a little warning bell that perhaps I was making a silly mistake in being so sorry for Gastineau and so ready to oblige him. The dreadful thing was that I could not be sure, yet it could have happened. I had not called at Peacocks Hall on the day I missed the Dormital, but I had seen Peter Gastineau. It was just after I had been to call on Miss Luffkin. I had left her safely in the house, for once, gargling her sore throat in the bathroom, and I came out to the car to find Gastineau standing beside it. I assumed he had just arrived after one of his little saunters down the road which were all the exercise he was able to take, but of course he might have been there much longer....

I was thinking about it as I reached my bed and fell asleep, and it was still in my mind when I woke a few hours later. The more I thought about it the more awkward it became, but at the same time my conviction that the blue paper was the same blue paper grew alarmingly. I half considered going to old Percy, and I think I would have done in the end had I not been so impossibly busy. As it was, the only immediate effect of the whole incident was that I forgot to order the ambulance until I was in the midst of a strenuous afternoon at the Friday Welfare Clinic. I had to make the call from the phone on the desk, and I remember thinking at the time that it was the most public telephone conversation I had ever had. Every mother and half the babies listened to me as if I was ordering a charabanc for an outing. There is not a lot of free entertainment in Mapleford, and people certainly make the best of what there is. By nightfall everyone in the place would know of Gastineau's visitor, her name, and where she came from and the exciting fact that I would see her in London, that fabulous city.

I don't know why it was, but I felt it was dangerous then.

Altogether it was a heavy week, and on Saturday morning it was a thrill to put away my solid tweeds and climb into a silk suit and a squirrel cape, to put on a silly hat which made me look twenty again, and to drive off to the metropolis fifty miles away.

I had lunch at the Mirabelle with Edith Gower, an old buddy of mine. We had heavenly food and one of those gossips which are good for the soul. Afterwards we went to an exhibition of modern art and met two of her friends who had pictures there, so just for a little while I wallowed in a world as far away from Mapleford as it was possible to imagine. It did me no end of good.

It was a quarter before four before I realized it and I had to make a Cinderella exit and fly for Barton Square. It is no good pretending that I did not regret my promise to Peter Gastineau just then. I wished him and his poor Madame Maurice, if not at the bottom of the sea, at least in the middle of next week. They would wait for me, I had no doubt, but even so there was none too much time as I had promised to have tea with Matron at St James's at five.

I found Barton Square without much difficulty, and the narrow, slightly tattered grey houses rose up like a cliff above me as I crept round it looking for the number. To my astonishment there was no sign of the ambulance. I hoped they had not run into trouble on the road.

Number 14 was a surprise, too. For one thing, it was shut up like a Bedouin lady in walking-out costume. Drab curtains covered the windows and there appeared to be no lights behind them. It was one of those narrow slices of building with steps to the front door, and an area with a lion's cage of a railing round it. I went up and rang the doorbell. I could hear its hollow clanging echoing through the hallway within, but there were no answering footsteps.

For some time I stood waiting, the cold wind whipping round me. Presently I rang again, and again I heard the bell, but still no one came. I was beginning to wonder if there could be two Barton Squares in the west of London when I thought I heard a movement in the basement below me. I suppose I had grown so used to admitting myself into patients' houses in Mapleford that I did not hesitate. I scrambled down the worn stone steps of the area and, skirting the ash-can, entered the tiny porch which I found there. The inner door was closed and, after knocking without results, I tried it.

My hand was on the knob when a most disconcerting thing happened. It turned in my fingers as someone grasped it on the other side, and the door jerked open, pulling me in with it so that I finished up with my nose less than six inches from another face immediately above me.

'Oh,' I said inadequately.

To do him justice, the stranger seemed just as startled as I was. He was a tall, middle-aged man with a gentle, vague expression. His good brown suit was loose for him, and he clutched a well-brushed hat and a carefully rolled umbrella. Just now he was hesitating, waiting for me to speak first.

I must have been rattled, I suppose, for I said the first thing that came into my head. I said: 'Have you seen the ambulance?'

The question shocked him. I saw his eyes flicker and he said in a quiet, pleasant voice which yet matched his vague expression: 'Oh, there was an ambulance, was there? Oh dear.'

I am afraid I am one of those people who can't help going to the assistance of the socially put out. Although I was half-way into someone else's house, and in the wrong if anyone was, I felt I ought to help him, he looked so worried.

'I'm Dr Fowler,' I explained. 'I've come to see a patient who, I understand, is to be taken into the country by ambulance. Her name is Maurice. Is this the right house?'

He peered at me in what seemed to be distress, and it occurred to me that I must make a rather odd sort of doctor in my all too feminine clothes, but apparently he did not doubt me.

'Do you know, I really can't tell you,' he said at last, adding sincerely, 'I'm so sorry. No one seems to be in the house at all except – well, perhaps you wouldn't mind coming to see for yourself?'

He turned and, highly mystified, I followed him into a labyrinth of those gloomy dungeons and subdungeons which our ancestors were pleased to call 'domestic quarters'.

The first, which was unfurnished as well as deserted, led to a second, smaller room fitted up snugly enough as a kitchen. There, stolidly eating her tea and toast, as if no one had been ringing a bell or standing on a doorstep, was a large clean elderly woman with the eyes and jaw movement of a cow in a field. She looked up as we appeared, smiled pleasantly, and just went on eating. It was, I think, the most unnerving welcome I have ever received.

As soon as I attempted to speak to her the mystery was solved. Still smiling, but with the complete indifference of one who knows something is hopelessly beyond her, she shook her head and with a forefinger pointed first to one ear and then the other. She was stone deaf, poor soul.

I opened my bag and was ferreting round in it for a pencil when a voice murmured in my ear.

'Well, you know, I fear that's no good,' muttered the man with the umbrella. 'She doesn't read English. I tried that.'

'What nationality is she?'

'That's it, I can't find out.' He sounded as helpless as I felt, and added as if he thought I ought to have an explanation, 'I just happened to call, you see.'

I didn't quite, as it happened, but it was the woman I was interested in. At that moment she broke the silence. After taking a draught from her cup, which looked as if it contained something boiling, she wiped her mouth and, leaning back in her chair, spoke in the very loud toneless voice of one who cannot hope to hear.

'All gone.' Her accent was unrecognizable and I could only just understand her. 'All gone.' She smiled again. 'No one.' She was trying hard and her hands illustrated the emptiness of the house above us.

'Where?' I was trying her with lip language and she watched me carefully but shook her head. It was frightful. We were two intelligences with no hope of communication.

'Who?' I tried again and she laughed.

I smiled back and shrugged my shoulders. There was nothing to do but go away and I had turned when her unnatural bellow filled the room again.

'Sick woman,' she shouted.

I swung round eagerly and nodded to show we were on the right track.

'Yes,' I agreed. 'Yes. Where?'

She sat thinking. I could see her doing it, her broad forehead wrinkled and her eyes moving. Once or twice she began to frame a word, but it was not an English one, I thought, and she always rejected it. Presently she rose and pushed back her chair.

'A-a-ah,' she began cautiously. 'Sick woman. Morter. Morter …'

'Motor,' muttered the man at my side. 'I think she means motor car.'

I nodded at the woman, who smiled, well pleased.

'Morter … whoosh … gone. Sick woman gone.' She sank down once more and pulled her plate towards her. We might not have been there.

The man with the umbrella accompanied me to the door, getting there first to hold it open for me.

'Dr Fowler,' he began, giving me a tremendous start because I had forgotten that I had introduced myself, 'there was a cream ambulance coming out of the square just as I came in.'

'Really? When was this?'

He considered. 'Now let me see. Yes. Yes, it must be just over an hour ago.' He was not at all happy, and his discomfort was nearly as evident to me as my own. 'It was caught up in the traffic,' he continued casually, 'and I happened to notice that it came from a place called Mapleford. Would that be the one, Doctor?'

'Yes,' I said absently. 'Yes, that's it. I wonder …'

I don't know what made me glance squarely at him at that particular moment, but I did, and what I saw set me back squarely on my heels. All the vagueness had vanished from his pale eyes and for

24

a split second they were shrewd and hard and frighteningly intelligent. The next moment he was his old, apologetic helpless self again, but I was frightened and I bade him good afternoon and hurried off up the area steps, feeling almost panicky.

Before I drove off to see Matron at St James's I spoke to the officer on point duty, and he confirmed that an ambulance had called on that side of the square at about three o'clock.

I was furious. By that time I was disgusted with the whole business, and there is one unalterable rule for a doctor who begins somewhat belatedly to scent mystery: that is for him to wash his hands of the affair as quickly and thoroughly as possible. I put the whole business firmly out of my mind and did not think of it again until nearly half past eleven that evening when I was driving home. By that time I was better-tempered. The night was glorious and I had time to think. I decided to give Gastineau and his lady friend a rest for a bit. It would be quite easy for me to plead overwork and get young Dr Wells, Percy's other assistant, to take them over for a while.

By the time I turned into the familiar road I had almost forgotten Gastineau, and I saw the light on in the cottage with dismay. Rhoda never stays up for me when I go to town. She goes to the cinema first and then to bed. She leaves me a jug of milk and a biscuit on the table, and sometimes a few enlightening remarks scribbled on the pad. If she was still up, something very unusual must be afoot.

I left the car just outside the garage and sneaked in by the back door. Rhoda was in her basket chair, knitting furiously to keep herself awake. As I appeared she glanced up and put a finger to her lips.

'Who?' I whispered.

'He won't go.' She nodded at the inner door and, taking up a final stitch, rolled up the vest she was making. 'It's that foreigner,' she murmured. 'He came creeping in just as I was going to bed. Said he'd been trying to telephone here all the evening and just had to come and see you to satisfy himself.' She paused, her bright eyes meeting mine. 'I can't say I think much of him now I've seen him.'

'Nor do I,' I agreed, keeping my voice down. 'Why didn't he go to Dr Wells?'

'Oh, he wouldn't. He said it was personal.' She was watching me with the suspicion of a mother, ready to defend but prepared for the worst.

'Rubbish,' I declared wholeheartedly. 'I'll go and send him home. I've never heard such nonsense.'

Her pink face cleared. 'That is a weight off my mind,' she said unnecessarily. 'I couldn't see what you saw in him. Besides, I've had a letter today from Southersham. It came by the second post and there's real news in it. Something *you'll* never guess.'

I am afraid I interrupted her. Rhoda would pause for a good gossip if the house was on fire. Just then my mind was occupied. This development was more than I had bargained for.

'I suppose you do mean Mr Gastineau?'

'That's what he called himself.' She conveyed it was probably a pseudonym. 'If you can get rid of him it's more than I could without taking my strength to him. Go and try. I'll pop the kettle on, and when you come back I'll tell you my bit of news if you're in a better temper.'

Peter Gastineau was sitting by the fire, his elbows on his knees and his long hands drooping between them. He got up stiffly when he saw me and took a step forward. He was struggling with nervous excitement and his black eyes had a light in them I had not seen before.

'I wouldn't have had this happen for the world,' he began. 'Doctor, you must be so angry.'

'Not at all.' I was not so inexperienced that I was going to let the party become in any way emotional. 'I am very tired, I am afraid, but is there anything I can do?'

'I hope so.' He spoke fervently. 'I am in a dreadful predicament. I am so frightened that I have made a most serious mistake.' He sat down again without being asked and I noticed a blue line round his mouth. 'I tried to catch you this morning, when I heard from London of the change of plan. You'd gone, of course.' He was not apologizing so much as stating the case, and I had the wind taken out of my sails.

'I gathered that the patient was removed earlier in the afternoon,' I observed acidly, and at once he was interested and even excited.

'Oh, you did see someone, did you? That is good. Who did you find there?'

'A deaf woman and a man who was visiting her. What happened exactly?'

He did not reply directly. The discovery that I had not merely found the door shut in my face seemed to engross him.

'If you saw somebody, made yourself known to them, that's something.' He spoke with relief and I found myself peering at him. He had changed somehow. There was something new about him, and to my annoyance I could not decide what it was. I wondered if he was stewing up for a nerve crisis. He caught my expression and pulled himself together. 'I am almost beside myself,' he explained awkwardly. 'As you know, since … since the war I have become such a lover of comfort and order and peace. Any change of plan makes me jitter. This morning the good woman who has been looking after Madame Maurice telephoned to say that the hour of departure must be changed. I was in despair, you were in London and out of reach. Finally I got hold of the ambulance people and with some difficulty got them to go earlier.'

He took a deep breath and leaned back. The idea, apparently, was that I should sympathize with him.

'Well, if you got her here, that's all right,' I said soothingly. 'There was no need for you to come up here tonight.'

He opened his eyes wide. 'But I came to fetch you. You must see her.'

'Not tonight,' I said firmly. 'That's out of the question. It's very late. Far better let her sleep now and I'll come round in the morning.'

He seemed astounded. I saw a glimpse of something in his face which startled me. I thought he was going to rave at me. It was a queer expression, very fleeting and familiar. I have seen it on the faces of tiny boys when they are suddenly deprived of something they want very much. It is elemental rage, I suppose. Anyhow he controlled it and said meekly enough:

'She is so strange. Neither Grethe nor I know what is wrong. It is a great responsibility.'

'Have you taken her temperature?'

'Grethe tried. It was impossible.'

'Is she delirious?'

'I am not sure.'

I put my temper under hatches. Here was a fine household to undertake the care of an invalid.

'Then you should have gone to Dr Wells, but it's too late now, I'm afraid. Look here, would you like to ring your housekeeper and see how she is?'

He shook his head. 'You must come back with me.' He paused and added devastatingly, 'Without you I cannot very well get home. I made certain you would come and so I sent my man back with the car. We could try to telephone for a taxi, I suppose.'

Now that was a trump card, had he known it. I could just see myself waking up old Chatterbox at the local garage and getting him to turn out to take Gastineau away from my house at midnight on my day off duty. I began to feel very angry indeed.

'Very well,' I said. 'Put on your coat and I'll run you back and take a look at her.' There was nothing else I could trust myself to say.

I got my own heavy tweed from the lobby and took him out through the kitchen to the yard. Rhoda gaped at me and I let them both see that I was not exactly pleased.

On the journey I said nothing at all, as far as I remember. After one or two ineffectual attempts to interest me in my new patient, he gave up and we raced on in silence.

There was a light in Miss Luffkin's front room which went out as we sped past, and I was unreasonably glad that the night had become so dark. All the lights were on at Peacocks. The old house looked as though it were celebrating something. Grethe, the house-keeper, a swart eastern European with the most eager eyes I have ever seen in a woman, met us in the hall. She spoke to Gastineau in a language I didn't even recognize and he turned to me.

'Madame Maurice is in the guest room. Will you come up?'

'Yes, I'll see her since I'm here,' I agreed ungraciously, but I did not take my coat off.

I followed him up the polished staircase, which was black with age and very wide, on to a large landing where Radek was waiting. I got the impression that this solid wedge of a man, with the heavy face and coarse yellow hair, had been sitting outside one of the doors, but I could not be sure. He too said something to his employer and Gastineau nodded and signalled him to leave us.

'She's here,' he said, and without knocking opened a door on the extreme right of the landing, facing the back of the house.

I went in first. It was one of those tremendous rooms which were designed to house a family. There was a coal fire in the grate and not much other light, and at the end of the plane of carpet I could see a big old-fashioned bed with a canopy and chintz hangings.

Two things impressed me the moment I entered. One was that the patient, whatever was wrong with her, was snoring more or less normally, and the other that there was a violent smell of alcohol in the room. I think I was saved from turning to box Gastineau's ears by the recollection of the story which little Mr Featherstone, the vet, had told me the week before. He said his Christmas evenings were always spoiled by dowagers who sent for him to see their apparently dying pets, and were furious when he had to tell them that if they fed a dog on plum pudding and brandy sauce they must not be surprised if they became tipsy.

I went over to the bed and looked down. It was so dark that I could only make out a little face and a cloud of hair on the pillow. I spoke without looking up.

'May I have some more light, please?'

'Of course.' His voice sounded odd, husky with intense excitement. I was concentrating on the patient at the time and although I noticed it I did not pay much attention to it until afterwards. He had gone round to the other side of the bed and now turned an unusually powerful reading lamp on the two of us. It almost blinded me. I waved it down a bit.

The woman lying before me was scarcely thirty and must, I reflected, be quite beautiful when her face was less flushed and mouth less slack. Her fair hair was bleached but very lovely and it spread round her head on the pillow like a halo. I don't know if I am particularly stupid or unobservant, but I do know that my training has taught me to concentrate only on certain details of a patient's face. It has happened that I have not recognized a woman whom I have been treating for weeks when I have met her some time later in the street. Anyhow, I know that on that night, up in the vast guest room at Peacocks, it was fully five minutes before the message which was hammering on the back of my mind suddenly got through my professional concentration and I looked at the woman and realized who she was.

Francia Forde.

I had never studied her photographs consciously and I had never seen her films, but now that I was confronted by her I knew it was she as surely as if I had lived with her half my life. In one way I suppose I had. It was one of those revelations which are at once terrifying and shaming. I saw just how much and minutely I must have thought about her, and just how avidly my subconscious mind must have seized on every little trick and detail of her face.

I found I knew the moulding of her cheek and the faint hollow beside her temples as well as I knew the lines round Rhoda's mouth. There were differences I hadn't expected, tiny blemishes the camera had not shown. This woman had not been doing herself much good just recently. There was a network of tiny lines, finer than a spider's web, on her eyelids. But she was still lovely. So lovely that the old helpless feeling settled down over my heart without my daring to question why or whence it came.

It was some seconds before I realized that I was being watched from the other side of the bed and I wondered if I could have given myself away. Gastineau couldn't have known anything about my private life, whatever the explanation of Francia Forde's appearance in his house might be. That was one thing I was certain of.

Fortunately I have a poker face by nature and my training has strengthened the gift. If I am scared or even very interested I am mercifully merely liable to appear preoccupied, and when he said at last, 'Well, Doctor?' I felt sure he had noticed nothing.

I returned to my job with relief, remembering that it was nothing to do with me who the woman was or why she was there. All I had to decide was what was wrong with her. That was not very difficult. She showed no inclination to awake, but she was by no means unconscious and when I shook her gently she flung away from me with an incoherent word.

'Was she like this when you collected her this afternoon?' I inquired.

'Not so sleepy.' He sounded doubtful and I wondered whether he could be really so stupid as he appeared to be.

'Yes, well,' I said, 'she's been taking a considerable amount of some sort of sedative, which you will probably find among her luggage if you look, and to put it bluntly she has also had a great deal of alcohol. You will doubtless find the source of that too if you use your eyes.'

I was falling back on an excessive formality because I was both annoyed and shaken.

'I should look under the bed valance, behind the curtains, and of course in her suitcases.'

He nodded. He was not going to pretend complete ignorance, I was glad to see.

'I can hardly believe it,' he said, coming round the bed, and walking down the wide room with me. 'It doesn't seem possible. She's a very fine actress, you know.' He shot a little quizzing glance at me on the last word or two, but I was in an odd emotional state just then and I didn't want to discuss her, or even to find out if I was right about her identity. I just wanted to get out of that dreadful room.

'Really?' I sounded uninterested. 'Well, I'm afraid I can't help her any more. Take away any alcohol or any drugs you may find. Give her bismuth or something of the sort in the morning, and if she is very excitable, one ounce and no more of whisky at eleven. By tomorrow night you should know whether the trouble is – er, chronic or not.'

To my discomfort I heard him laugh very softly.

'You're very businesslike.'

'I'm also very tired. Perhaps you'll forgive me if I get away now.'

I moved towards the door and he came after me.

'When will you come again?'

'You may not need me any more,' I said cheerfully. 'There's nothing very wrong with her. This may not be a regular thing. But if it is, you'll need rather different advice from any I could give you. Good night, Mr Gastineau. No, don't come down. I can find my way out.'

He hobbled to the stairhead with me and looked down as I

descended. I heard his murmur just above me and the words were so extraordinary that I thought I must have mistaken them.

'Courage,' I thought I heard him say half to himself and half to me. 'That was the only thing I doubted.'

I glanced up sharply but he was simply smiling and nodding.

'Good night, Doctor. It was very good of you. Thank you. Good night.'

I did not realize I was so shaken by the whole business until I got out into the air. As my hands gripped the steering wheel I found they were trembling. This alarmed me as much as anything, for my life is based on the premise that I am a sensible, unshockable sort of person. I am one of those who have never thought mystery, doubt, or drama in any way exciting. I hate the lot of them. My instinct is to scramble stolidly to my feet whatever happens to me, like one of those toys which are weighted at the bottom, and the result is that I seldom get rattled and am made twice as bad by noticing it when I do.

As soon as I got the car going it occurred to me very forcibly that if Gastineau's Madame Maurice was really Francia Forde (I admitted there was a strong chance I had made a crazy mistake here) there was something very odd indeed about her arrival in Mapleford, and the sooner I made a graceful escape from the affair the better.

I was reflecting on the most practical way of arranging this, and was thinking that Wells would be a more sympathetic ally than Ludlow, when I was pulled up by someone who walked out into the road and waved a torch at me. I trod hard on the brakes before I realized that I was just outside Miss Luffkin's house.

There she was, wrapped up like a bundle of laundry, her thin excited face peering out at me from under a sou'wester tied on with a Liberty scarf.

'Oh, Doctor it *is* you.' I was aware of her eyes noting that I was hatless and had a silk suit on under my ulster. 'I've been so worried about those poor people down at Peacocks. I saw the ambulance go by. Is someone very bad, Doctor?'

I have sometimes thought that Lizzie Luffkin's curiosity is quite as pathological as her popeyes, an overactive thyroid gland. I don't believe she can help it Even she must have known that the solicitude in her voice was unconvincing. The sight of the ambulance must have acted like a red rag to a bull on her, and not knowing the explanation for five or six hours must have been pure agony.

'Nothing serious,' I said with forced heartiness. 'Just an old friend of Mr Gastineau's come to convalesce.'

'Oh, I see, a friend.' Her disappointment was so obvious that it was funny. She clung to the door of the car, eager for just a scrap more gossip. 'You are out very late, Doctor.'

'Yes, I am, aren't I?' I shouted above the engine I was revving. 'But so are you. Good night.'

I shot away into the darkness, hoping I had not been too abrupt and should pay for it. In ten minutes I was home and I put up the car and walked into the kitchen. If Rhoda was sometimes a thorn in my flesh, there was nothing like that about her now. She was the one person in the whole world whom I knew to be unshakably on my side. As always, whenever I needed a really sober-minded confidante, she was there.

I told her who I thought was at Peacocks Hall. I can see her now turning away from the stove, the kettle in one firm red hand. There was no smart comeback, no undue surprise.

'Are you sure?'

'No, and I can't believe it. It's too ridiculous. Have you got that photograph you were showing me the other day?'

She got it for me at once out of her own private drawer, the middle one of the dresser, and spread it on the table for me to see.

I stood looking at it carefully for some time. I could see where it had been touched up, where the line of the jaw had been sharpened and the eyelashes drawn in. But the other facts were all there. It was not a usual face, not even one of a type. The contours were definite and convincing, the features line for line the same.

'Is it?' Rhoda came to stand beside me and put a heavy hand on my shoulder, a possessive gesture she seldom permits herself.

'I think it is,' I said slowly. 'It's either her or a double. It's not sense, though, Rhoda. How could she be here calling herself Maurice?'

'*He's* calling her Maurice,' she corrected me with typical

reasonableness. 'Besides, it's not quite so funny as you seem to think. You've not seen the paper today, have you?' She was ferreting under the radio table, where she keeps current reading matter, as she spoke, and soon came back with a copy of her favourite daily. 'I noticed this when I was reading at lunch-time.'

It was a small news item, one of those five-line affairs tucked into the foot of the column.

STAR To REST. Friends of Miss Francia Forde, the screen actress, say that the star is to take a few days' complete rest in the country after the ardours of making still pictures for the 'Moonlight Girl', a new advertising campaign due to begin in the Press on Monday.

I read it through two or three times before it made any sense to me.

'That's all very well,' I said at last. 'But I don't see why she should come down here in an ambulance. I don't see why Gastineau should tell me this Maurice story or why she should be staying with them.'

'Perhaps she's hiding.'

'Who from? She's very well known but she's not one of the American top-liners. There aren't armies of fans hounding her.'

Rhoda had become very thoughtful. If I had been more myself I should have noticed that tightening of the lips and the lowering of the thick determined brows, and might have been on guard.

'You're not satisfied, are you?' she inquired, and the slightly hopeful note in her tone irritated me instead of warning me.

'Well, of course I'm not,' I burst out angrily. 'How can I be? I'm persuaded to send an ambulance to London to fetch a woman who appears to be no more than very tipsy, and when I see her I recognize her as ... well, as somebody other than the person she is represented to me to be.'

'Ah,' said Rhoda, taking a beaker from the dresser with the idea of pouring us a hot drink to take to bed, 'you are like your father when you talk like that. I can hear him this minute. My word, he'd be wild!'

'The extraordinary thing is that she should come *here*,' I went on, ignoring the reference to Father, although it had its comforting side.

She paused, jug in hand, and turned a pink face to me.

'Coincidences do happen. That's life. I've seen it a hundred times. Some people call it fate and some people call it religion, but whatever it is there's no denying it happens.'

I always find Rhoda rather difficult to bear when she gets on this theme. It is one of her favourites and there is no stopping her. I took up my beaker and edged for the door.

'You can run,' she said warningly, 'you can run, but it'll catch you. This is a coincidence, and it's more of a one than you know. You get some sleep.'

In my ignorance I felt this remark of hers was the only one that contained any reason at all, and I went off to bed feeling that at least there was some solace there.

Despite my worries, I felt the slow anaesthesia of sleep creeping over me the moment I pulled up the blankets. Just before I slipped away into unconsciousness I remembered two things. The first was that I had not asked Rhoda what news the letter from our old home had brought her, and the second that in my preoccupation with the patient I had not tackled Gastineau about the scrap of blue paper I thought I had seen on his desk. Even in my drowsing state this last seemed a formidable proposition, and I sailed away into oblivion without making up my mind how to to tackle it.

The next day began quite normally for a Sunday. That is, I was up very late and only partially by mistake. I fear I leave the worst of my paperwork – and there is no end to it in these days – to Sunday morning, and I settled down to a mountain of hospital reports on patients I had sent there, about a quarter to eleven. I had not forgotten Francia Forde by any means, but I was trying to get her out of my mind. It was not just Francia. She brought back too many unbearable memories altogether. I was still stunned by the knowledge that she had got so close to me.

The only unusual element that morning was provided by Rhoda. Once or twice I wondered if she was ill. She bustled about as if she was thinking of spring cleaning, and for ten minutes we had a wrangle because she objected to my clothes. I was very comfortable in slacks and a twin set, and her remarks on my 'slovenliness' and my 'nice new red wool upstairs' completely bewildered me. In the end I got the better of her by insisting on taking her temperature. It was normal but her pulse was slightly quick, and I recommended a sedative. She left me alone after that but I heard her go out to the back gate several times, which was puzzling, for no one goes calling in Mapleford on a Sunday.

The sound of the car pulling up in the road outside filled me with sudden apprehension that Gastineau had come for me again. He seemed to have no idea that a doctor might have any hours. Also I guessed that his patient, if not in any danger, might well be feeling pretty sick by this time.

I got up and tiptoed across the room to peer out of the small window overlooking my minute front garden, so that I should get fair warning.

I pulled the curtain back half an inch and the next moment stood petrified, every nerve in my face tingling as if I had pressed it to a network of live wires.

John Linnett was standing at the small iron gate.

For a long time I simply did not believe it. I watched him hesitate, glance nervously at the cottage, and then fumble with the latch through his heavy driving glove.

He looked much older, and there was a touch of apprehension in his expression which I had never seen there before. It may sound absurd to say so, but I knew it really was John because of the changes in him.

The car he had come in, a low roadster covered with dust, stood in the lane behind him, empty, so he was alone. Of course. The sudden explanation of his sudden arrival broke over me like a wave. He had come to find me because Francia was at Peacocks, and I was supposed to be attending her. My scattered wits came together with a jerk. I felt my expression setting and becoming hard and brittle and very bright. If I had had any sense at all, I suppose, I should have expected him to appear on the scene sooner or later.

I threw open the window at once. 'Hallo, John.'

'Ann.' He came stamping over the garden, his coat skirts flying and his hands oustretched. I saw how thin he was, suddenly, and how the bones of his face stood out. 'My dear girl, thank God you're all right.'

It was the most unlikely and most unexpected approach, and it floored me as nothing else would have done. He took my hands through the window and looked anxiously into my face.

'What's happened? What's the matter? I came at once, of course.'

The whole thing was beyond me. My new hard cheerfulness cracked completely. I was only aware that he was there, trying to get into the house, and, apparently, through the window.

Rhoda opened the front door. I heard her say something to him and the next moment he was in the room, filling it. The nervous energy which I remembered in him so well had become intensified. His narrow eyes were eager and still terribly anxious.

'You look all right,' he said with relief. 'You haven't altered at all. In fact you're better. Lost your puppy fat. What is it, Ann? What's happened? I got the telegram early this morning and I've been driving ever since.'

There was a passage of stupefied silence from me, and a movement from Rhoda lurking in the doorway.

'I sent it.' Her tone was flat and her face expressionless, save for a faint gleam of belligerence in her eye. 'I put your name, Miss Ann, because I thought that Mr John might not remember mine. As soon as you came in last night and said you weren't satisfied I knew it was my duty.'

The barefaced wickedness of it took my breath away, but the thing that foxed me utterly was how she'd known where to send. She answered that one as if I'd asked the question.

'I got a letter yesterday from my neice in Southersham. I was going to tell you about it but you were too busy to listen. She told me that she'd heard down there that Mr John was attached to the hospital at Grundesberg in Northamptonshire, so last night, when you'd gone to bed, I got on the telephone and sent a telegram to him there.'

I said nothing. There was nothing to say. She gave me a defiant stare and opened the door.

'I've got the lunch to see to,' she said as if I was thinking of disputing it. 'I'm doing something special because I expected Mr John. You still care for pancakes, I expect, sir?'

'I do,' he said without thinking and returned to me. His expression was not only anxious now, but somehow frightened. 'I thought *you* sent,' he said. 'I thought *you* wanted me for something. The telegram just said, "I think you had better come at once, Ann Fowler." and gave the address.'

It was his dismay that got me. The utter disappointment came out so clearly that if I had been only half as sensitive where he was concerned it would have reached me. I found I knew him as if he had never been away.

'If you've driven from Grundesberg this morning you must be exhausted.' I said hastily. 'Sit down and I'll get you a drink. We'll thrash this out in a minute.'

He laughed and it was a laugh I had known from childhood.

'I haven't even shaved. The thing got me out of bed at dawn. What's the mystery? What aren't you satisfied about?'

I had my back to him, since I was fixing a highball on the sideboard.

'Rhoda got scared by something I said last night,' I began with a casualness which was not convincing even to me. 'I was called out to a new patient and she turned out to be … Francia Forde.'

'Oh.' His disinterest was startling. 'Is she down here? I thought I read somewhere that she was setting up as an advertising model.'

I swung round to look at him blankly and he took the glass from my hand.

'I've not seen her in four years,' he said slowly. 'I shouldn't get involved in any of her machinations if I were you, Ann. She's a dangerous piece of work.'

I don't drink whisky as a rule, but I had poured a highball for myself and now, in sheer absent-mindedness, I swallowed it almost whole, nearly choking myself. I had tears in my eyes and was gasping for breath and I said the first thing that came into my head.

'John, what happend to you?'

He met my eyes steadily but he was ashamed, even frightened, and desperately miserable.

'God knows, Ann.'

That was all, but I knew about it suddenly, or I knew a very great deal.

Rhoda came in to set lunch at that juncture. She was very busy being the model housekeeper, keeping her eyes downcast and wearing the wooden expression of one who has withdrawn completely from any awkward situation she may have precipitated.

Because I wanted to talk to him so badly and found it so easy I asked John about Grundesberg.

'Understaffed and overcrowded. The usual story in that kind of district,' he said easily. 'Just the place to catch up on one's general work. I've been there nearly eighteen months, ever since I was demobbed.'

'But I thought …' I began before I could stop myself, 'I mean I thought you came out in 45.'

'No,' he said coolly. 'I got some extended leave then and set about making a goddam fool of myself in a pretty big way, but after that I sneaked back into the army and went to the Far East.'

'Hence the – silence,' I murmured.

He said nothing at all. He did not even look at me. Rhoda saved us by a remarkable entrance, the silver soup tureen which we never use held high.

That meal was a revelation to me. I knew she had her secret store cupboard stocked against Christmas (or another war, perhaps) but I had no idea that it could produce anything like that. She waited on us, too, putting on a remarkable act which was part Maitre of the Ritz and part Nanny at the party.

John began to enjoy himself. I had seen it happen to him so often in our childhood. The prickles drew in and the silences grew fewer. He began to laugh and to tease us both indiscriminately. No one mentioned the telegram, I think we forgot it deliberately. This was a dispensation, a time of sanctuary, something that might never come again.

After the meal we sat by the fire while the shadows grew long outside. There was so much to tell about the present that there was no need to speak of anything else, and we were chattering, and eating some filberts which Rhoda produced, as contentedly as if we were back in my schoolroom at Southersham.

I spoiled it. We were talking of his life in Grundesberg and he was giving me a highly comic if horrific description of the lodgings he shared with the other house surgeon when I said suddenly and without any excuse at all:

'Are you still married to that woman, John?'

It was like breaking a gaily coloured bubble. The light went out in our little make-believe Sunday afternoon of a world.

'Yes,' he said, and added flatly, 'I suppose so.'

I said nothing more, and after a long time he began to talk. At first I hardly heard what he was saying because I had made the panic-stricken discovery that his being here made the kind of difference to my life that colour makes to a landscape. It made sense. I had never before dared let myself believe that that could happen.

'If I stop telling you I shall stop making excuses for myself,' he was saying, 'and there aren't any. When I realized exactly what I had done, I decided that I was mental and I went right away. I meant to stay away, and I did …' He turned on me with sudden anger. 'Damn you, Ann. I was all right until I got that telegram.'

'So was I.' It slipped out before I could stop it.

I could hear the words breaking like a little crystal dish on stone.

He lunged clumsily out of his chair and caught me as I sat, pushing his rough cheek into my neck and holding my shoulder blades with heavy, well-remembered hands. There was no helping it, no stopping it. I put my hands into his hair and held him close while my heart healed.

Percy Ludlow had to tap at the french windows twice before we heard him at all. The room was fairly dark, but he is not exactly blind and he was pink and apologetic when at last I got over there to admit him.

He had walked across the meadow with a packet of the endless papers which dogged our existence, and at first he was disposed to thrust them at me and depart, but I forced him to come in and be introduced.

'This is Dr Ludlow, John,' I said. 'I told you, I'm his assistant. And this is Dr Linnett, Dr Ludlow. We were brought up together in Southersham.'

Percy gave me one of his sidelong glances.

'I formed the impression that you were old friends,' he said primly. 'I can't think why I haven't heard of you before, young man. She's a very close young woman, Dr Fowler, almost secretive.'

I thought that at any moment he was going to inquire how long 'this' had been going on, but I got him into a comfortable chair and was on the point of seeing about some tea when Rhoda came in without ceremony.

'You didn't hear the phone, did you?' she said. 'It's the gentleman from Peacocks, and that you must go down to see her. He said he'd come for you if he didn't hear.'

'Eh, what's that? Is that the foreigner?' Percy startled Rhoda, who had not seen him.

'Mr Gastineau.' I glanced sharply at John to see if he would recognize the name, but clearly it meant nothing to him. He was standing in front of the fire with his chin up and the most obvious and reckless expression of delight in his eyes.

Percy grunted. 'A woman down there now?' he inquired.

'I understand it's a Madame Maurice,' I explained cautiously. 'He brought her from London yesterday and fetched me up late to look at her. My impression was that she was mainly tipsy.'

'More than probable.' He jerked his chin up to show his complete distrust of all the millions in the world who had not got themselves born as close to Mapleford as possible. 'Perhaps you'd better run down, though, eh?'

This was just like him. He would reproach me for visiting Peacocks at all and then insist that I answer the first telephone call at speed. It irritated me because I had been expecting Gastineau to ring all day, and, since I was convinced that there was no one very ill there, I was going to cajole Wells to take the call for me. Wells is an outspoken young man and I felt he might do everbody a bit of good. Percy made all this impossible. I knew once I started to explain he would infer that Gastineau had been making passes at me, and nothing I could say would convince him otherwise.

Rhoda piled on the agony by remarking that the 'foreign gentleman' wouldn't take no for an answer.

Percy nodded at me. 'You change into a Christian skirt and pop down and settle the trouble,' he said cheerfully. 'Dr Linnett and I will have a smoke until you come back. It won't take you ten minutes.'

I have given up wondering at Percy's impudence. I knew he was dying to get the lowdown on what he clearly thought was a new romance of mine. I felt John was going to have quite an experience, and I hoped he was up to that kind of catechism.

With a stab I realized that the chances were that he would say more to Percy, who was another man and a stranger, than he would to me, and that perhaps I would have to hear some of it second-hand. Yet I thought I could guess most of it.

At any rate, I got into my red wool and a coat faster than ever in my life, and was out on the road in less than five minutes.

I drove as if I was flying. The whole world seemed to have suddenly turned inside out and become marvellous. I knew nothing of John's story except the one thing that I suppose really mattered to me. He was in love with me still. I never doubted it. Whatever had happened was nothing to me. Whatever was coming to me, I did not care. Whatever the difficulties were, I felt certain we'd get over them. There was happiness ahead, real useful lives and happiness. It never occurred to me to remember I had something to forgive.

I was singing to myself, I think, as I drove down the lane. Certainly I waved at Miss Luffkin's house whether she was at the window to see me or not, and I pulled up outside Peacocks with a screech of brakes and a flurry of gravel.

Radek opened the door to me. His English was more than sketchy but he bowed to make up for it and said: 'Come, please,' and led me to the staircase.

I ran up it, I remember, striding across the landing behind him with an eagerness I had not known since my student days.

Grethe opened the bedroom door to me and I noticed that she was very pale. It was not so dark as on the night before. There was still some light from the windows and there was a lamp by the bed, but when Gastineau rose up from the shadows by the fireplace he took me by surprise. I had not expected him to be sitting there in the semi-darkness.

It was as I caught sight of him and was about to speak that I heard something from the bed that sent a chill through me. I turned away from him abruptly, so that he stood with hand still out-stretched, and went over to it.

Francia Forde lay flat on her back, the light from the reading lamp full on her face.

She was breathing very slowly, with the deep stertorous respirations of coma, and her face was almost unrecognizable, it was so congested. I took her hand and it was flaccid and limp as a doll's.

No one came near me as I made my examination. I was quick, but as thorough as I knew how to be, and every new discovery filled me with more and more alarm.

She had no reflexes. I could not believe it. I tested her again and again, motioning to Grethe to come closer and give me the help I needed. It was no good. I tried her eyes and found the pupils semi-dilated, which puzzled me. Her temperature was up a little, not very much.

My bewilderment increased. This was no logical continuation of the condition in which I had seen her eighteen or so hours before. My experience was not vast like Percy's but I was competent. I should never have made a mistake of that magnitude. At midnight this woman had been suffering from acute alcoholism, not very serious and one of the simplest things in the world to diagnose. Now she was in a deep coma which could have only one end, unless a miracle intervened.

I put some questions to Grethe, who answered them promptly, and my suspicions grew into terrifying certainty.

'How long has she been breathing like this?' I inquired.

The woman shrugged her shoulders and looked blank, so I put the vital inquiry into words.

'What has she taken during the day? What drug?'

This time Grethe decided not to understand me at all. She appealed to Gastineau and he came forward into the circle of light.

'This morning she was very excitable,' he began softly, 'almost demented. No one could do anything with her. Then at last she dropped into a sleep. At first no one worried, but at four o'clock Grethe came up and was frightened, I think.'

She nodded vigorously and turned away. I didn't realize that she'd gone out of the room until I heard the door close softly.

'I shall need her,' I murmured. 'Will you call her back please? I am afraid Madame Maurice is very ill.'

The news did not surprise him. His quiet dark eyes met mine.

43

'I will ring in a moment. Before that, though, there is something I should say to you, Doctor.' He looked towards the bed. 'You know who this is, don't you?'

I was silent a fraction too long and I heard him sigh.

'Of course you do. You recognized her last night. Francia Forde, one of our leading film stars. A face that is very well known.'

He startled me horribly, not because he had told me anything new but because of a definite change in his attitude towards me. I took refuge in my most professional manner.

'I hardly think her identity is of any great importance just now.' I said briskly. 'What does matter is her condition. I tell you frankly that she has taken something since I saw her last, something – er – something of a strongly narcotic character, and if we are to save her life it is vital that I should know what it is. Do I make myself clear?'

I realized that things were going very wrong as I finished speaking. He showed no sign of any kind of feeling. He was not alarmed or worried or even particularly interested.

'You may be right,' he said gently. 'She was in a very strange mood when I persuaded her with such great difficulty to come with me into that ambulance which you so kindly arranged to send.'

I could hardly credit it, but there was, I was sure of it, a very definite emphasis on that last observation. It shook me. I certainly had hired the ambulance for him and because of one thing and another half the town was aware of the fact. However, there was nothing awkward in that unless …?

The idea which had come into my head was so melodramatic that I discounted it at once. People were kidnapped from time to time as I knew from the papers, but when they were, surely they were never brought to ordinary places like Mapleford by ordinary people like Gastineau?

He had been watching me for some little time and presently he said something which set me back on my heels, while the hairs prickled on my scalp.

'I came to live in Mapleford solely because of you, Doctor. Did you know that?'

'No,' I declared, 'and I can't think –'

'Do forgive me for interrupting you.' His voice was gentle, even pleasant. 'I know how anxious you are to get on with your work. I just want to tell you that I felt sure you would recognize Francia Forde when you saw her, and I also felt that you would appreciate my introducing her here under a name that was not so well known as her own. There is some sort of etiquette in these matters, I think.'

'I had never seen Miss Forde before last night,' I began boldly.

'No.' He smiled at me as if he were explaining some small social matter. 'But you knew of her and you had good cause to – what shall we say – think of her quite a lot?'

There was a long silence. I think I was more terrified in that minute than ever before in my life.

He remained looking as I had always known him, bent and stiff and quietly polite.

'I think I am right when I guess that had you known who my Madame Maurice was you would have hesitated to associate yourself with any illness she might contract. You do realize how far you are committed, don't you, Dr Fowler?'

Did I? Francia Forde was dying from a dose of poison, either self-administered or given her by this terrifying man in front of me. If there was ever any inquiry at all, it must emerge at once that it was *I* of all people who had cause not only to hate her but, since this afternoon, to be anxious to get her out of the way. As I cast around me, every circumstance in the past few days seemed to conspire to point at me.

I got a grip on myself. 'I think I must ask you to get other advice.' I heard the well-worn formula creep out in a little thin voice I scarcely knew. 'Since you're – you're so well informed, you'll understand that in the circumstances I really – really couldn't take the responsibility.'

'But of course you could and of course you will.' He spoke to me as if I were some kind of frightened child, scared of an exam. 'You'll do your utmost for my poor friend Madame Maurice, widow of an East European refugee. I fear it may be a long business. Pneumonia may intervene even, and if at last the worst should happen, then we know that a constitution weakened by alcoholism does often succumb to any acute pulmonary infection. Isn't that so?'

He was talking like a medical book, trying to put a formula into my mouth which could appear on a death certificate.

I gaped at him. Only the dreadful breathing from the bed convinced me that I was awake and facing reality.

It was an invitation to connive at murder. More than that, it was a threat, with my career and even my life as the alternative.

'This is nonsense.' I murmured. 'You're making an idiotic mistake. I must ask you to go to the telephone and call another doctor. Someone must treat this woman immediately, but it can't be me.'

'Don't you think so?'

As he spoke he stretched out his hand and slipped something into mine.

I looked down at it. It was the Dormital bottle and it was empty.

Part Two

The great bedroom with its glistening black beam stretching across the low ceiling, and its diamond-paned windows letting in the last of the light, became very still.

The fire stirred and flared and a coal fell on to the hearth with a ghost of a clatter. Peter Gastineau did not move. He stood a foot or so away from me, looking at me steadily with his expressionless eyes. Downstairs someone was rattling crockery and there was the sound of footsteps and a door closing.

I remained looking down at the little bottle in my hand. I had never thought so quickly or so clearly and it was natural that I should have done it in the way I had been taught.

In this predicament I was thinking medically, sorting out the things I knew for certain from the things that were as yet doubtful, and putting myself in the background and the life of the patient first. Now that I knew what the trouble was, and understood what had happened to the snoring bundle of humanity on the bed, every other consideration slid into second place. There had been fifty tablets in the bottle, each one five grains. I raised my eyes to Gastineau.

'Where did you get this?'

'From a shelf in the bathroom.' He pointed to a door which I had supposed to lead into a cupboard and turned back to meet my gaze impudently. 'I had never seen it before, of course.'

He was being the worried host again, completely acquiescent, leaving everything in my hands. Our conversation of a moment before might never have occurred.

As any doctor can explain, I ought at that moment to have fled. That move was the one thing that might have saved me. If I had done anything but stay – run to Percy, the police, anyone – I might just possibly have saved my own skin, but the woman would have died.

I didn't run. I thought she had an outside chance. People had survived larger doses.

As for the man in front of me, the fact that he was a potential murderer, that the Dormital was the Dormital I had lost, that he had trapped me deliberately, all these things still remained half proved. Had they been medical facts I should not have been justi-fied in acting upon them from the evidence I had so far. I decided not to now. Besides, let me be honest, I was not afraid of Gastineau. I thought I knew him and could manage him. So I made up my mind and walked straight into nightmare.

'We must get a nurse at once,' I said.

He sighed. It was a little sound of pure relief. That ought to have settled it. It was my last chance, my last warning. I ignored it.

'Where is the telephone?'

'There is one in the hall and an extension in my sitting-room. Is there anything I can do?'

'Yes, please. Get me Mapleford 234 and I'll follow you down.'

As soon as he was out of the room I went to the door and discov-ered, as I had hoped, that the key was still there. I took it and locked the patient in, and then I went downstairs. I suppose I thought it was going to be as easy as that.

The hall telephone was near the entrance and as soon as I came up Gastineau stepped back and handed me the receiver. He did not leave me, though. I could hear him breathing as he hovered in the background just out of my sight. The number I had given him was Nurse Tooley's and as I heard her voice my heart rose.

'It's Peacocks Hall, Nurse,' I began, speaking very quietly and hoping that she would use her wits. 'Could you come down at once and bring a night bag? I think you had better have your calls put through to Nurse Phillips. You may be out some time.'

'Something serious? I'll be there in a jiffy, Doctor.'

I blessed her calm acceptance of whatever was coming and trusted I wasn't dragging her into danger.

'Is there anything I can bring?'

'Well, yes' I said. 'Could you go round to the surgery and – Nurse?'

'I'm listening, Doctor.'

'Could you bring the – *equipment* we used on young George Roper some little time back? Do you remember?'

I heard her exclamation.

'The day he ...? Oh dear, yes. You've got someone listening, I suppose? Do you expect trouble, Doctor?'

'I don't know,' I lied, 'but it's very urgent. If you'll go to the surgery and bring *everything* I'll get Mr Gastineau to send his car down there for you.'

'I'll be there. Don't worry.'

'Bless you,' I said, and hung up. Then I put my head round the angle of the wall. 'Will you send the car, please?'

Gastineau was standing a few feet away, his hands in his pockets and his head bent. He glanced up sharply and there was a faint smile on his mouth.

'Do you really think it will do any good?'

It was that quiet man-to-man query, suggesting we were accomplices and emphasizing the fact that we were alone, which gave me my first jolt after making my decision to stay. I checked the retort which rose to my mouth and, feeling like a criminal, shrugged my shoulders.

'We must do everything we can.'

'But of course, Doctor.' He shot me an odd, half-admiring glance. 'I will call Radek. You shall give him the instructions yourself.'

There was nothing whatever I could do for the patient until Nurse arrived with her grisly pumps and so I waited until I saw the man go and then I fetched my bag from the car and went upstairs again. There was no change and I expected none. Her heart was keeping up and I was certain I'd been right in deciding that there

49

was no question of sending her to hospital. There were no pulmonary symptoms so far and I was not going to risk any by moving her an inch. Everything that was to be done, and there was plenty, would have to be performed right there in the room.

It had grown dark and I drew the curtains and turned up the lights, very glad of them somehow in that ancient shadowy bedchamber which must have seen generations of births and deaths in its four hundred years.

There was something which had to be done before Nurse arrived and I set about it. I went over the room like a police officer, searching it minutely for anything I could find. As I had expected, any suitcases which might have come with her had been removed. The drawers in the tallboy were completely empty. There was nothing in the wardrobe or on the chintz-skirted dressing table, not even a powder puff, a comb or a hairpin; nothing at all.

I investigated the bathroom and found that it literally was a cupboard, one of those enormous presses which are often built into the alcove of a fireplace in very old houses. It had been tiled in green and fitted up very cleverly with a tiny window high up over the bath. There seemed scarcely room for anything to be hidden there, and yet I found something. Down on the floor, in the angle between the bath and the pedestal of the washbasin, was one of those flat plastic envelopes. It had not been noticed because it was the same colour as the tiles, and it was standing on its side flat against the wall and half-hidden by a pastel-shaded towel. I pounced on it and pulled back the zipper. Inside there was a soggy mess of face towels, soap, and odds and ends.

The first thing I pulled out was a nail brush, rather an elaborate affair, but sticky, of course, as everything else was. I turned it over with two fingers and stood looking at it. There was a monogram on the back, stamped into the ivory and picked out in green: F.F. Francia Forde.

So I was not dreaming and the thing was true. There was something about that utterly personal label which drove the facts home to me as nothing else would have done. Whatever the explanation of the whole crazy business might be, it truly was she and somehow or other I had got to save her life.

It was at that point that I heard someone try the door, and immediately afterwards a somewhat startled knocking. I thrust the brush back into the bag and dropped it where I had found it. If I had had the sense to go on examining it I might have been in a rather different frame of mind but as it was I hurried out and opened the door to find a startled Nurse Tooley, with Radek, bundled up with gear, behind her.

I had seen Nurse Tooley arriving on a scene of trouble at least a dozen times in so many weeks, but as usual she gave me the same thrill of pure thankfulness. She kept Radek quiet and got the bags into the room without letting him enter. Her movements were light and neat and yet as powerful as a tractor. As she bent I saw her solidness and the width and power of her haunches under the stiff and pristine belt.

The moment the man had gone she closed the door very quietly and, with an eye on me, twisted the key softly in the lock. Then she pulled off her cloak, jerked the strings of her bonnet, and shot a long, searching glance at the bed.

'Now, what have you got here?' she demanded.

I let her look and saw the deep frown appearing on her forehead. When she looked back at me I noticed with a pang that she was scared.

'What has she taken, by all the saints?'

'Some form of barbituric,' I said briefly, and it was the first time I had ever been evasive with Nurse Tooley.

'Indeed now.' She was startled and disapproving. 'I had in me mind something more homely, like the boy Roper you were mentioning.'

She was referring to a hectic afternoon we had spent together dealing with Mrs Roper's youngest, who had eaten deadly nightshade berries and had worried us both stiff before we had got him through.

'I wish it were,' I said involuntarily. 'But the initial treatment's the same.'

'Ah, it would be,' she agreed with that heartening acquiescence I knew so well.

We got to work immediately. Nurse had obeyed me literally and had 'brought everything'. We did not have to appeal to anyone in the house. We had a fire and we had hot water; the rest she had brought with her.

I suppose it was nearly two hours before we said any word which was not purely to do with the job in hand. Long before then, whatever poison was left in the patient had been already absorbed. I completed the work and watched anxiously for any sign of improvement.

Francia lay flat on her back, her eyes closed, her breath still stertorous, and as I listened to her heart my own sickened. Despite the stimulants I had given, it was not quite so strong.

There was only one thing to do and that was to wait for a while. Nurse was clearing up at the far end of the room. I knew that at any moment now I must make her some sort of explanation and as I hesitated I saw out of the corner of my eye the Dormital bottle standing where I had left it on the corner of the chest nearest the bed.

There were one or two small ornaments on the glistening wood, a Spode bowl and a little lustre jug amongst them. I picked up the bottle and slid it into the jug for safety. It was practically a reflex action. I had no intention of doing anything secretive, but as Nurse turned round and caught me with my hand outstretched I coloured. There was nothing I could do to stop it.

She did not show any sign of noticing. Her own face was as placid and sensible as ever and she pulled a chair to the fire.

'Rest yourself, Doctor,' she suggested, her Irish voice soft and easy. 'It's terrible hard work you've been doing and there's nothing more to be done for her, poor soul, for a time at any rate.'

It was a straight invitation to talk, and I knew that with her I could take it or leave it as I chose. I went over and sat down and she eyed me with concern.

'You *are* tuckered up,' she observed. 'You're as white as linen. Wouldn't you like to run back for a minute or so, if it's only to have a bite of supper? I can well sit here, and if you think it's advisable to have the door locked, well, I can lock it.'

There was no query in her tone. I could explain just as much or as little as I liked and I knew then just why I had called her in and nobody else. She was my insurance against any weakness which might lie within me. I knew that with her beside me I'd just have to do what was professional and correct, whatever the consequences. I respected her and I trusted her as I didn't seem to trust myself. She was a bridge I'd burned behind me.

'I don't want the patient left alone,' I said at last, 'unless the door is locked and the key is in your pocket or mine.'

This was a pretty startling statement and could only mean the obvious. She took it with a nod.

'Just as you say. 'There'll be no one comes anywhere near the poor little thing while I'm about.' She paused and added the one thing which could have shown me just how completely in the picture she was. There'll be no windows left open by mistake to give her pneumonia while I'm around.' And she leant forward to make up the fire, the red glow shining on the white linen of her cap. 'Well now, why don't you treat yourself to half an hour at home?'

I shook my head. John was at the cottage and frankly I did not dare to think about him. His appearance had made the present situation so appallingly dangerous that I felt that the only thing to do was to keep him out of my mind and trust to God that he would not enter into anybody else's. I relied on Rhoda to explain where I was. His own intelligence would tell him that something fairly serious was amiss, and I trusted he'd do the sane thing and get quietly back to Grundesberg. Personal matters were not thinkable at that moment, and the new warmth which suffused me and was making me so reckless gave me a guilty feeling I certainly wasn't going to analyse.

Nurse Tooley folded her hands in her starched lap and raised her neat head.

'Would this be the young party that was brought down from London in the ambulance there was all the talk about?'

I felt my heart miss a beat. 'Talk?'

She smiled at me apologetically. 'There's one thing I don't believe in and that's gossip,' she murmured. 'It's an evil in this town, God knows. But you know there was a bother about the whole business, don't you?'

'I knew the time was changed at the last moment,' I said cautiously.

'Ah, that put them out to begin with, no doubt, but they had

53

trouble at the house, you know. There was no one there but a woman no one took a fancy to, and the patient was in a highly peculiar state.'

She cast her eyes down and let me think what I would.

'There was no one who could do anything with her except this Mr Gastineau, who had come with them, and there was a misunderstanding about yourself not being there to meet them.'

In her attempt to let me down lightly she succeeded in painting a scarifying picture, and I could just imagine how the tale would run round Mapleford.

Her pretty voice continued softly.

'But it's all completely all right because everyone knew it was you, Doctor, who was arranging the matter.'

I was trying to decide what would be the most sensible comment to make when she forestalled me.

'But early this morning when the stranger came round asking questions, everyone was interested, naturally,'

I don't think I could have moved had I dared. I had heard of people feeling that their blood had turned to ice water and for the first time I could believe it.

'What stranger was this?' I hoped my voice sounded more normal to her than it did to me.

'From what Mr Robins the Superintendent said, he was very pleasant but kind of simple.' She made the words sound kindly and I suddenly knew who she meant although there was no reason why I should have guessed it.

'Was he carrying an umbrella?' The words were nearly out of my mouth but I checked them. The man had succeeded in rattling me in London, but never so much as now.

Nurse Tooley was laughing. 'Mr Robins took pity on him and told him where to get rooms, poor soul. He seemed to have just stepped off the train without making any arrangements. What people will do!'

I got up. That final exclamation of hers had gone straight home. What people will do! I knew what *I had* to do. The decision had arrived ready-made in my mind some few minutes before. The time had come.

I gave Nurse the necessary instructions with regard to the patient and told her to call me the moment she thought she noticed any change, and then I let myself out into the dark upper hall and went downstairs. The old house was very quiet and oddly serene. Its very naturalness made the horror around me seem worse and more peculiarly my own. It was as though I had brought it there. I knew my way about, of course, and, making as little noise as possible, I walked into the sitting-room and across it before Gastineau was aware.

He was sitting in his chair by the fire and the room looked just as it always did, very comfortable and civilized. The desk was just as untidy as when I'd seen it last and the little drawer which Gastineau had closed so quickly was still shut. It looked as though nothing had been touched.

I walked straight over to it, ignoring him, and pulled it open. There were all kinds of rubbish there, string, paper clips, a roll of tape, but no blue pamphlet.

The man behind me did not move. His eyes had been on me ever since I entered but he had not stirred. His stiff legs were turned to the blaze and his hands remained in his lap. As I shut the drawer he smiled at me.

'You did notice? I wondered, but I wasn't sure. It was a bad moment for me. I thought I would be on the safe side.' He nodded at the fire pointedly.

I pulled up a chair opposite him and sat down, and as I did so I caught a glimpse of myself in a long narrow mirror on the farther wall. It startled me. I looked much younger, much more feminine and less impressive than I had thought. I wondered if he really did see me as just a pretty girl. If so, it was an image that had got to be dispelled.

'Look here,' I announced as unequivocally as I knew how, 'I want an explanation.'

His eyes met mine and I was aware of a sort of quietude, a contentment which I had not seen there before.

'But of course you do,' he agreed. 'How understandable that is. But you know I don't think it is wise.'

It was the last attitude I had expected him to take. I had to struggle to keep the initiative.

'That's for me to decide.'

'Perhaps so.' He offered me a cigarette box from the telephone table at his elbow, and when I refused, took one himself.

'What do you want to know?' He was pleasant and conversational. We might have been talking of anything in the world.

'When did Madame – Miss Forde go to Barton Square?'

'A little over a week ago.'

'Why did she go there?' If he preferred to do it this way I did not mind. I was not moving unless Nurse called me.

'I took her there,' he said at last. 'We had been dining together.'

'And left her there?'

'Yes.' He laughed at my expression and I had to take a grip on myself. I had known patients who had played the fool like this when they were monkeying with the truth.

'Explain', I snapped.

He hesitated for a long time and finally shrugged.

'You are a good doctor, I think. You probably saw for yourself that she had recently taken – what shall we call it, a little sedative.'

'In fact you drugged her.'

He spread out his hands. 'Well, that is a theatrical way of putting it. I gave her an opiate. It is a prescription I have had for many years and have used myself when I had much pain. When she became sleepy I took her to Barton Square, where I had a very good friend who looked after her ...'

'And kept her prisoner?' I demanded, aghast.

'Not at all. She was persuaded to stay.' He spoke easily and rationally, and it occurred to me that he had had experience of being questioned. There was something skilled in his little retreats and omissions. 'She waited until I could make arrangements and come to fetch her.'

'Do her friends know where she is now?'

For the first time I saw him waver. 'Perhaps not,' he said at last. 'You see, Doctor, there is a little secret about Francia. It is the thing which tempted me to – well, to persuade her to come here in the way I did persuade her. Just before her last film was made she had some sort of *crise de nerfs* and it was discovered, with dismay, that she had taken refuge in alcohol. It was all kept very dark, you understand. An eminent specialist prescribed. She went into a nursing home and she was cured. Splendid. The incident was forgotten. The new film was made. Everyone was delighted. And then this magnificent offer from Moonlight came along, and she was photographed from morning to night, very successfully, I believe.'

He paused, and I saw something so cold and so terrible in his face that I had to master an actual fear of him.

'I have kept a very careful eye on her for some time and I was one of the few who knew about that breakdown,' he went on at last, adding calmly, 'It occurred to me that such a thing could so easily happen again....'

'That's abominable!' I exploded, and he watched me placidly.

'Do you think so? It was not very difficult to arrange at Barton Square, I assure you. She was angry and alarmed and the alcohol was there. I did it because it was so convenient. You see, I felt certain that when she vanished those nearest to her would jump at once to a certain conclusion and would probably keep quiet. On the other hand, if they did not, and by some bad luck she was found before I was ready, well, it would appear to be just as they had feared.'

The sheer wickedness of it appalled me. I leaned forward.

'And you brought her here in an ambulance because you knew no one would query it, getting a doctor to order it for you to make yourself doubly safe?'

'No.' For the first time he came back at me and his dull eyes became bright and alive. 'You are forgetting. I got not *a* but *the* doctor to order it for me, and to go to Barton Square where she was noticed. I should not be surprised if you called considerable attention to yourself when you saw no ambulance there. Did you ask a policeman?'

I didn't answer that. 'A doctor or the doctor, it makes no difference.'

'But it does.' The gentle voice was soothing, and it filled me with sheer terror. 'Of course it does. Come, you are a realist, you are not a fool. We have discussed this already. You know where you stand.'

He was getting the upper hand. It was becoming his interview. I sidetracked to get it back again.

'Who was the deaf woman I saw at Barton Square?'

'The Ukranian servant of my friend. She would have been alone in the house when you arrived.'

'And who was the man with the umbrella?'

Gastineau was puzzled by that. I could see it in his face.

'Where did you find him? In the kitchen?'

'Yes. What's more, I think he's followed us down here. He's been asking questions at the ambulance station,'

This information did not alarm him in the least. He swept the news away with a flicker of a finger.

'It may be someone who is employed by my friend in Barton Square. Women are inquisitive and sometimes jealous. There is nothing in that.'

To my horror I discovered that I was finding him reassuring.

'What was your reason?' I demanded suddenly. It was the shock of mistrusting myself which made the question come out so brashly. All the time I had been wondering about it, but to ask it outright meant that I accepted – well, the thing I wasn't accepting.

He understood me at once. It was still the most frightening thing about him that we did understand each other so well, as I had noticed long before. He looked down at his knees, the wooden stiffness of his legs, and peered up at me from under his lids without moving his bent back.

'I was a tall man at one time,' he remarked unexpectedly and with a detachment which I found unnerving. 'I walked a great deal. Mountain climbing was my hobby. I was also very sensitive to my surroundings. Sordidness, ugliness, anything dirty or cruel disgusted me physically.' He stopped, his flat eyes still watching me. 'If you want to know you must listen to this. It won't take very long.'

'Go on,' I said.

'There was a time in my life,' he continued quietly, 'when I was in business in Stockholm. It was just before the war. During that time I was able to do certain little services for my own country. I shall not explain them, but you must understand that they were secret. And, since I was able to enter into the high circles in Germany and Austria, of some little use. Do you understand?'

'You were a spy,' I suggested bluntly.

'No. If that were true I should be dead by now. No, I was in effect a confidential messenger, no more.'

'I see.'

He nodded and continued. 'I was in love with a woman who was very much younger than I. She had come to the country with a dancing troupe which had been stranded, leaving her with a British passport and not much else. When I first saw her it was in the summer and she was trying to persuade a business friend of mine to give her a job dancing and singing in his restaurant. She had no voice and her shabby little clothes hung on her like paper streamers on one of those wands you buy on a fairground.'

There was no actual change in his tone, which was still quietly conversational, but there was a force there which I recognized. It was an emotional thing. I knew it only too well.

'I was not very rich,' he said slowly, 'but I was not poor, and there was something indefinable about her which attracted me. I got her her job and I saw that she had something to wear. She accepted anything I offered eagerly, her passion to get on somehow at all costs amused me. I saw a great deal of her after that and gradually a terrible thing happened to me and I fell in love with her.'

He was still watching me. 'Not everybody loves,' he observed at last. 'With some people it is a ghost of a thing, a flare in the night which is bright and transfiguring and then ... gone. But with others, and I think you know all about this, it is a most dreadful power, frightening and devouring and inescapable.'

I tried to shut him out of my sympathies.

'I just want the facts,' I murmured as if he were describing a set of symptoms.

'But that is *the* fact,' he protested. 'You know that as well as I do. I loved this girl in that particular way, and because she was the kind of woman she is I was soon near ruin and I had to tell her so. I do not think I have ever horrified anyone more, even you, dear Doctor.' He laughed a little, but not with amusement. 'Fortunately, I still had the little money on which I now live tied up in England, but by then the war had begun. The time came when I had to make one of my regular journeys to Berlin. Because I was in love with her I trusted her with a secret connected with my trip. It was only a little thing, mercifully – I carried no papers. It was no more than that I had to go to a certain man and tell him that the answer was yes. In my complete infatuation, perhaps because I was insane enough to imagine it might make her think more of me, I let her know I was not going solely on business.'

I knew what was coming. It was clear in his dark ugly face. There was nothing to guess, even.

'Yes,' he agreed, as if I had spoken, 'she sold the information. I was of no further use to her so she took the last there was to be got out of me. She whispered the news at a party where she was dancing, wearing a dress I had chosen for her and jewels I had given her. The man she told paid her in cash. And as for me, when I reached the little house in the German capital, I was arrested. The rest I will not speak about!'

The last words came out with passion and brought me half to my feet. I hardly recognized him in the blazing, bitter wreck before me. He thrust out his hands, which were already malformed, and his gesture embraced the rest of his warped and tortured body.

'You *know*,' he said. 'There is no more for me to tell you about that. You are a doctor. You can comprehend something of that imprisonment.'

I said the one thing that I could say to that. 'Are you sure?'

'Sure it was she? Sure it was done for money and to get rid of me? Yes.' It was final, a very softly spoken word.

I have said somewhere that I myself am frightened of hatred and that I have always fled from it lest it should consume me. As I looked at him I knew what had happened to him as surely as if he had shown me a gangrenous joint. He *was* the ash of hatred. It had got him and poisoned him and made him mad.

He went on talking quietly again now and almost pleasantly.

'I could not face discomfort and hideousness again. I could not risk any kind of imprisonment, anything ugly or terrible. I had to find a way to punish her that for me was quite safe. I had to have help. So when that other woman in Barton Square, who has always watched my affairs so carefully, showed me a cutting from a magazine which she had saved, and I found out that there was another person who had cause to hate Francia as much as I did ...'

'No.' The word was jerked out of me and it sounded frightened. He went on as if I had not spoken.

'When I discovered that not only did such a person exist, but that she was a doctor, someone in the ideal position to make what I had to do perfectly simple and perfectly safe, then I felt that there was justice in the world, and I – came here to Mapleford to find you.'

'Yes,' I said cautiously, feeling my way as one does when the disease is new to one and shocking. 'But when you saw me didn't you realize that it wouldn't work?'

'When I saw you,' he said contently, 'I recognized you, or rather I recognized something in you. You were drowning yourself in work, hiding in it, but you were not quite escaping, were you? I saw that if I put the idea to you you would do your best to have me certified insane, but I guessed that if the *fait accompli* were presented to you suddenly I should get my way and you would help me.' He threw the butt of his cigarette into the fire. 'And I was right,' he said.

'No.' I spoke as quietly as he had done. He had ceased to terrify me. I had begun to see him as a pathetic pathological case with which in other circumstances I could even have sympathized. 'You're making a mistake.'

'I don't think so. You have imagination. You know what will happen to you if you do not do your part. There are too many coincidences for you to explain in any police inquiry. Besides, this is the woman who stole your man. Since then you have not even considered anyone else. Your neighbours have noticed it "The little doctor has taken a knock. She hasn't forgotten it." Isn't that what they say?'

I ignored the last part of that and tried to reason with him. He was sane enough in every particular save one.

'Don't you see,' I said gently, 'all this happened some years ago? If I was upset then, I did nothing about it. Why should anyone believe that I should seek out Francia Forde now?'

I saw the doubt creeping over him. His own hatred had been kept alive so long by his sufferings. He had identified mine with it.

'But you stayed tonight.'

'I hope to save her.'

'You won't.' It was as though he knew something I didn't. For a second he had me off balance. 'You knew it tonight,' he said. 'That was why you sent for the nurse you felt you could trust. I could tell from the way you spoke to her you were certain she would never give you away. Perhaps she is too stupid or perhaps she is too dependent on you. It is one or the other.'

'You're wrong.' Now it was my words which were really convincing. There was triumph in them; I couldn't keep it out. 'I chose Nurse Tooley because I trust her more than I do myself. She's my sheet anchor.' That was the first time I frightened him. He understood exactly what I meant, as I had known he would.

'You wouldn't have dared.' He was appealing, he was hoping not accusing, and he went on talking still with the trace of uncertainty. 'It was the only thing which made me wait so long. You give this profession of yours the passion you ought to give a lover. It is a religion with you. Yet you'll ruin your career if you don't go through with this.'

'Should the patient die I shall have to risk that.' I believed it, and I said it, and it sounded true.

He lay back in the chair and stared at me. There was astonishment there, that and chagrin.

I don't know what would have happened then. There's a chance he would have cracked, or he might have gone for me, I don't know…. At that precise instant something happened which defeated me. It was the unkindest trick pure chance ever played. The telephone bell began to ring.

Gastineau was between me and the instrument and he took up the receiver.

'Yes. Yes, I will tell her, she is here. Who shall I say is calling?'

I was watching him and I saw the change in his face. The blood raced into its greyness and his eyes grew bright. He turned to me with a smile of victory.

'It is for you. Dr John Linnett.'

It was nearly half a minute before I took the receiver. My first impulse had been not to take it at all. When I did, my hand shook and I held my elbow to keep it still.

John's voice came through strong and natural and faintly apologetic.

'Ann, this is to warn you. I'm running down to say good night.'

I moved back as far as I could from the man in the chair. The cord was very short.

'Oh no,' I said firmly, 'no, I shouldn't do that.'

'Why not?' I knew that tone of John's. I had heard it a thousand times, from nursery days on. It meant he was going to have his own way. 'I shan't keep you a minute,' he said. 'I'll be at the front door in something under a quarter of an hour. I shall ring the bell like a proper little practitioner and ask for you, and you're to come out. Do you hear? Got that? Just say "yes", and tell whoever's listening it's the Ministry of Health.'

'No,' I said again, but he rang off.

I looked up at last to find Gastineau considering me speculatively. I said nothing. There was nothing I could say, and presently I turned and went out of the room. As I reached the doorway he spoke.

'At any rate we know each other a little better, Doctor.'

I left him sitting there and went up the stairs again and across the deserted upper hall. From the grandfather clock in the corner I saw that I had not been away more than twenty minutes. I could have believed it twenty years.

Nurse Tooley had got the door locked and she arrived in something of a flutter in answer to my tap.

'Oh, it's you, praise be,' she murmured. 'I was wondering if I'd call you.'

I looked at the bed eagerly but she shook her head. 'No change at all, poor soul, no change at all. The heart's keeping up though.'

'Thank God,' I said fervently. There was not a lot more I could do. While her heart remained strong and there was no sign of lung trouble it was best to let the body do what it could for itself.

Nurse Tooley kept her bright eyes on my face. She was more flushed than usual and there was a hint of defiance in her which was new to me.

'Will you look here, Doctor?' She pointed to something on the dressing-table and we went over towards it together. It was the green plastic envelope which I had found in the bathroom and had not had time to examine properly. Nurse had been more thorough. The entire contents was laid out neatly on a folded towel, ready for me to see.

'It's the only thing in the world the poor thing has with her,' she confided to me in a whisper, 'or so you'd imagine from the naked-ness of this room.'

I glanced at the exhibits and looked again. The usual parapher-nalia was all there, but there was something else, something new which I had not found in my interrupted search. It was a little heap of small white pills and the sodden screw of paper which had once contained them. There were twenty-two of them, battered and sticky but still recognizable. I could make out a roman numeral stamped on the surface of the one I picked up.

I could guess what it was before I touched it with my tongue and tasted the bitterness.

'What is it, Doctor? Luminal?'

'I don't know.' I spoke woodenly because my heart had sunk with a thud. This explained the mystery of the deep and prolonged coma, which had been puzzling me. It also explained Gastineau's belief that Francia would die. 'It's one of them.'

'It's one of them.' Nurses's conviction echoed my own. 'Medi-nal, Dial … something. You see, she's been in the habit …'

I cut her short. She had gone straight to the point, as usual. That was what this discovery meant. Francia Forde was in the habit of taking barbituric acid in some form, and one of its peculiarities is that it is cumulative. It remains in the system a considerable time. Therefore the sudden dose of Dormital must have merely added to the sum already in her body. There was no knowing what the total might be.

That it was a habit was clear. The patient who is given a few grains by his doctor to take in case of insomnia hardly keeps them loose in a sponge-bag. This contempt indicated a very considerable familiarity. I supposed she had been given them after her 'breakdown'.

While I was digesting this appalling consideration, Nurse Tooley made a remark which took some seconds to register on me.

'Well, at any rate we know what it is. That's a tremendous comfort if anything should happen to the poor thing.'

It was the way she said it which startled me. There was a note in her voice which I had never heard there before. It matched the hint of defiance I had noticed in her manner. At last I recognized it. She was guilty about something.

My eyes strayed across the room, past the vast bed with its tragic little burden, and over to the chest. The lustre jug had been moved several inches nearer to the wall. I turned to Nurse and looked at her. She became very red and the involuntary thought shot through my mind that any prosecuting lawyer would have the time of his life with her if ever he got her on the stand. She was not designed for subterfuge.

When I went to the chest and looked the jug was empty.

'Nurse.'

Her back was to me. She was poking the fire and making a blaze. The flame and her face were just about the same colour. She took a minute to make up her mind and then straightened her back, the iron poker still in her hand, so that she looked like something allegorical in a village pageant.

'I soaked off the label and put it in the fire, and I smashed up the bottle on the hearth and put the pieces down the drain. So now you know.'

I couldn't believe it. The statement took all the breath out of my body. I must have goggled at her. She came a step or two forward, still grasping the poker.

'Now look, Doctor dear' – her accent had become as broad as a beam – 'I'm an old woman by the side of yourself and I'm imploring you. There's never one word will be passed between the two of us or any other living soul on the subject again. There's no one knows better than I do what people will do. They'll pick up something out of your bag and leave it lying around for the first poor crazy thing that comes to the house to pick up.'

She was so earnest that her kind eyes were full of tears and she trembled till her apron crackled.

'I know. I've seen even more than you have. But you're a fine

65

doctor, conscientious, and as brave as a lion, and I'm not going to see you held up while the Coroner makes damaging remarks on carelessness and suchlike rubbish. As soon as I saw those little pellets in her sponge-bag I said to myself, "Here's something that will do, sent by the Lord".'

Had I heard it at any moment but that one I could have laughed. As it was, I nearly wept. This was the first thing that she or I had done in the whole business which was actually wrong. We might have been silly but we hadn't been criminal. Without this I could have told my story and stuck to it and held my head up and prayed that the truth would save me. But this complicated the issue. This destroying the bottle proved that at any rate we weren't half-witted and that we knew what was happening.

'Holy Mother, have I made a fool of meself?'

'No,' I said hastily, trying to forget that I'd been relying on her for moral support, 'No, it'll be all right ...' and got no further because a tap on the door interrupted me. Nurse went over and came back with a note.

'The foreign manservant's waiting outside for an answer,' she murmured.

The letter was from Miss Luffkin and it was typical.

My dear Doctor,

Very worried indeed to gather someone so ill. What can I do? Do not hesitate to ask anything. Would milk pudding *help*? Have some *real rice*, sent in parcel nephew America. Have telephoned Dr Ludlow, since did not care to interrupt your work. He says not to worry as you are very capable. Know that, of course, but feel you are so slight and young. Forgive me, I see you have that good nurse with you so suppose you can manage, but perhaps Dr Ludlow will run down. *Always remember I am here.*

Ever yours sincerely,
Gertrude Elizabeth Luffkin

P.S. Have spoken on phone to Miss Farquharson, Mrs Dorroway, and Betty Phelps in the village. They all say you must let them know if there is anything they can do to *help*. Shall run down with this myself.

It was the final line which I found most alarming, and I went to the door to speak to Radek. He seemed to share my anxiety, for he pointed to the floor below and put a thick finger over his lips. I took his tip and pencilled, 'Nothing now, but thank you. Please don't worry, but get some sleep. A.F.' on the back of the envelope, and sent him down with it. I felt safer when the door was locked again.

I went back to the bed. Percy might turn up if she had been worrying him. It would hasten matters if he did. I had made up my mind to be quite frank with him and to take what was coming.

I went over the patient again. The breathing had not changed, the pulse was faint, and the temperature had risen half a degree. She was bathed in perspiration. The lungs were still all right.

'What a pretty woman,' said Nurse, her homely face full of pity. 'She's put me in mind of someone I've seen somewhere. Maybe one of the Holy Angels in the pictures. It would be that fair hair, no doubt. Do you know who she is at all?'

'Yes,' I said. 'Her name is Forde.'

It meant nothing to Nurse but it carried full weight with me. Until then I had striven to achieve the impersonal attitude which a doctor must preserve if he is to do any good and yet not tear himself to a rag. The chance remark had broken it down, and from that moment on her identity was as vivid to me as if I had been confronted with her alive and well. I could see her walking on those long slender legs, turning that perfectly shaped yellow head and smiling, perhaps.

I checked myself. This was not the time to bear even the recollection of jealousy. The new information made things just as bad as they could be. I began to see just exactly what was most likely to happen. The probability was that in the next twenty-four hours the coma would become even deeper and the heart, despite my stimulants, would slowly, slowly fail. Then, in the dawn perhaps, defeating all our efforts, while Nurse and I looked at her, both of us impotent and exhausted, it would flutter and be still. We should try artificial respiration. We should try everything. We should wear ourselves to shreds. But it would be as hopeless as I ought to have known it would be, and I should do what I had to do and tell the police.

I had no illusions. I could see the rags of my career fluttering down over me like dead leaves. If that was all I should be lucky. If Gastineau stuck to the story he was clearly intending to tell I should find myself on a criminal charge, *for this was Francia.* I hated her. I still hated her, God forgive me. Somehow or other I had got to save her life and have her still tied to John. Otherwise very probably I should find myself arrested for murder.

I was not going to be able to save her. That conviction crept into my consciousness like a very small thin knife entering a vital part. There is no other way of describing it. It gave me that physical sense of extreme danger and despair which is like nothing else.

'Look out!' It was Nurse. She came round the bend and caught my arm. 'You've overdone it, Doctor me dear. I don't want you on my hands as well. Put your head down. Wait, I'll get a chair and have you round in a jiffy.'

I drew away from her and attempted a laugh. 'I'm all right,' I said, 'honestly. Look. Perfectly steady now. It was a little hot in here.'

'I believe you're right.' Her relief was tremendous. 'You gave me quite a turn for a moment. Upon me soul, every shred of colour went out of your face. You looked like a corpse. I'll get meself down to the kitchen and see if anyone in this benighted house can make a Christian cup of coffee.'

It seemed a most sensible suggestion and I returned to the bed as she went out. But she was back in a moment, very startled and put out.

'It's himself, the foreigner, standing on the landing. He wants a word with you in private,' she whispered. 'He said he'd not got as far as knocking and I think it's true,'

'I'll go,' I murmured. 'Stay with the patient.'

Gastineau was waiting for me, and it was evident that something had happened. He was angry and his stiff hands were trembling.

'What have you done?' he demanded. 'The police have been on the telephone.'

'The police?' I had not known I could start so guiltily. 'What about?'

'That is what I want to know. I told them you were busy with your patient, who was very ill, and they asked would you ring back.'

I glanced at the clock. It was nearly ten, late for ordinary business calls from the police or anyone else. Gastineau was eyeing me suspiciously.

'Have you no idea at all?'

'None.'

'Have you communicated with them in any way?'

'No.'

His catechism had the merciful effect of annoying me and restoring my wits.

'I can't imagine what they want,' I said briskly. 'We'd better go and see. You can listen to the conversation if you want to.'

He gave me the half-admiring glance I had seen from him once or twice before and came awkwardly down the steps behind me. His experiences had crocked him very badly, I reflected. He must have been continually in pain.

I made for the telephone and had almost reached it when Radek came hurrying past me from the kitchen to answer the front door-bell. As he swung the wood open I looked up and all thought of the phone or the police went out of my head in a wave of dismay. John was standing on the step, his coat collar turned up and his shoulders dark with rain. He saw me at once and did not smile.

'Oh, there you are, Dr Fowler,' he began with becoming formality. 'Can I speak to you for a moment, please? I have a message for you. It's rather urgent. Will you come out to the car?'

I was prepared for Gastineau to protest and braced myself to avoid an introduction at all costs, but when he made no movement forward but limped back to the living-room I knew that the thing I dreaded most of all had happened. He had recognized either John's voice from the telephone, or his face from a photograph, and so from henceforth John was implicated however much I tried to save him.

Meanwhile, John had stepped into the house and put the rug he had brought round my shoulders. He said nothing but bundled me off and I was outside and into the car before I could protest. He shut me in and went round to the driving seat, opened the door, and glanced not at me but at the dark well behind me.

'Well, this is the place,' he said cheerfully to someone in the blackness. 'If you want Peacocks Hall this is it.'

I dragged away the shrouding rug which had all but blinded me just in time to see a tall, apologetic figure climbing out.

'How stupid of me. Thank you very much, sir, thank you. Dear me, I had no idea we had arrived.'

I recognized that misleading helpless voice on the first syllable.

'Very good of you,' it was saying. 'I shall go round to the back door, I think. Thank you so much. Good-bye.'

He looked back, saw me, and raised his hat politely in recognition before he disappeared in the downpour, still clutching his unopened umbrella.

I think that was the final shock which broke me. I heard myself babbling, apparently from a long way off.

'Oh why did you bring him here? Why? Who is he? *Who* is he?'

'Here … hey, old lady, what's up?'

A very strong damp arm took a grip round my shoulders. 'What's the matter?'

'Where did you find him?' I was gibbering, powerless to control myself.

'That old boy? On the road, just outside your cottage. He hailed me and asked me if I knew of a place called Peacocks. I told him to get in and I'd take him there. I shoved him in the back because he was so wet and I wanted to keep this pew dry for you.'

This reasonable explanation all but paralysed me.

'But that's the man who was at Barton Square,' I chattered. 'That's the man who followed …'

'Stop it.' The flat of his hand caught me sharply across the wrist and the stinging pain brought me to myself. I heard my sob of relief as I regained balance. The time-honoured cure of hysteria had saved another patient.

John's grip round me tightened and he pulled me to face him in the faint glimmer from the dashlight. The familiar bone of his face and the tones of his voice were sources of actual physical strength to me. I felt, absurdly, that I was home again.

'Listen, Annie.' It was the name he gave me to tease me when I was in disgrace with him in the schoolroom. 'I've had a chat with Rhoda and I know who your patient is. Tell me, *what is she up to?*'

'It's not that.' I had got myself in hand again. 'You must go at once, John. Get back to Grundesberg and don't tell a soul where you've been.'

'Damn good idea,' he agreed. 'We'll both go.'

'No. This is serious, John. She's going to die.'

'Francia?' He whistled softly. 'Oh, I see what you mean.' There was no deep concern there. To my disgust I found I'd listened for it. 'What's the trouble?'

'An overdose of barbituric acid, various forms.'

I felt him go stiff at my side.

'Hell!'

'Exactly.' I spoke very softly and urgently. 'That's why you've got to vanish. It's for my sake quite as much as your own. You do see, don't you?'

'Coroner's inquest and stink generally. And me calling on you? Oh, Lord, what have I let you in for? Yes, you're right Ann. The only thing I can do is to beat it.'

I think it was my very silence which gave me away. I was so anxious for him to escape it all I could hardly breathe. He guessed. He knew me too well. His grip grew tighter.

'Ann, speak up. Why did she take the stuff?'

I didn't lie to him. I couldn't. Besides, he'd have to know sooner or later. I moistened my lips.

'She didn't take it. She had it given her.'

The words sank into the silence and their tiny echo hung in the darkness for a long time. John moved. It was typical of him, as I remembered, that in the face of real trouble he should become quiet and gently matter-of-fact. He removed his arm from my shoulder and laid his hand over mine.

'Just give the facts,' he said softly. 'The whole thing. Start at the beginning. Don't try to go too fast.'

I gave up trying to resist. It was like telling myself. I went through the whole thing, keeping my voice normal, even conversational. It was just one doctor telling another about a case.

I hid nothing. I let every damning circumstance have its full value – the Dormital, Nurse's destruction of the bottle, the ordering of the ambulance, the visit to Barton Square, and the man I'd seen there.

He listened to me in silence to the end. Then he bent down and kissed the top of my head very lightly.

'Added to which, you and I were discovered by old Dr Consequential lying in each other's arms this very afternoon.' He made the statement with finality and opened the door of the car.

'What are you doing?' I demanded.

'Coming in.' He leaned over the seat and hauled a battered leather bag out of the back. 'I've seen a couple or so of these cases. I'd better stay.'

'That,' said I, coming out of a trance, 'is pure madness. You can't attend your own wife, John. You're jeopardizing everything.'

'My dear girl,' he objected, 'everything is jeopardized, as you call it. You and I might as well be in the dock this minute.'

'I might,' I agreed. 'I've realized that for the last half hour. But not you. You can prove you'd not heard from me since 1945, until you got Rhoda's telegram yesterday.'

He made no reply to that but continued his manœuvres.

'Come on,' he said.

'I won't let you do this,' I said. I was obstinate. 'I refuse to allow it. I won't let you into this case and ruin yourself for my sake.'

He came round to open my door for me and bent to help me out. His face was expressionless.

'Then perhaps you'll let me do it for hers,' he said distinctly.

It was the same technique as the slap, but applied emotionally. Even though I recognized it, it had its effect. It reminded me exactly where I stood. A man had jilted me and made a fool of me, and four years later he had walked into my house and held out his arms. Without the faintest hesitation I had pitched myself neatly into them. It wouldn't be difficult for me to discover that I'd got exactly what I deserved for that. It broke down my resistance very effectively.

'I must phone the police as soon as I get in,' I said. 'I told you.'

'Yes. Any idea what that's about?'

'No. Unless this man you brought here is anything to – to do with them.'

John considered. 'I rather think not. Better get in and find out'

We went quietly back to the house. There was no one in the hall and as he slipped off his wet things I got on the phone. I was answered at once by Sergeant Archer and he appeared to have been waiting for me. I recognized that catarrhal voice and was reminded painfully of our last encounter at the road accident, when I had been so abrupt with him.

''Ullo, Doctor, that you? Mapleford Division of the County Constabulary 'ere. It's a little matter of a dangerous drug.'

'Yes,' I said faintly.

'Dormital. I'll spell it, if I may.' The thick voice was heavily official. 'D, Ho, R, M, I, T, A, L. One two-ounce bottle containing fifty five-grain tablets or cachets. Is that right?'

'Tablets, not cachets.'

'Tab-lets.' He was writing, taking his time. 'Thank you, Doctor. Reported lost at 3.00 P.M. on the 12th inst. Sorry to bother you when you're busy, but records are records and have to be kept. Now it 'as come to our knowledge in a highly irregular way that there is every likeli'ood of you 'aving found these 'ere tablets by this time –'

'What?' I felt my scalp prickling.

'Pardon, Doctor.' He was heavily polite. 'Dr Ludlow was having a chat with our Inspector Brush and it was said …'

I breathed a little more easily. I saw what had happened. Percy had told Brush not to worry and Brush had told Archer not to worry, but Archer had seen a chance of getting his own back on the pretence of getting his records straight. I did not even hear the end of the sentence. What I did hear was his next question. It came clearly across the line.

'Have you in fact found these tablets, Doctor?'

Don't lie. Whatever you do, don't lie. Every instinct I possessed seemed to be screaming at me. I could have screamed myself, I think, but presently I heard my own voice, very crisp and formal.

'Yes, I have. A few hours ago. Since then I have been very busy, as I am at this moment. I will make my report in writing tomorrow morning. Good-bye.'

I hung up and walked out into the hall. I felt as if the rope were already round my neck.

John was waiting for me, his dark-red eyebrows raised. I gave him a murmured explanation and he frowned.

'Awkward. Still, the only thing you could have done in the circumstances. Lord, what a mess! Why is your old boss so anxious to keep quiet about the stuff?'

'He has a horror of scandal.' I was looking at his face and I saw his wide mouth twitch and the flicker in his eyes. It was the most characteristic grin in the world, expressing pure humour, sardonic and his own. It brought the reality of his return home to me more vividly than anything else had done.

'Unlucky man,' he murmured. 'Now, where is your avenging lunatic?'

I pointed to the living-room door. 'And the kitchen quarters are down at the back.' I said. 'That man who came with you …'

He shook his head. 'None of that is our affair. We're doctors, not policemen. Where's the patient?'

He was right, of course. I felt rebuked for even thinking of anything else and I led him up the staircase to the dark landing. Nurse admitted us with suspicious promptness.

'There you are, Doctor,' she began with relief, but stopped abruptly as she caught sight of John. He followed me into the room and she closed the door behind us. I made a brief introduction, murmuring something vague about a second opinion, and they shook hands, but her eyes turned to mine with a question in them. She was far more jumpy than I was, and she had not even begun to grasp the horror of the situation, poor darling.

I smiled at her as reassuringly as I could and we both watched John, who had walked over to the bed. It was a difficult moment for me. As must have appeared already, my trouble is that I am human.

I followed him slowly, Nurse behind me, every starched yard of her crackling. The bed was a pool of light in the shadowy room. Francia was still completely comatose. Her mouth was open, her flesh dark and terrible. Only her breathing had changed. It was shallower now and very fast. John bent over her, his fingers on her pulse. His eyes were mere slits and his face blank as a wall.

I knew that look. The mantle of impersonal professional interest had dropped over him, shutting out every consideration save one. The woman before him was nothing to him but a faulty machine whose troubles he might be able to cure. I guessed that he had scarcely recognized her. But at the same time I made a bitter discovery about myself. To me she was no interesting machine. To me she was Francia Forde, and while John was present so she would always be.

The routine went on. John scrubbed up and made his examination, with Nurse assisting and growing more and more approving at every stage. I approved myself with what was left of a balanced intelligence. I had never seen him at work before and I understood then why his career had been thought so promising. He had thoroughness and the authority of knowledge, and never for one moment whilst he was at work did a single extraneous thought appear to pass through his mind.

When at last it was over he straightened his back and his face was very grave.

I prepared to make my report to him. Nurse brought the tablets she had found in the sponge-bag, and I sent a flush of horror through her cheeks by describing the Dormital in detail. We went into the time factor and Nurse showed her charts. Finally we came to my treatment so far. John kept his eyes on my face, putting in questions and nodding at my answers, and all the time we might have been two other people.

As I finished I saw that he had become haggard. He looked older and even thinner. As I looked at him my own courage began to ebb. The nightmare which was the future settled down over me, more terrible now than it had ever been, since he was in it. Until John had arrived I could have forgiven the woman on the bed. Now, as I looked at her, I found I had not even pity.

'Very sensible and very thorough, Doctor.' He gave me a brief smile as he spoke and it occurred to me that even I was no longer a real person to him either. I tried to achieve some of his detachment.

'Is there anything else?'

'I have used strychnine.'

There was a long silence. I knew that some authorities advocated large doses at comparatively frequent intervals, but the danger was tremendous.

'I thought of it only as a last resort,' I said at last.

He moved his head sharply towards the patient. His voice was very quiet.

'I don't think there's all that time.'

Nurse stood behind him, digesting every word, and I saw her nod to herself vigorously. So it was two to one, and I was overruled. Nurse's opinion carried weight with me. If she saw death, it was coming: I had no illusions about that. She had more experience of it than either of us, and there is something about it which does not belong to doctors or books. Its ways are known only to those who have watched for it and seen it steal in again and again through the years.

When John spoke of the size of the dose I felt the sweat break out on my forehead. I had hesitated to give a sixteenth: he was mentioning a sixth. I was on the other side of the bed watching Francia all the time he was talking, and I thought I saw a faint deterioration, an almost imperceptible change. I knew then there was nothing for it. We should have to take the risk.

We made the decision, John and I, with Francia Forde lying senseless between us, and the whole picture was very clear to me. Once we were committed there was a lot to be done, and I found that it was a return to our childhood, and that once again John, with his careful hands and cautious eyes, was the leading spirit and I his faithful assistant. Nurse found it extraordinary. She kept looking at us, her plump face curious but impressed.

Once, when she and I happened to meet at the washbasin, she ventured to remark on it.

'A grand man. A grand man,' she whispered. 'You'll have known him before, no doubt?'

'All my life,' I murmured back, and let her make what she would of it.

At the last moment there was a hitch. The kettle of freshly boiling water went over in the hearth and Nurse, in a flurry, hurried downstairs for another. John and I were left waiting. It was a trying moment and neither of us spoke. The room seemed to have grown larger and more bare, and I could hear the tick of my wrist watch where it lay on the mantelshelf.

Nurse was a long time and presently I began to walk up and down the rug, aware that my hands were growing wet and that my eyes were sticky. John did not move. He was quite steady. He was looking absently at the expanse of chintz curtains over the windows, his eyes introspective and the muscles of his jaw relaxed and easy. He was worried but not keyed up in any way. I was ashamed of myself.

Nurse returned with a rustle, a steaming kettle in her hand.

'This is a madhouse,' she whispered. 'The servants have gone to their beds and there's no one in the kitchen but a perfect stranger talking to that dratted old cat of a Miss Luffkin of all people.'

I nearly dropped the glass tray I was holding and John, noticing the involuntary movement, drew back the needle in his hand.

'We'll see to all that later. Steady, Ann, please.'

The quiet voice jerked me back to sanity and for the next three minutes nobody spoke at all. In complete silence we tried the last resort, so bold, so dangerous.

I saw the soft flesh of Francia's upper arm pinched between John's fingers. The blue shaft slid deftly under her pale damp skin. Firmly the plunger went home. He dabbed the puncture with the spirit-soaked wool, laid her limp arm gently at her side, and drew the coverlet up to her chin. Then he went to the shelf and glanced at the watch.

'Twenty-five minutes before twelve,' he said, looking at me. 'Nothing to do now but wait … and pray.'

I turned down the light by the bed and he went off to the bathroom to wash. Nurse was standing beside me and I leaned towards her.

'Did you say Miss Luffkin was downstairs?'

'Did you ever!' Her eyes were round with indignation. 'Standing there with a milk pudding, every hair of her twiddled into a question-mark. That woman will be snooping in purgatory. The whole town will hear everything, you know. What she saw, and what she didn't. What she thought and what she didn't have time to think. I said to her, "You be off to your bed or that bronchitis of yours will get you and the doctor and I will be too busy to see to you." She soon went. I put the pudding on the side and shut the door after her.'

'And the man?'

'Oh, him? I don't know what he was doing there at all. He wasn't answering her questions, I do remember that. Just stood, holding his pipe politely, as far as I remember. I was busy, you see, getting the kettle to boil'

'Did he ask you anything?'

It was evident that she had not taken him very seriously. She was so used to running into unexplained people in the houses where she went to nurse.

'I don't think so,' she said at last. 'I remember him saying, "I expect you're busy," or something idiotic like that. He was only waiting, that was all.'

'Yes.' My word was hardly as light as a breath. She was right of course. He was only waiting, whoever he was, and I made myself look at the still figure in the bed.

'That woman you were talking about just now.' John had come back without my hearing him. 'Is that the alarming old duck who rushes out with a torch and stops cars?'

'That'll be her, sir.' Nurse spoke with conviction. 'She's lonely. That's the best you can say for her. Did she have the cheek to stop yourself?'

'She did, but I couldn't help her, I fear, and she retired discomfited.'

'So much the better.' Nurse radiated satisfaction. 'She's in the dark, that's what's got under her skin. She's often said to me, "I'm not inquisitive, Nurse, but I've got to know."'

A faint wry smile touched John's mouth as he met my eyes.

'The vultures gather,' he said softly. 'Nurse, if there's another room available I should like you to lie down for an hour or two. Dr Fowler and I will watch the patient, but we ought not to need you until about 4 A.M.'

She dared not object. John had made a tremendous impression on her and her instinct was unquestioning obedience. But I could see she didn't like it.

'I'll go down and see what room she can have,' I said quickly, and went out before anyone could demur.

The grandfather clock struck midnight as I crossed the landing, and I thought how melodramatic it sounded. It had a very deep chime with an asthmatic wheeze or death rattle between each stroke.

The lights were bright downstairs but the lobby struck chill as I reached it. I crept out of the kitchen. I don't know what I intended to say to the man with the umbrella, if I was anticipating some sort of showdown, or if I just wanted to be sure I had not gone out of my mind and it was really he, but when I pushed open the kitchen door there was no sign of him. Yet the lights were on and it was very warm and bright in there under the heavy beams. The stove was open and a chair by the table had been pushed back as if someone had just risen, but the room was empty.

The back door was closed but not locked, and I went on out into a maze of dark pantries and washhouses not wired for electricity. In the middle of an outside passage I fell over a suitcase. It was perfectly ordinary, leather and shabby and fastened with heavy straps. It was just standing there, plump in the way.

I did not shift it, since it was hardly my affair, and I went back to the kitchen. There a shock awaited me. The chair had been moved. I had left it where I found it, some feet out in the room, but now it was back in its place, its seat neatly under the table. Also, hanging in the warm air, clear and unmistakable, was a blue wisp of tobacco smoke. Yet I had not been more than a few feet out of the kitchen and I had been listening, straining my ears, but I had not heard a sound.

I hurried into the hall and there everything was the same, bare and bright and cold.

Gastineau's voice startled me when I knocked at the living-room door, even though I expected it. He was not in his usual place by the fire, and I glanced round the room nervously. Presently I found him, sitting in a high-backed wing chair which had been pulled up to the desk.

He was tidying a chaotic heap of papers which had covered it, and the wastepaper basket at his side was nearly full. He had moved when I came in and I saw the unspoken question in his eyes. Its eagerness shocked me and I spoke stiffly.

'Miss Forde's condition is unchanged. I came to ask you if I could have a room for Nurse. If she can get a little sleep now it will help.'

'A long day tomorrow, eh? Take any one you like, Doctor. They're all empty.' He spoke brightly. 'The servants sleep at the back, where they have their own staircase, and I shall not go to bed.' He leant back in the chair and pointed to the desk. 'You see? I clean out my pigsty. It is about time and it is as well to do something useful when one is waiting.'

There was the same abominable frankness, the same suggestion that we were allies. I was still recoiling from it when his next remark caught me unaware.

'Dr Ludlow telephoned but I begged him to excuse my calling you down as you were busy. I took the liberty of telling him that you had brought in Dr Linnett.' He paused briefly and added, 'He was relieved, and I imagine he has gone to bed. So you see, we are all three here.'

I realized just a little too late that he had checked John's identity very neatly and that this was a gentle reminder that we were all three in it together. Angry with myself and frightened, my only consolation lay in the fact that I saw he was on edge himself. I guessed our combined efficiency was a bit more than he had bargained for. I wished I felt even that much confidence in it.

'Nurse can have any room, you say? Thank you. Good night, Mr Gastineau. When there is any further news I shall let you know.'

I got out on that and went up again, my knees feeling weak and unreliable.

I found a room with a bed in it which wasn't damp, and I called Nurse out to it. She was very weary but loath to rest while I was still on my feet, but she did as she was told. The sickroom was quiet and airy. John was by the bed as I entered and I went over to him.

'So far so good.'

His narrow eyes were bright in the light of the lamp.

'The lungs are sticking it, that's the mercy. Good vetting of yours, Ann.'

'No reaction yet?'

'No. We'll have to wait. Come and sit down.'

We sat by the fire in the chairs which Nurse and I had pulled up earlier in the evening. John lay back, his dark red head resting against the chintz. His chin was on his breast and I could see the profile that the film people had gone so crazy about when they made the move which smashed his life and mine. I imagine that we both had the same thought just then. It amounted to a simple question: when, if ever, would he and I be able to sit quietly before a fire and speak freely again? If Francia died – and although I shrank from facing it the chance of her recovery seemed very slender now – the answer was, irrevocably, never. Neither of us would do the cheating, betraying our oaths, or laying ourselves open to blackmail. The story was very simple to guess. There would be a few weeks of agony, gossip and uncertainty, and then.... what? Who was going to believe the literal truth from either of us? Would I, if I were on the jury?

John turned and caught my eye. The warm light made his face crimson.

'I fell for the movies,' he said abruptly.

The intimacy was so very precious to me that I dreaded saying something wrong. Far out of my childhood, a scene at a Christmas party crept into my mind. I saw myself in white silk knickerbockers lashed to a lamp-standard mast.

'The boy stood on the burning deck,' I murmured.

He chuckled. The tears of laughter welled up and stood in his eyes.

'O God! you were funny.'

'"Eh-eh, the lassie did her best."'

'Father said that, I remember. Oh, you were so angry! You kicked the audience.'

I laughed. 'I made a fool of myself, I know. I still remember that with resentment.'

'Do you?' He was staring back at the fire. 'You didn't make such an ass of yourself as I did, Ann, in Italy.'

I took all my courage in my hands.

'It was a bad time just then, just after the war. Victory and nothing else, not even peace.' The words came out lazily, I might have been half asleep.

'That was just about it,' he agreed wearily, his forehead

wrinkling. 'We were just kicking our heels. I was sick of stinks and suffering and useless sacrifices, and these film people were frightfully amusing. I couldn't follow half of what they said, but it all seemed very complimentary. There was one little chap like a sallow Hotei....do you remember?'

I nodded. I could see the fat little Chinese god of plenty sitting on Mrs Linnett's bedroom mantelshelf. John was following my thought.

'I couldn't bear to come back to the empty house, Ann.'

'No. Better not. Hotei was white, by the way.'

'This little guy wasn't. He was grey. I don't know what he was or how he got there, but he was the big noise in the outfit and they were getting special permission to make films outside Florence. I was to be his big discovery, and he went through the Command to get me the necessary leave like a knife going through butter. That's how it happened.'

There was a long silence. I wanted to tell him that it did not matter how it happened, and that I could guess. I wanted to say that I wasn't a fool, and I could imagine what it was like to see a chance of getting away from weary horror, and that I could forgive anybody, let alone him, from shrinking from revisiting that pretty, shabby old house in Southersham where every click of a door latch must have brought him leaping up to meet someone who could never be there again. But I didn't say anything.

Behind us in the dark was the one thing which needed explanation. My throat grew dry and I fidgeted.

'Francia Forde was with them?' I murmured, and held my breath.

'She was about.' His face was hardly so handsome with those deep lines in it.

'You fell for her too?'

'That was a mistake. I knew it. I was a fool.' I felt him draw into himself and the shutters come down between us. 'That's something I can't tell you, or rather, something I won't tell you. Do you mind?'

Mind? Mind? When we had so little time!

'Good heavens, no,' I said. 'I'm dying to talk about myself. I've fallen for whooping-cough.'

'Have you?' His interest came back like a light playing over me. 'It's a tremendous subject. Most of the men I see in these days are still prescribing conium and ipecacuanha.'

'Oh, I can do better than that.' I climbed stiffly on my hobby-horse, while all the time behind us in the gloom lay Francia, hovering between life and death and holding in her limp fingers everything that to us was worth living for. Gradually our talk changed to the diseases of children, and before we knew it our old dreams were out again, hanging like beautiful swathes of coloured material from the cornices.

'I've had my eye on Nurse Tooley for our clinic,' I said.

'What, this one?' He was very interested. 'Yes, she's quite exceptional, isn't she? I noticed that. What's she like with kids?'

'Marvellous.' I started to say and the word had caught and died in my throat. I bent my head over my hands. There was nothing I could do. The tears ran down my face, over my chin and on to my coat. I stove my body into the chair and struggled with myself, and his hand crept over my elbow and on to my wrist, where it settled like a band of steel.

'Ann....oh, Ann.'
It might have been the end of the world.

I heard it first. My ears, attuned to the faintest nuance in his voice, the slightest sound in the house, picked up the altered breathing from the bed. As I sprung to my feet the other sound came. It was deep, breathy, and quite horribly loud.

We were both on the other side of the room in an instant and John's fingers fumbled as he felt for the lamp switch. Francia lay as we had left her. She was on her back and her hair, like golden seaweed, lay spread across the pillow. But for the first time since I had seen her her eyes were open and as the light reached them they fluttered closed again. Her lips moved and very slowly she turned her head away. My heart turned slowly over in my side, or that was what it felt like. Hardly daring, I put out my hand and took her wrist. The pulse was not so fast. It fluttered no longer.

I looked at John on the other side of the bed. His face startled me. He was radiant. Pure joy looked out of his eyes as he watched her. His lips were half open as if he were helping her, forcing her, to speak.

She woke like the Sleeping Beauty after a thousand years. She was still drugged. Her eyes tried to focus and gave up. Her dry lips moved and she struggled with the clouds which held her. Her will to live was tremendous. I felt it in her pulse. She was fighting manfully. One could only admire her.

I gave her a tiny sip from the cup beside me and she swallowed greedily.

'Francia.' John spoke sharply in the quiet room.

Her great eyes fluttered open and she looked full at him. Recognition was complete. There was even surprise.

'John,' she said in a silly little baby voice, and her small claw of a hand, which still had crimson lacquer on its nails, closed pathetically over his.

In another moment she had gone again. He released himself gently and stood up and wiped his forehead. The dazed, delighted expression was still in his eyes and his voice had a catch in it.

'We've done it' he said. 'She'll do. That's Phase One. Now, Ann, wake the nurse.'

I could do nothing at all. I turned and went blindly out of the room with a mind which must have been in much the same state as the patient's.

When Nurse came hurrying in, fastening her belt and looking strange and older without her cap, he was walking about the room like a lunatic.

'Broth,' he said abruptly. 'Anything hot and fluid and nourishing. She'll wake up starved in a minute. You did this, Nurse, you and Dr Fowler.'

'You must take the credit yourself, sir.' She was beaming at him and for the first time I saw little beads on her wide bumpy forehead. So she had been scared too, had she? 'She is so frail, you see, I thought …'

'Yes,' he said, looking down, 'so very little.'

I hardly heard him. I went into the bathroom and met a drawn, hard powderless face with red eyes peering at me out of the mirror.

My hair looked as though someone had been trying to pull it off me in a bunch, and my white coat was wet round the neck. My bag was in there and I did what I could with myself, but my hands were shaking and there was something funny about my eyes. They had grown, for one thing, and looked like a tragedy queen's in full make-up.

When I came out, John had fixed himself a high seat where he could command the bed, and he was sitting there, one hand on her pulse, his gaze fixed steadily on her face.

'Damned near normal,' he said over his shoulder. 'Do you think I'd raise the house if I burst into song?'

I bit back what I was going to say and made myself very busy.

'I wonder if I ought to go and help Nurse?'

'No. She'll find anything that's there. Nurses like that have six senses. They find sustenance in deserts and under flowerpots. You leave it to her.'

'And the patient to you?'

He didn't even notice my tone. 'Yes,' he said contentedly, 'and the patient to me. Look out.'

Francia stirred again and he gave her water, and I washed her mouth. She was gaining every minute, and every minute I was seeing more and more clearly the sort of person I thought she must be. Her beauty was but the half of it, I suspected.

John cut into my thought. 'Of course you don't know her, do you?' he said cheerfully. 'You wait.'

On the last word he bent over her again, and so mercifully did not see my face.

Nurse returned triumphant with a smoking bowl on a tray.

'Just tinned soup,' she apologized, 'but it's a good kind. Mr Gastineau had to come out and find this for me himself, or I shouldn't have got a thing. I've told him to send down to the town, wake somebody up and get me some meat extract.'

John waved her to the hearth. He was still in ecstatic mood.

'Keep it hot a minute. She won't be so long now.'

Since there was absolutely nothing for me to do, I sat down in the larger of the two chairs by the fire. My idea was to think out the next step. What were we going to do about Gastineau? The problem of Francia seemed to have been settled. John was attending to that.

The heat crept over me and the relief from the strain of the last thirteen hours was very relaxing. Sleep hit me like a hammer. I felt it and hardly struggled against it. My last conscious thought was that there was nothing, nothing that I could do.

I awoke feeling that I was sailing slowly up an enormous lift shaft, and opened my eyes to see the cold light turning the chintz curtains grey. In the room, very far away, someone was speaking. It was a voice I had never heard before, female and husky and affected, and it said, unless I was still dreaming:

'Not t'irsty, t'ank you.'

I sat up and saw Nurse Tooley looking down at me, a harassed expression on her shining face.

'Well, it's a wonderful thing to be able to sleep,' she remarked. 'I've heard you say so yourself, Doctor. Good morning to you.'

'I say, I'm sorry.' I got up and stretched my cramped legs. John was still at the bedside. I could see his shoulder blades, sharp and weary-looking, showing through the white linen of his coat.

Raised now, on a heap of pillows, her hair combed and her eyes wide open, lay Francia. As I went over I realized that something was different and before I reached the bedside I knew what it was. The entire atmosphere had changed. During all the terror and misery of the night we three had been comrades, linked by a single outlook. Now that was gone. A stranger had arrived.

John got up. He was exhausted and there were dark rings to his eyes.

'Take over, will you? I don't want her to sleep for a bit. See what you think of the general condition.'

'You're going to leave me?' The patient, who was as weak as a fish and still had the drug about her, managed to convey a sort of halfhearted seductiveness and her little hands moved.

'Just for a while.' John spoke firmly and kindly and exactly as any other doctor would have done. 'Dr Fowler will look after you.'

'Vewy well.' Her great eyes rolled away from him and came to rest on me. 'Can you move me? I'm tired. One of my shoulders hurts. I don't know which one. Well, find out, can't you?'

Her speech was still slurred and she must have been only half there, but it was perfectly plain that she had one manner for men and another for women, neither of them guaranteed to have been successful, I should have thought.

In the next twenty-five minutes I learnt about Francia Forde, and an hour later I could have written an essay on her, and I was a less jealous but infinitely more puzzled woman. She was the most unsubtle person I had ever met and she had one interest – Francia. She was practically without subterfuge; and greed, which is of all the vices the one most instantly apparent to the average human being, gleamed out of every word and every movement and every look. Her hands were greedy, her eyes were greedy. The moment she was not acting, rapacity appeared. Poor little thing, she didn't even hide it.

Whatever I had expected, it had not been this. Gastineau's story was completely convincing in every particular save the important one. It seemed impossible to me that he should have loved her. Yet, when I remembered that the incident had taken place at the beginning of the war, ten years ago, when she must have been still in her teens, perhaps it was not so difficult. She must have looked like a flower. Perhaps even her greediness had been pretty, like a child's.

The thing I did not understand at all was John. He was sitting with his back to me in the chair I had slept in, and I saw his dark head above it. If he had been taken in, even for an hour by *this*, he simply wasn't the man I thought he was.

I left Francia to Nurse and went to him. He considered me with narrowed eyes and did not move. His arms were folded and he looked like a sleepy bird.

'What are we going to do with her?' He did not speak aloud but mouthed the words very elaborately, so that I was bound to follow them.

After a bit he tried again. 'Can't leave her here, can we?'

It was the one mood I had not expected. We were in a fine old predicament, the two of us.

'I'll find out.' I spoke with decision. The problem of Gastineau was yet to be solved. Our duty was plain. We ought to remove the woman and inform the police, and yet I shrank from it. I was not a detective … or a judge either. Yet one could hardly leave him loose, perhaps to try to kill again. However, I could make him talk. He owed me that at least.

I went out of the room, stepped on to the dark landing, closed the door very softly behind me as a doctor should, and froze.

Seated near the top of the stairs was the man with the umbrella. He still had it with him, neatly rolled, hanging over the back of the chair. His hat was on his knees.

He rose as I appeared and favoured me with one of his apologetic stares.

'Good morning, Doctor. May I hope that the patient is a little better?'

I was not afraid of him any more. I made the discovery with a stab of delight. Indeed, eyeing him now, it seemed absurd that I ever had been, he was so meek and gentle-looking.

'Yes, thank you,' I said cheerfully, and was about to pass when he made a most surprising remark.

'I fear everyone else has gone,' he said. 'That was why I thought it best to come up here.'

'Gone?' I repeated stupidly.

'Oh dear.' It seemed to his favourite expletive. 'I made sure you knew. Otherwise I should have certainly ventured to warn you. But since you had seen Mr Gastineau destroying his papers I made certain you had guessed his intentions. He and his servants went off in the car soon after the nurse came down for broth. I think she told someone to go for meat extract, but as they all took their suitcases I really don't suppose they will be back.'

It was the longest speech I had ever heard him make. He towered over me and his pale eyes were frighteningly intelligent as they looked down into mine.

'I sincerely hope I've not been unhelpful, but since I heard you trip over the manservant's trunk in the back kitchen I really thought that you were aware that they contemplated flight.'

His excessive formality might have been funny at any other time.

'Where were you?' I demanded.

'I – er – I moved,' he said obliquely. 'I didn't want to introduce myself just then.'

'Who are you?' I nearly said, 'Who on earth are you?' but I had the impression that might have hurt him.

He was very dignified. He produced a card at once, with relief, I thought. Engraved on the pasteboard in fine flowing script were the words:

Re acquaintance Ltd
Mr Roland Bluett

'Oh, a detective agency!' I exclaimed in triumph, and a flush appeared on his high cheekbones.

'We don't call ourselves that, Doctor,' he protested gently. 'We are a very old established firm. We specialize in finding lost people with the maximum amount of discretion. Most of our work concerns lost relatives, of course, but this ... this was rather different. In this case we represent Messrs Moonlight, a rather larger concern than our own if not quite so long established.'

'I see,' I agreed slowly.

He sighed. 'I'm so glad,' he said simply. 'I did so fear you might have formed a wrong impression. My clients were merely anxious to make certain that nothing of – er – how shall I say? ... an unfortunate nature would appear about Miss Forde in the very same newspapers which had arranged to carry their advertisements. You do see, Doctor, that would have been most embarrassing?'

'Do you know how near it might have happened?' I felt unkind as soon as I had spoken. He looked both intelligent and appalled.

'I gathered it,' he said earnestly. 'I've been on tenterhooks, believe me. But my position was particularly difficult since the lady was in the care, and not the very good care, I fear, of her husband.'

My heart jumped violently but I didn't understand him. I stood looking at him blankly until he said primly: 'Miss Forde was married to Mr Gastineau some years ago in Sweden. We have verified that.' He conveyed that as far as he knew a marriage in Sweden was legal, but not of course so good as it would be in England.

Even in my shaking-kneed condition I felt that he and Percy should have met.

'Are you sure of this?'

'Oh, without a doubt,' said Mr Bluett firmly. 'Otherwise my position would have been so much easier, wouldn't it? You would have found me at the front door, Doctor, not the back. It was the return of Mr Gastineau, virtually from the dead, which has made most of our trouble.'

'But I thought Miss Forde was married to – to someone else,' I said huskily.

He regarded me with horror and said the last thing I had expected.

'Now that really would be intolerable. I know there was an unfortunate publicity story which appeared before she was famous, about some runaway – er – escapade in Italy, but believe me, that was pure fiction. Miss Forde herself assured my clients when they were checking her credentials that there was nothing in it. They understood that she was a widow, Mr Gastineau's widow. When they learnt that she had vanished after going to dine with her husband, who had so suddenly reappeared, they were naturally anxious, so they put matters in our hands.'

'Because they feared that she might be on the verge of a breakdown?' I murmured cruelly.

He met my eyes very steadily.

'On the verge of a breakdown,' he repeated meekly, and the vague expression crept over his eyes again.

I said nothing. My mind was seething with a thousand questions and it was some seconds before I heard his polite inquiry.

'When do you think she will be well enough for me to take her back, Doctor?'

When it did sink in I nearly fell over.

'Take her back?' I whispered.

'Naturally.' He was surprised by my stupidity. 'Quite frankly, now that I have found her I have no intention of leaving her side. My clients are in the process of spending two million pounds in publicizing their product in advertisements which – er – incorporate her face. Now that Mr Gastineau has gone, she will hardly want to stay here. I should like to take her back to her flat in London.'

I didn't know what to do. I stood there shaking, wondering whether to tell John at once, wondering whether to clasp dear Mr Bluett by the hand, wondering whether to sit down and cry with relief. The thing that settled the matter was the most unexpected incident in the whole of that hectic week-end.

Downstairs in the front hall somebody coughed loudly and, looking over the banisters, I found myself facing Percy Ludlow and Sergeant Archer. They were both cold and miserable and Percy looked furious. As he saw me he heaved a noisy sigh.

'Ann! Thank God for somebody sensible. Come down, can you? Give this feller some sort of statement'

Mr Bluett had faded into the background like a shadow so I went down to them alone. Percy had his hands in his coat pockets and was stamping on the tiles to keep his feet warm. It was clear that he had been dragged out of bed, for he was unshaven and there was a muffler round his throat.

Archer was in much the same state, except that his uniform hid his lack of collar, and both men were covered with mud. The sergeant was more quiet and paler than I had ever seen him, and it took me some minutes to grasp that this new attitude of his was partly deference and partly shock. Percy surprised me by taking my arm.

'You look tired. Had a bad night? Patient doing?'

'Not bad,' I assured him. 'Sitting up.'

'Eating?'

'A little.'

'That's all right, then. Sorry to bring you more trouble, but we can't get on without you. The two survivors can't speak anything but monkey talk.'

'Survivors?'

'Yes.' He blew the word into a bubble. 'Another blessed road smash. And I tell you what, Ann, and I don't mind saying it in front of a policeman, he can take it down if he likes, it's solely the fault of that fool woman.'

'What woman?'

He exploded. 'Why, Lizzie! She was the only woman on the road. Lizzie Luffkin, silly old besom. She admitted to running out

91

to a fast-moving car and shining a torch in the eyes of the driver. I ask you! I hope she gets a reprimand from the court – in fact I'll see she gets it. Car turned clean over. One man died instantly.'

'Who?' I asked, although I think I knew.

Percy patted me. 'Your patient, my dear. Sorry, but there you are. I think I'm right. Osteoarthritis, far advanced.'

'Yes, that's Gastineau.'

'That's all I want to know, Doctor.' Archer was gentle. 'Just the name and approximate age. I can't get a word of sense out of the others.'

Percy stayed with me and when the policeman had gone tried to comfort me, I don't quite know why.

'Poor feller,' he murmured, standing on the doorstep, his legs wide apart, his old eyes roaming the morning scene. 'Poor, poor feller. But still, arthritis. Joints badly affected. He hadn't much to look forward to, had he?'

'No.' I spoke more softly than I had intended. 'No, he hadn't. Nothing at all,'

Nurse and Mr Bluett stayed with Francia, and before I left Peacocks I rang Mr Robins again and arranged for the Mapleford ambulance to take her back to London but not to Barton Square. Mr Bluett, who revealed a remarkable resource, fixed for a London nurse to travel with her.

No one appeared to notice that it was a little odd that Gastineau and his servants should have decided to go driving in the dawn with a earful of luggage. Mapleford was so aghast at the accident, and so intrigued by its cause, that it missed the obvious, and the only person who would have been certain to seize on it was not saying very much just then. Poor Miss Luff kin had taken to her bed with the outspoken Wells as her medical attendant.

I took John home to breakfast and Rhoda met us with a look which said plainly as words that we could tell her what we liked, but as she saw it we'd been out all night. However, since John was so thin, she spread herself over breakfast, and while she was cooking and singing 'Careless Hands' with expression, I snatched a bath and he telephoned Grundesberg.

We sat in the sunny window with coffee, home-made bread, and the butter which Rhoda had given her by a woman who knows a cow, and we did not look at each other. The world was quiet and warm and green and I was happy and hungry and curious.

John was happy too. It glowed in him and made him different and exciting, and not at all as I had known him as a boy.

After a long time he said abruptly:

'I had a talk with Mr Bluett, and if he's right about Francia Gastineau you'll have to have me led around by a keeper, Ann. Choose someone kind.'

'Is he right?'

'I don't know.' He spoke very slowly, putting out his hand to find mine. 'The thing that makes it credible is the otherwise unbelievable attitude of Messrs Moonlight and Company.'

'Why?'

'Well, my dear girl, a concern of that size doesn't merely choose a pretty face, however famous. It's a serious business, that sort of advertising. They must have examined her record very carefully before they risked using her in a scheme as vast as that. If she said she was Gastineau's widow they'd have spotted any legal second marriage, or so I should have thought.'

I turned round to him, put my hands on his shoulders and looked into his face.

'It's time I had that story, John.'

His face was close to mine, but there was no deeper colour in it and his eyes were thoughtful rather than ashamed.

'Now we've saved her silly little life for her, I don't seem anywhere near so sore,' he observed unexpectedly. 'That was why I was so thrilled when I saw her reviving, I suppose. My God, she made a monkey out of me.'

'What was this?' I burst out with some asperity. 'A shotgun wedding?'

That annoyed him and his arms closed round me to make certain of me while he talked. In some ways he had not changed since he was ten.

'I didn't write and tell you about the film offer because I knew that you'd never approve of my giving up medicine, and I wanted to get it all fixed before you could advise against it,' he announced

93

with all the peculiar irritability of a man making a confession.

'Very wise,' I murmured.

He sighed and pushed my head down on his shoulder.

'I told you. I fell for the movie offer and I helped push the thing through with the army. The company was going to make a film with the old French stage star, Mme Duse, a wonderful old dear, Ann. She had a face like a duck but she could make you laugh or cry at will. I was to be the young army officer, bursting with charm and verisimilitude, who was to make hay with her daughter's heart as I came charging in with my men to liberate 'em all.'

'Yes, I see all that.'

'I don't think you do,' he said grimly. 'I was so dead keen and so were all my buddies in the regiment. Some of 'em were to be loaned for small parts, and we were like kids about it all. The war was over and this was the first pleasant thing to happen to us for years. Unfortunately I was teacher's pet and I didn't know the ropes at all. There's a hell of a lot of jealousy in that business, Ann.'

'I believe you,' I laughed and he pushed my head down again.

'It's not quite as you think, all the same. The movies are a much more chancy business than most, and publicity seems to mean such a hell of lot to everybody. You see, until the little director chap discovered me, and got a story with me about my being given indefinite leave because I was just what they wanted and typical and all that, until then the *daughter* was supposed to be the second most important person in the show.'

'Oh, I see. And she was to be played by Francia?'

'Exactly. Francia had been spotted playing "bits" in Sweden and had been sent over for the part. She was a go-getter in her way. At least she wouldn't let anything stand in it. But unfortunately when she arrived I had appeared on the scene, and seemed all set to steal her thunder.'

He paused. 'Mind you, there was not a great deal of thunder to go round. We only had what Mme Duse left. However, the director had become sold on me and he had the script-writers enlarge my part. The result was that it didn't look as if Francia's big chance was going to get her very far.'

'Did she make it clear that she resented that?'

He grinned. 'Not to me. I suppose I was the only soul in the outfit who had no notion what was happening. My idea was to act. I didn't know there was any more to the job. God, I was green! Francia began by snubbing me, and then, after she'd had a good look around, suddenly made a dead set at me. I wasn't attracted and I kept out of her way. That's why what happened took me completely by surprise.'

He hesitated. 'I think I exasperated her,' he said at last. 'Anyway, just as all the preliminary publicity was going out she gave a party. I couldn't get out of going. I drank what I was handed and after that it was the Bristol Splice trick pure and simple.'

I wriggled my head round to look at him and sat up.

'What's that?'

He was sneering, his fastidious nose contemptuous.

'The Bristol Splice is the trick that in the seventeenth century the ladies of the town used to play on those prudent sailors who had left their pay with the mate, my dear. I didn't remember the end of the party, and when I did wake, with my head on fire, it was the day after tomorrow so to speak. I was in a country hotel bedroom, Francia was dancing about in a negligee, and a friend of hers – one of the lads who wrote publicity – was showing a pack of Italians, who he said were newspapermen, a picture of Francia in a wedding dress and an Italian civil marriage certificate. Everybody was drinking our health.'

'What did you do?'

He smiled angrily. 'Oh, same like the sailors, I'm afraid. It's a time-honoured reaction, except that I had the presence of mind not to talk. I knocked out the publicity writer and, while Francia was reviving him, dressed hurriedly in the bathroom and lit out of the window. So ended my movie career.'

'But, darling,' I protested, 'didn't you go back to the film people at all?'

He shrugged his shoulders. 'Where was the use? I'd got it into my head that the certificate was genuine. I made certain I was trapped. If I made a row I damned myself and the film, and if I didn't, well, I had Francia on my hands. Besides …'

'Besides what?'

He gave me a curiously timid glance from under his lids.

'I thought I was probably better at medicine. Oh, have a heart, Ann! I'd come smartly out of the rose-pink fog. I was sick to death of the whole lot of 'em.'

I sat thinking. He might at least have told me. And yet I knew a little of the odd mental conditions which appeared in men who had suddenly been released from years of active service. For a time some of them had developed the self-consciousness which would have been considered excessive in a Victorian miss of seventeen.

We were still holding hands and I moved a little nearer to him.

'You'd better find out about the marriage now.'

'Good lord, yes.'

I couldn't resist it. 'Lucky I waited,' I observed.

He pulled me close to him and kissed me squarely on the mouth.

'I had my eye on you all the time.'

'What?'

'I found out where you were when I got back. Then I had to get a job and I had to make good at it. Last week I thought the time had come, and I set about breaking things to you gently. I began by letting it be known in Southersham that the prodigal had returned. I knew someone would pass it on.'

I sat up at that.

'Do you mean to say that you were conceited enough to expect me to approach you?'

He pulled me back again and chuckled.

'Hang it,' he said, 'I got a telegram.'

Rhoda stopped the fight by appearing in the doorway, the morning papers in her hand.

'See here.' Her voice was packed with admiration. 'Look at that Miss Francia doing her washing. Doesn't she look lovely? All over a whole page!'

Safer than Love

Part One

I suppose the most frightening thing in the world is the moment when one realizes that courage isn't going to be enough. One plods along cheerfully, convinced that one hasn't got a breaking point, and then, quite suddenly and at the most unlikely moment one sees it, not yet quite on top of one but not so far ahead.

That was why I crossed the road before old Mrs Wycherley caught sight of me. I had nothing against her, poor old darling. She was kindness personified, and the canon's sister, but I knew that in less than five minutes I should be seeing her sad eyes peering out of her unpowdered face, should be feeling her gloved hand on my arm, and, out of a warm cloud of cologne and mouthwash, should hear her soft voice saying: 'How *are* we today, my dear? Forgive me, but you look so *young*' And I felt I couldn't stand it.

Mrs Wycherley always said that. At first I had assumed that she was worrying because I didn't start a baby, but just lately it had dawned upon me that she was only guessing, with the rest of the insatiably inquisitive town of Tinworth, and was inquiring if I *could* be happily married. So far I had always been brightly reassuring but this morning, the moment I saw her black drapery bearing down upon me, I turned and fled across the glistening surface of Tortham Road, panic-stricken. It alarmed me all the more because I had not dreamed that I could ever be that sort of person. Until then I should have said that I was a young woman who didn't hold with panic. I hurried down the Tortham Road, giddy with the shock of the discovery.

Every provincial town of any size in southern England has its own Tortham Road under some name or other. It is the good road, the residential street leading off the main shopping centre where, in their heyday some eighty years ago, Victorian merchants built their little mansions. These still squat there, portly and inconvenient, each boldly individual in style to the point of mock-Gothic turrets or pagoda-topped conservatories, and each muffled like a sleeping beauty in thickets of laurel and rhododendron. Now, of course, they are nearly all nursing homes, or converted flats, or schools. Our school, the one of which my husband was Headmaster, was at the far end of Tortham Road and our estate marked the end of the town and the beginning of the fields. The main house, dominating the four others put up to form dormitories for the boys, really was a mansion. It had been modernized, but the broad Georgian façade, glowing in rose brick at the far end of wide lawns, had been built by a retiring Tinworth banker at the time of the great merger, and it still bore his name.

Buchanan House was a first-class private preparatory school, and little boys came there as boarders from all over the country to be made ready for Tortham College, which could hold its own with – well, if not quite with Eton, at least with most of the others.

Tinworth was delighted with Buchanan House. As a market town with a side line in the manufacture of agricultural imple-ments, it did not set out to be particularly intellectual itself, but it liked its school and liked it all the more because there was nothing state-aided about it. Parents paid and paid highly, and their money went out into the town's trade. Ratepayers, startled by the demands of the County Council for the new education account, felt that was as it should be.

As headmasters go, Victor was young. He was in his late thirties and was thought to be brilliant. Indeed, if all I'd been told was true, Tinworth was prepared to credit him with the brain of an Einstein and the knowledge of an encyclopedia, but that did not prevent it from speculating with uncanny insight about his private life. I was beginning to realize that after my six months of marriage to him.

I was walking very fast, almost running, the shopping basket I carried for show swinging on my arm and my straw hat flapping. I was forgetting my dignity and trying to forget everything else, including the atmosphere I had come out to escape, not to mention my latest irritation, which was the news that Andy Durtham, of all people, was going to take a locum job here in Tinworth for Dr Browning while the old man went on holiday.

Dorothy's letter, mentioning this somewhat startling news amid a host of other gossip from St Jude's, where she was still a Sister, was in my pocket. It had only arrived that morning, but as usual there was no telling when she had written it. Dorothy wrote letters as some people knit woollies, now and again when the mood took her. It was sometimes possible by carefully noting the changes of ink in the closely scribbled pages, to discover if any particular item was some months old or comparatively recent, and I was just wondering if I could pull the untidy bundle out and examine it again there and then in the street when I saw Maureen Jackson thumping down the sidewalk towards me.

Miss Jackson was the Headmaster's secretary and, I suppose, about five years older than I was. The notion that the Head's wife was always older than the Head's secretary had made our relationship, I thought, vaguely awkward at first, but she appeared to have decided to 'settle all that' in her cheerfully efficient way by treating me always with bluff kindliness, as if I was not quite right in the head or a foreigner. So far I had not attempted to enlighten her, because she was Tinworth personified and I was trying very hard to get the hang of Tinworth.

Miss Jackson was the daughter of the town's best auctioneer and estate agent, quite a powerful person in that community, and her relatives seemed to spread into every conceivable branch of the town's affairs. Her grandfather had been Mayor seven times. Her uncle was the owner of the great ironmongers and agricultural engineers in the High Street. Her mother was an Urban District Councillor, and at least two of her brothers were Justices of the Peace.

She came thumping towards me, big, bony, and not uncomely,

with a pink-and-white face and clear cold-blue eyes which were somehow typical of Tinworth in their bland self-satisfied intelligence. She was known as the 'thundering English rose' by the junior masters, whom she used to treat with offhand tolerance. I understood her work was excellent, and she certainly took Victor's acid rebukes with amiable forbearance.

'Morning!' she shouted at me when we were within hailing distance. 'The vac is heaven, isn't it? Or don't you like it?'

Her last question brought her level with me and she did the thing all Tinworth seemed to do, pausing and looking into one's eyes and investing ordinary trivial questions with direct inquiry. As usual it put me slightly at a disadvantage. To say outright that I'd temporarily forgotten that the day before yesterday all the boys and most of the masters had gone home for the summer holidays, and that yesterday the majority of the domestic staff had dispersed also, would be about as silly as mentioning that one had forgotten a recent earthquake or an invasion in arms. On the other hand, if one said that as far as one's own life was concerned it appeared to make no difference at all, I knew a shadow of suppressed excitement would float over that bovine countenance of peaches and cream and she would want to know why. To do it justice, Tinworth never minded asking.

'It's very pleasant,' I said, adding idiotically, 'Are you going to the school?'

'Of course I am. The letters still come, don't they? I should have thought you'd have known that.' There was no impudence in the last observation. It was just another inquiry, a sharp inquisitive inquiry if I'd really forgotten I'd once held down a high-powered secretarial job at St Jude's Hospital myself. Her blue-eyed stare was filled with pure curiosity. I said nothing at all so she had to go on. 'I expect the Headmaster's out of his room by now, isn't he?'

'He was there when I came out,' I told her, adding drily, 'with Mr Rorke.'

'Oh.'

I don't know quite how people bridle, but if it means that an expression both disapproving and self-righteous, if admittedly justi-fied, comes over their faces, Maureen bridled.

'I'd better hurry along. Good-bye, Mrs Lane.'

The thud of her feet was still in my ears, and I had only just had time to remember that at least she had not asked me outright where we were going for our summer holiday, when I saw my next hurdle. Bickky Seckker was advancing demurely down the path towards me, his gold spectacles glinting in the morning sun.

Mr P. F. Seckker was senior classics master at Buchanan House, and the fact that he'd been just that for more years than anyone would like to mention probably accounted for much of the school's reputation. His nickname, a reference to his initials, which were the same as those on a favourite brand of shortcake, indicated his standing with successive generations of boys. Very few masters achieve such an innocent soubriquet.

When I first met him I had assumed he was a very ordinary elderly bachelor, a little old-maidish and perhaps the least bit seedy, but as the months went on I had revised my opinion and was fast coming to think he was the kindest soul I had ever met in my life. He smiled at me, hesitated, made sure that I really did want to stop (which I didn't, of course, but I would have died rather than hurt his feelings), and came out with the one most unfortunate remark which from my point of view he could have made.

'I don't know when you're off for your vacation, Mrs Lane, but my sister and I will be at home here at Tinworth all the holidays and my sister – I mean we – would be delighted if you'd drop in to see us just whenever you feel like it.' He was a little shy, as he always was with what he was apt to describe quite suddenly as 'a very, very pretty woman', and he twinkled and glowed at me as if he were twenty-four and not I. 'Nothing formal, you know,' he chattered on. 'We are too old, and like most other people too poor, for formal entertaining, but my sister was talking to you on Speech Day and she thought that, well, you never know, you might care sometime for a cup of tea in our wailed garden.'

He paused abruptly and to my horror I realized that my face was growing scarlet.

'I – I'd love that,' I said. 'I would like it better than anything. I'm not sure – quite – when we're going away.'

'Naturally.' Now that I had betrayed embarrassment, any shyness of his own was thrust aside and he took social command with all the charm and ease of his kind. 'Of course. Well, you must come when you can. We shall be delighted. I love this warm weather. It suits Tinworth. Some people think it's an ugly town, but I don't. We've got history here, you know. The site of the Roman camp at Mildford is perfectly fascinating. I shall show it to you one day. Much better than half the things one travelled all through France to find.' And then, abruptly, as if he were a gauche old person surprised into speech, 'That blue gown of yours makes your dark eyes darker and puts quite a blue light into that black hair of yours. There, isn't that forward of me?'

The old-fashioned word made me laugh, as I think he knew it would.

'No,' I protested. 'It's charming of you. I feel better and younger already.'

'That would be impossible,' he assured me gravely. 'Until I show you the Roman camp, then.' He raised his polished cherry-wood stick in salute, since he was hatless, and strolled on, leaving me shaken to find that even old Miss Seckker, who was considerably his senior and certainly half blind, should have noticed that I might need a little human comfort in the sanctuary of her garden. Yet I was glad I had met him and was grateful for his compliment.

It was at that precise moment as I turned away that I saw Andy. He was speeding down the road towards me in a well-worn open sports car. We looked straight at each other for an instant as he passed and then I heard the shriek of brakes and the revving of the engine as he swung round in the wide road. In the last few hours I suppose I had envisaged meeting him again in half a hundred possible places. For some reason I had assumed that it would be at some very crowded social gathering, the Agricultural Show perhaps, or one of the eternal sherry parties Tinworth likes so much. I'd even prepared an opening gambit: 'Oh yes, of course I know Dr Durtham. We met at St Jude's. How nice to see you again, Andy.'

To find him pulling up beside me in this vast and now apparently empty street called for an entirely different approach and I was so amazed and so pleased to see him that I couldn't think of anything at all suitable.

'Hullo, animal,' I said.

'Hullo yourself,' he said briefly. 'Get in.'

They say it is impossible to forget anyone you've ever been truly in love with, but it is astounding how easy it is to put out of one's mind the things about them which one loved. One of the things I had succeeded in forgetting about Andy Durtham was his force. He was a big, rakish, intensely masculine person, dark as I am and not ill-looking in a tough untidy way, but his chief characteristic, and I suppose charm, was vital energy. It was a bit overwhelming and there had been a period when I had found it alarming. It seemed to radiate from him almost noisily, as if he were an engine ticking over. He was young, of course, only just qualified.

'Get in,' he repeated, holding the door open for me. 'I want to talk to you.'

'I was going to the High Street.'

'Then I'll take you there. Come on, Liz.'

I had been called Elizabeth so thoroughly by this time that I had forgotten how much I disliked the abominable diminutive. It just sounded friendly today. I stepped into the car and he sighed, let in the clutch, and turned round in the road again.

'Hey,' I protested, 'where are you going? I said the High Street.'

'We're going there, by Morton Road and the by-pass. That's the way I know best. I've only been here a week.'

'A week? I didn't know.'

'Too bad. Nobody tells you anything, do they? But I'm going to, and it's going to take me just about seven minutes, so – we'll go by the by-pass.'

I did not speak. Andy was returning to my conscious mind with a rush, and with a new and painful vividness I remembered why I had written to him and not phoned or arranged a meeting when I finally decided to marry Victor.

'Yes, well,' he said, and his mouth twisted down at the corners as it always did when he was embarking on one of his more outrageous performances, 'lean back and relax, because you're going to take this in if it's the last thing I do. I've been thinking about this lecture very thoroughly for some months and here it comes, piping hot.'

He turned and peered at me from under bristling eyebrows.

'First of all, I suppose you know you've lost twenty pounds.'

It was such an unexpected thrust that it took me by surprise. Until that moment I had been enjoying him, like a beautiful draught of fresh air. Now I was annoyed by his impudence.

'Don't be a boor,' I said. 'I've lost eight.'

'They were the eight which held your looks. The wan white waif act doesn't suit you. Don't touch the wheel. You'll break our necks. Still, I'm glad to see you're not completely devitalized in spite of all I've heard since I've been here.'

I had made no real attempt to touch the wheel, of course. I wasn't a child, and we were travelling very fast and passing all the people I'd met before, but I must have stiffened and I felt the blood in my face.

'How extraordinary of you to take this locum job down here,' I said abruptly. 'When did you leave St Jude's?'

'In my script for this conversation you don't speak.' He was not looking at me. At that moment we were negotiating an unexpectedly narrow turn. The Vicarage car was parked on the corner, as usual, and a milk tanker was attempting to pass. We were held up for a second or two and I found myself face to face with the vicar, who was dithering in front of his aged bonnet with a starting handle. He stared at me, recognized me with open astonishment, and was groping for his hat with his free hand when I was whisked unceremoniously from under his nose.

'You merely listen,' Andy continued, squaring himself as the car leapt forward down the villa-lined length of Morton Road. 'You have made a basic psychological mistake and, having got it clear in my own mind, I intend you to see it. It may not do you much good but you've no idea how it's going to satisfy me! Look, Liz, you never forgave your mother for making a mess of her marriage, did you? You always secretly thought she could have saved it. That's why you made the idiotic mistake of trying to play safe.'

He was speaking with utter sincerity, his tone urgent and forceful, and if instead of speaking he had suddenly pressed a blade directly into my heart I think the pain he gave me must have been exactly the same.

'No,' I said violently, because I wouldn't and couldn't let it be true, 'that's insulting nonsense. For heaven's sake let me get out of here.'

He put on a little more speed and he bounced out into the stream of traffic on the by-pass which Tinworth uses so freely to relieve its own tortuous streets.

'You were in love with me,' he went on doggedly as if I had not spoken. 'Probably you are still, whether you know it or not. But if it's not me it's someone like me, and it always will be.'

He was not looking at me, which was merciful, for we were in traffic, and he ignored any sound I made but continued the harangue exactly as if I were some recalcitrant patient to whom he was in duty bound to report on a considered diagnosis.

'There's a great deal of rubbish talked about the kind of love I mean,' he said. 'It's sublimated and sublimized and sentimentalized and generally kicked around, but the one ordinary elementary fact which is self-evident is that it is an affinity exactly like a chemical affinity. You know the definition of that. You must have typed it for old Beaky Bowers at St Jude's often enough. "*The peculiar attraction between the atoms of two simple substances that makes them combine to form a compound.*" Now I don't suggest that love *is* chemical. I only say that it is *like* it and quite as irrevocable and inescapable. You love something because you need it. It is made up of the things you have not got. You recognize your need instinctively, and instinctively you go for it as soon as you find it. Be quiet. Listen. You can get out when I've finished.'

Since I could do nothing else I sat bolt upright, staring in front of me, the furious blood burning in my face. Since I couldn't keep my hat on in that air stream I took it off and held it in my lap. I tried not to listen, either, but one might as well have tried to ignore an avalanche.

'People keep saying that one is attracted by opposites,' Andy's lecture continued, 'but that is one of those sweeping half-truths which are so misleading. What they mean is that if one hasn't got quite enough of a particular characteristic oneself one is automatically attracted by the person who has a little too much of it. When one finds someone who appears to balance out *all* one's own excesses and deficiencies, one falls in love with her – er, or him.'

He turned to me, his vivid grey-blue eyes dark with intelligence, and dropped his professional manner.

'You must know what I mean, Liz. You've got the warmest heart in the world, but with it you tend to be cautious, intellectual, and reserved. I tend to be headstrong, intuitive, and confiding. You're levelheaded to a fault, I'm on the verge of being wild.'

'Wild –' I was beginning, but he stopped me.

'You're unconventional and oversensitive and gentle. I'm basically unconventional and – well, rough. Cruel, if you like.'

Andy's sincerity had always captured me, holding my attention, forcing me to think along lines I would not normally have chosen. It performed its exasperating magic again now.

I was attracted to you, my lad, because you were alive, I thought, and somehow I don't seem to be very much alive alone. There was no point in saying it aloud, of course, and certainly I was alive enough myself at that moment. I was outraged by him. The tastelessness, the utter impropriety, the insolence all the old-fashioned words crowded on to my tongue, making me temporarily incoherent.

'You happened to need someone like me,' Andy was saying with steady insistence, 'not in spite of my faults but because of them. You couldn't help it.'

'At that rate, nor could you.' Of all the words in the world those were the last I had intended to say. They were silly and dangerous, but in the last few seconds he had got under my skin.

'And so what?' He turned his head and I saw his eyes had become as hard as marbles. 'We're not talking about me. I've had my own problem and I've settled it. I sail in three weeks' time. I'm perfectly all right. I'm simply explaining your position to you because I don't think you've seen it.'

'Sail?' I said, as if it were the only word I'd heard. 'Where are you going?'

'Newfoundland. There's a hell of a lot of work to do there, it's a rough, hard, free country and it'll suit me. George Brewster and his wife are going too. She'll have to do the secretarial work for both of us. It'll be hard going but worth it, I think. Anyhow, all that is beside the point. I'm clearing out of the country and I just wanted to explain the whole thing to you before I went. You didn't give me an opportunity at the time and I don't suppose I should have been able to see it so clearly then if you had.'

'There's nothing for you to explain.' My lips felt stiff as I spoke. We were entering the lower end of the High Street and I gathered my hat and basket with what I felt was a gesture of finality. 'I had merely made up my mind what I thought would be the best for both of us.'

'You'd done nothing of the sort, you know, Liz.' Instead of pulling into the curb he put on a burst of speed which shot us out into the main stream of the morning shopping traffic. I saw several faces I recognized, all of them surprised, but I had no time even to acknowledge them. Andy proceeded to wind his way expertly through the throng of familiar cars, talking all the time in his forceful, forthright way.

'I had a night out with the boys, got in a stupid rag, and finished up at a police station. There was a row at the hospital and I got an imperial raspberry,' he was saying cheerfully. 'It wasn't very clever of me, but it's a thing that happens to young doctors who haven't left medical school quite long enough. It did me no harm, probably a bit of good in the long run because it scared me and showed me I wasn't quite as intelligent as I thought I was. But the harm it did, the real harm, Liz, was that it frightened you.'

I made an inarticulate noise but he took no notice of it.

'It frightened you out of all reason, all proportion,' he said. 'I ought to have understood it and been prepared for it, but I wasn't. You've grown up obsessed by the broken marriage of your parents which spoilt your childhood, and you were determined not to make the same mistake. Therefore, when you saw yourself as you thought in love with a drunken ne'er-do-well (I'm not blaming you, woman, I'm simply clarifying your mind for you) you panicked, and to save yourself from love you took a safe offer which happened to come along at that particular moment.'

'If you'll stop I'll get out,' I said.

'Can't park on the corner. Besides, I haven't finished. We'll go round again. This is the last time I shall ever speak to you and I intend to get this right off my chest.'

We swept out of the main street towards the Tortham Road again and I was suddenly glad. If this was to be a once-and-forever fight I had something to say myself. It welled up inside me in a great wave of self-justification. It was the thing I'd been wanting to explain to the whole of Tinworth – to the world for that matter – for solid months.

'I married as I did because I was determined to make a success of it,' I bellowed, and realizing I was shouting, lowered my voice abruptly. 'You're quite right, in one sense,' I went on, trying to sound reasonable and succeeding only in conveying my savage irritation. 'I did remember Mother. I did remember how a romantic love affair had become a jealous bickering match. I did remember that love can die and a woman and her child can be reduced to dreary misery in the process. I didn't want that kind of marriage. I didn't want the humiliation of any more divorces. Mother's was enough for me. I did remember all that, and therefore I married where I felt I could make a good honest job of it. I wanted to be a good wife and I wanted to stay married. Now do you understand?'

He did not answer immediately and when I looked at him his head was turned a little so that I could only see the angle of his jaw. His face was darker than ever and I was very much aware of the hard angry muscles under the coat sleeve at my side. We were roaring up Tortham Road again by this time and he did not speak until we swung round past the Vicarage once more. Then he said mildly:

'Then it wasn't altogether the row?'

'No, of course it wasn't. That simply cleared my mind, and, as you said, Victor happened to come along at the same moment.' I felt I was gaining my point and couldn't understand why it didn't make me feel happier.

Andy brought the car to a crawl and looked at me curiously.

'You just honestly don't see it, do you, Liz?' He made the observation almost gently. 'You don't want to, of course. That's why you're deceiving yourself. You were afraid of love, old lady, that's what you were escaping from. You wanted something safer.'

His stupidity and obstinacy made me absolutely furious. I had never felt so helpless. For three quarters of a year I had been clarifying my mind in private upon the subject, until I felt I knew all about everything I had ever felt or ever could feel. Now, when I tried to express it for the first time to another human being, it seemed to be going all wrong. To make matters worse, until that moment I should have said that Andy was the easiest person in the world to whom to tell anything. It was his greatest gift, both as a doctor and as a man.

'Look here,' I said, making what I felt was a last attempt to get through the wool, 'call it an ideal, if you like. I had set my heart on a steady, sober, ordinary sort of marriage, something I could make something of.'

'And have you got it?'

The question came out quite naturally and without the least hint of malice. It hit me, of course. I felt the blood go hot in my face. It rose into my hair, making the roots tingle.

'I think so,' I said. 'I mean, of course I have.' There was a pause and I added idiotically, 'Term time is liable to be very busy for Victor.'

He cocked a shrewd eye at me and I realized all over again how very well we two were acquainted. It wasn't going to be easy to hide much from Andy.

'And you haven't had much except term time so far, have you?' he was saying slowly. 'As I hear it, you were married just two days before the spring term began. Your husband had to spend a short vacation at the end of that term on a course at a Swiss university where you couldn't accompany him. And now here you are at the end of the summer session and he's due to go on a mountain-climbing expedition – experts only.'

This shook me and I showed it. I couldn't help it. My mouth fell open. For the past twelve hours or so I had thought that I was the only person to know about this latest bombshell of Victor's, but if Andy had picked up the information in the week he'd been in Tinworth it seemed I was rather late off the mark. I was so amazed I forgot to be humiliated. Some sort of preservative sixth sense was working, however, and I spoke promptly.

'Victor has explained. That was arranged a Long time ago. You

111

seem to know a great deal about us.'

'Only what everybody tells me.' He gave me a sudden disarming grin. 'This is my first experience of a provincial town. You seem to have got yourself in a fine old parrot house, ducky. They're wonderful, aren't they? Every man his own detective. No mystery too small! Do you *like* them, Liz?'

'I don't know any of them very well, yet,' I said evasively. 'They're all right. Not terribly exciting.' My mind was beginning to work again. I told myself it was all very unfortunate meeting Andy, and he was behaving abominably, but here was a chance to find out exactly where I did stand with the town. At least I knew him well enough to know he wouldn't lie. I began with great caution. 'There isn't much outside entertainment in a place like this,' I said. 'People talk about their neighbours because there isn't much else to interest them. Sometimes they get things rather wrong.' I hesitated. He didn't speak. 'I don't know what you've heard about me?'

'About you?'

'Well, about us generally. What is the gossip? You seem to have the impression that there is some. Let me straighten it out for you.'

He had the grace to look uncomfortable but to my relief he didn't avoid the direct question.

'There's no gossip, exactly.' He bent forward to push a bundle of untidy memo slips and prescription pads back in the locker in the dashboard, so that I could see only his cheek. It had coloured a little. 'There's no "talk", old girl, nothing to worry about'

'No, but what do they actually say?'

'Oh, they're only intrigued,' he said at last.

'About Victor's marriage? Do they mind him marrying? Do they object to a city girl?'

'Oh no, no, nothing like that. You've got it wrong, Liz.' He was looking at me earnestly now, desperately anxious not to be clumsy and hating being involved. I knew it served him right but I was almost sorry for him.

'Well?' I persisted.

'It's the set-up which they find so interesting,' he began at last. This husband of yours is a well-known local man who for years seemed set to remain a bachelor. He seems to have run his life and his school to a very firmly fixed schedule. The school runs like a machine and his own holidays have followed the same hidebound pattern. At week-ends he plays golf hard and actually has a cottage near the links to save time. On the Easter vacation he goes on some university course designed to fill it. In the long summer holidays he goes on an expedition up a mountain with a team of which he is the president, and at Christmas he has a three weeks' cultural whirl in London or Paris. Tinworth knew all about his programme and was used to it'

He eyed me to see if I was agreeing with him and I made my face impassive.

'Well,' he went on, 'think of it. One day this lad turns up with a beautiful young wife who appears to have been something of an organizer herself, and who looks and sounds as if she might have some ideas of her own. Naturally everyone sits up waiting to see the changes.' He paused and gave me one of his shrewder stares. 'As far as they can see, there haven't been any changes. He seems to be living exactly the same sort of – well, somewhat self-absorbed life he always did. Tinworth is dying to know what you're making of it, that's all.'

It was his tone on the last two words which made me look up. Until then he had told me nothing that I did not know rather too well, except that I had not realized that Tinworth saw things quite so clearly; but something in that last little phrase struck an alarm bell in my mind.

'It sounds as if it wasn't all,' I murmured, and added, 'You never were any good at hiding things.'

'I'm not hiding anything.' He spoke a trifle too loudly but a set- tled obstinacy had spread over his face and I knew I should get nothing more out of him. 'I've said too much anyway,' he insisted. 'I was merely trying to point out that although your neighbours down here do seem to be a pack of chatty old geese, I don't think they're entirely unreasonable. After all, people always do sit round a marriage and watch who wins, that's natural.'

'They think I'm losing, I suppose?'

'They think you needn't lie down under the steam roller and quite frankly neither do I. There's no need to lose all that weight, surely? And usen't your hair to have a wave in it – at the sides, I mean?'

That did it. It was that bit of silly masculine clumsiness coming just at the right moment which saved me from going to pieces and telling him the whole story. I might so easily have tried to explain what it felt like to drop feet foremost into just such a machine as he had described, and just how impossible it was to reason with or to cajole a man who never had a moment to hear one. I might also have indulged in the bad taste of recounting what happened when one tried to stage a full-scale row, as I had on the evening before when the news that 'of course' the alpine expedition would take place as usual had been given me so casually. I might also have dilated upon the difference between a man who is merely cold and one who seemed to have nothing to be warm with ... a man one couldn't even make angry. As it was, I was so hurt, I said nothing whatever.

Andy turned the car slowly into the High Street again and edged slowly in to the curb.

'It hasn't turned out as I meant it to,' he said abruptly. 'I've been obsessed with the desire to get things off my chest, and now that I've done it it doesn't seem to have got us anywhere. Honestly, I didn't just want to add to any difficulties you may have, Liz.' He was silent for a moment and then said awkwardly, with the idea of making amends, no doubt, 'I think you'll like to know that nobody blames you for the whirlwind courtship. This fellow, he – er, your husband, has tremendous charm and drive, they say ...'

By this time I was shaking with some emotion which I vaguely supposed was anger. I heard myself cutting in with a very stupid and revealing statement:

'At least the confirmed bachelor did ask me to marry him, Andy. In all the excitement over our private affairs, no one seems to have offered an explanation for that rather important point.' I was looking full at Andy as I spoke and I saw his expression. He looked suddenly guilty. So the gossips had a neat little explanation for that too, had they? Whatever it was, he was not repeating it. He hopped out of the car and came round to open the door for me. Standing on the pavement, we shook hands very formally. 'Good-bye Andy,'

I said. 'I don't suppose I'll see you again.'

He stood looking down at me gloomily and there was nothing but emptiness all round us.

'No,' he said at last, 'no, Liz, I don't suppose you will. Sorry about all this. Silly of me. Good-bye, old lady, good luck.'

We each turned away abruptly at the same moment and I walked off down the crowded pavement, unaware what I looked like and without seeing anyone at all. Yet when I reached the chain store on the corner I went in and bought myself one of those cheap home perm outfits. It was something of a gesture because Victor considered all beauty treatments a waste of time and slightly vulgar, and I had had no money to spare for them since my marriage.

I was standing in the queue at the cash desk, still feeling as if there was a good stiff layer of ice between me and the rest of the world, when Hester Raye pounced upon me.

There may be Hester Rayes in other parts of the earth, but she has always seemed to me to belong quite peculiarly to a certain small section of present-day society in southern England. Her husband, Colonel Raye, was Chief Constable of the county (the police always seemed to choose a retired army man to command them) and she herself had sprung from army stock. At fifty she was still good-looking. Neither time nor experience had bequeathed her any tact whatever, and her intense interest in other people did not seem to have taught her anything important about them at all. She ploughed through the small-town life of Tinworth like an amiable tank.

Her smiling eyes, which looked so misleadingly intelligent, shone into mine.

'Buying yourself something to make you look pretty? That's right, never give up. I never have.' it was a typical pronouncement, guaranteed at best to be misunderstood, and at the same moment she gave my arm a squeeze which would have startled a bear. 'I was talking about you only the other day to someone – I forget who, but it was someone quite intelligent – and I said then I did hope you wouldn't let your husband dry all the life and youth out of you – for you're quite beautiful, you know; you are really when you take trouble – but that you'd stand up to him and get a little life of your own however selfish he is. He's *so* charming, isn't he, and *such* a villain ...'

I had heard her talk as frankly as this to other acquaintances and I had wondered how on earth one responded to the bland; patronizing gush which yet had a sort of outrageous bonhomie in it. Now I understood the fishlike stares which I had observed on the faces of her victims. There was no protection one could devise against her at all. She was a product of the twenties, when it had been fashionable to say the unforgivable thing, and like the little girl who grimaced in the nursery story, the wind had changed and she had stayed like it. I remember thinking vaguely that it was quite clear that she meant well, and perhaps that was why no one had ever gone berserk and killed her.

'Are you going back now? she demanded. 'Because if you are I'll give you a lift. I've got the car outside. I've often seen you walking down Tortham Road and I've said, "I bet he doesn't even let that sweet girl drive his car in the morning." No, don't run away. I want to make you promise you'll come to the Flower Club meeting tomorrow. I've gone to fantastic lengths to get Judith Churchman down to lecture on the modern trend in flower decoration, and I just must have a big audience. You did promise, you know.'

'I'll be there.' I realized I had shouted at her a second too late to do anything about it. The avalanche of dropped bricks had been too much for me altogether. I must have looked rather wild as well, for to my dismay she decided I was having a nerve storm.

'Oh, you poor child,' she said, her grip on me tightening. 'Come along. I insist. I'll drive you home. You're terribly brave to put such a good face on things, you know. Everybody says so.'

'Then I think everybody's making rather a silly mistake.' I walked along beside her as I spoke and climbed into her car. There had been more cold venom in my tone than I thought I could summon and I noted her startled expression with deep satisfaction. 'People who discuss couples whom they don't know at all often make utter and rather offensive fools of themselves, don't you think?'

She did not answer. The colour had come into her face and she made a great business of starting up and getting out into the traffic.

However, I had reckoned without her powers of resilience. Before we had gone fifty yards she was herself again.

'You don't know how you surprised me or how pleased I am,' she announced with gay naïveté. 'We'd all been pitying you, you know. Wasn't it dreadful of us? I expect it'll make you furious, but it's terribly funny really. Of course we've all known Victor for years, that's why. You've got him right under your thumb, have you? Good for you, my dear. He's going to give up that old summer expedition and take you somewhere, is he?'

'He's not going on the expedition.' The words came out with a conviction which was completely unjustified, particularly in view of the few chill words Victor and I had had on the subject the evening before. Victor never had a row. That was one of the few things I had come to learn about him so painfully in the past few months. He simply stated his intention. Usually that was enough. However, as soon as I spoke to Mrs Raye that morning I realized that I had started some intentions too, and I knew that the expedition would have to be the issue which settled things between me and Victor for good and all. She gave me an odd little glance and I met it steadily, in fact our eyes watched each other until hers dropped. After a while she giggled.

'My dear, how wonderful! Just to see you about, you know, one wouldn't dream that you had it in you. You sounded positively sinister.' She laughed, as far as I could tell with genuine amusement, and settled down to be cosily confidential. This really is quite terrific and I'm terribly glad because we've all been thinking that it was rather mean of Victor getting married suddenly like that to silence all the talk, but then we never realized you *knew*. We all thought that you were the complete little innocent, you see.'

She was watching the road ahead and did not see my face, which was fortunate. She drove with the same calm effrontery with which she seemed to conduct her social life, and while she forced her way through a bunch of traffic I had time to grasp what she was telling me.

Victor's sudden decision to find a wife had been occasioned by his desperate need to silence some sort of gossip which threatened, presumably, his position at the school. That was the part of the story which Andy had forborne to mention. I knew it was true as soon as Mrs Raye spoke. It explained so much about Victor and my life with him, and made so clear and even forgivable the attitude of the townsfolk towards me. So that was it. That was the solution to the one mystery which, until now, had given me some sort of justification, some sort of hope for my ridiculous ideal for a safe, sound marriage, based on something more solid than the dangerous sands of love. Now I could see exactly the sort of fool I'd been.

To my relief I discovered that I was quite past feeling hurt. I had had more than I could take already that morning, and now I found myself in that quiet grey country which is on the the the other side of pain. I was hard and uncharacteristically shrewd and quick-witted.

'Oh, I think any bachelor in a small town like this is hopelessly vulnerable to gossip,' I remarked lightly, 'but I hardly see poor Victor as the local Don Juan, I'm afraid.' In my tone there was just enough contempt for the wild life of Tinworth to arouse her. I found that once one decided to pull no punches she was almost simple to manage. She rose to the bait at once.

'Oh, don't you be so sure,' she said, quite forgetting who I was, apparently, in her anxiety to make her point. 'He's been awfully well behaved lately, of course, but *last winter* ...! Well, there never is any smoke without fire, is there? Besides, you can't tell *me*. What about that little hidey-hole he has out on the road to Latchendon?'

The cottage by the golf course?' I said wonderingly.

'Golf course!' she exploded. 'What other man wants a cottage to play golf in?'

It occurred to me that she had something there, and that either I'd been born blind or was ripe for the half-wit home. But to do Victor justice, I'd been shown over the place, which was a very primitive little affair, and had understood it was merely an escape from the school for an occasional semi-camping week-end. I knew he'd lent it to a couple of masters once or twice during term, and it had been used for school picnics. It had certainly never struck me as being anything in the light of a love nest. But now that she mentioned it, I could see that it was perhaps a rather odd place for him to possess, little more than a couple of miles out of town.

'What is he supposed to take up there?' I demanded. 'Strings of dancing girls?'

I suppose the bitterness showed through. Anyway, it was not an intelligent thing to have said, for she gave me a sudden wary glance and began to retract, stumbling over herself in her anxiety.

'Oh, I'm not saying there was anything wrong, my dear. I only spoke of the talk, and how grateful he must be to you that that's all died down. Tinworth isn't narrow-minded. After all, none of us are saints, are we?'

She gave me a roguish smile which belonged all to the 1920s and pulled up beside the school gates.

'I thought *your* boy friend was very handsome this morning, for instance. Had you met him before? You seemed to be getting along very well.'

She caught me off guard and I felt my expression growing horror-stricken. She laughed outright at that and touched my arm.

'Round and round the town, every time one came out of a shop there you were tearing down the road with your heads together. You can't say you don't know who I mean. He's doing a locum for Dr Browning, isn't he? Somebody pointed you both out to me this morning and said so, I forget who. Well, don't cut the Flower lecture tomorrow, will you? So long, my dear, and I shall tell everybody that we were quite wrong about you. I think you're quite wonderful …'

The car slid away without my having to say anything at all, which was merciful in the circumstances.

The rose-red buildings looked forbidding and forlorn as schools do out of term time. The shaven grass was well worn and although there was no litter or untidiness about, yet the place had all the shabby sadness of a deserted nursery. I walked along the side path, aware of the heat haze and of the loneliness, but principally conscious that I had no place there. This was not my home. However much I tried, it would never have room for me.

I passed under the main arch which had been constructed through the house into the quadrangle behind without seeing a soul, but instead of going straight to the Headmaster's Lodging, which was in the centre of the block on the southern side, I passed by it and went on to the narrow gate behind the chapel. I had got to have things out once and for all with Victor, but I wanted to be quite sure of myself first. There must be no tears or other signs of hysteria in that interview, and I needed a little more time to collect myself.

Behind the chapel lay all those utility buildings, old and new, which did not fit into the main architectural scheme. The boiler houses were there, and the glasshouses and the swimming pool, the disused stables and the laundries, all huddled together in a fine muddle of old elegance and new necessity. I went into the stables, and as my footsteps sounded on the bricks there was a single shrill bark from the farther loose-box. Izzy was in my arms a moment later, bounding up on his short legs, his hard brindled body wriggling in ecstasy. This wild greeting nearly broke my heart, it was so uncharacteristic of his dour Scotty personality. A year before he would never have lowered his dignity by anything more than a discreet wagged tail at my arrival, but then at that time we had never been apart during his lifetime. This kennel business was part of Victor's discipline. He had been very nice about it but very firm. I had seen that if the boys were not allowed pets in the school I could hardly expect to have mine at large, and so very comfortable quarters were arranged for Izzy and I took him for walks every day. It was very nice, but just not our idea of life, that was all. Poor Izzy and poor Liz, both victims of the same silly mistake. However, this was the end of all that. I had decided it.

I set Izzy down and left the door of the box wide.

'Come on, I said, 'you get a bath after lunch. You smell like a dog.'

He peered at me from under his fierce old-man eyebrows and the little black eyes which had earned him his pet name were shining and hopeful. He bounded a little, very clumsily as Scotch terriers do, and then parked himself at my heels in complete content. Where I was going, so was he. I felt much better with him behind me.

We came back together and were crossing the yard when the door of the shower room, which was next to the pool, was shattered open and a most unexpected person came reeling out almost on top of us. It took me a moment or two to recognize Mr Rorke, our much-discussed science master. It was generally understood that Rorke, although admittedly brilliant, possessed what was euphemistically described as an 'unfortunate failing'. Until now I had never taken the story seriously. I had only seen the gaunt white-faced scarecrow of a man at meals in the dining-hall, and perhaps twice at the dreary functions which were described as the 'Headmaster's coffee party', and then he had seemed to me to be a harmless and even a pathetic figure. I had supposed somewhat vaguely that his transgressions took the form of quiet tippling in the secrecy of his room, and was quite unprepared for this spectacular performance so early in the day. Moreover, he appeared to have attempted to remedy matters by taking a shower, at least from the waist upwards, but as he had omitted to remove even his jacket for the operation his condition now was pitiful. I never saw a man in such a mess. His hair hung over his eyes in a damp mass and he was shaking violently. Izzy drew back and began to growl and I hesitated, uncertain whether it would be kindest to offer assistance or to ignore him altogether. To my dismay he paused directly in my path and shook a wavering acid-stained hand at me.

'You too,' he shouted, 'you too.'

I did not quite gather the rest of the sentence. It sounded as if he prophesied that I should or should not be sorry, I was not sure which.

'You go and change and lie down,' I commanded, summoning all the authority I could muster. 'You'll feel better.' But my tolerance faded suddenly and the smile was wiped off my face.

Through his tousled hair his eyes peered at me with an intensity which was intelligent and menacing. I drew back involuntarily and he swung away and lurched off down the yard towards the back gates. I looked after him, wondering if I ought not to do something to see he came to no harm, or if it would be unwise to interfere. Izzy settled the matter by prodding me firmly in the ankle with his wet nose. It was one of his most characteristic gestures and meant 'get along out of here'. It reminded me that I had troubles of my own to attend to, so I collected myself and went along to the Lodging to find Victor.

As Izzy and I entered the light, white-painted hall where the parquet shone with hygienic cleanliness, the silence of the building descended on me like a tangible cloak. In the normal way the house was full of hurrying people, and the chatter of typewriters from the school office never seemed to cease. But all was quiet now and still in the sunlight. It was a queer little dwelling, designed for its purpose by the architect who had converted the mansion. On the ground floor there were two rooms, one on either side of the square hall. One was the office, the other was the Headmaster's study. On the floor above was a drawing-room for the Headmaster's entertaining, a very small dining-room, a bachelor bedroom and bath. One floor higher still was a little suite of three rooms for the use, presumably, of any family the Headmaster might want to tuck away up there. Until my arrival it had been deserted. Now I lived there, for the most part of the time alone. There was no housekeeping. We came under school management. The school servants kept the house clean. We fed in hall with the boys during the day, and in the evenings our meal was sent up from the school kitchens and served with due ceremony by the head steward. Victor had always lived like that and had seemed horrified when, early in the present term, I had suggested that I might install a small kitchen of my own. I suppose I ought to have put my foot down over some of these points, but when one is fighting against the conviction that one has made a really big mistake, one is apt to be unduly cautious about making small ones, so I had concentrated on trying to make a go of things, on fitting in and giving way. It had got me exactly nowhere. I was getting that into my head at last.

Well, if it was to be settled once and for all, the sooner the better. I pulled myself together and walked into the study. I did not knock, as I usually did in case Victor was interviewing somebody. Term was over and I was in my own house.

But there was no one at the big desk which spread so importantly over the far half of the carpet. The tall windows draped with formal curtains were closed. The room was airless and deserted. It was anticlimax and I was turning to go out again when a smothered gasp from the fireplace on my left brought me wheeling round towards it.

Mr Seckker was kneeling on the hearthrug, surprised in the very act of burning something in the empty grate, for a thin blue wand of smoke still wavered up the chimney as I looked. For a second he stared at me, dismay on his prim, wrinkled face, but he recovered himself at once and hopped up with quite remarkable agility to stand smiling at me with all his wonted courtliness, although he took care, I noticed, to step between me and the fireplace.

'Oh, it's you, Mrs Lane,' he said easily. 'I thought for a moment it was the Headmaster returning. I don't know that I shall wait for him after all. I can come up tomorrow.'

'Is Victor out?' I said in surprise. 'I've just come back from the town. I didn't meet him.'

'Then he must have gone the other way, musn't he?' he said, twinkling at me. 'I was in my classroom and I saw him drive out of the gates – when was that? Let me see, half an hour ago perhaps. I came in here to bring him some books and settled down to wait with my pipe. I flicked a match into the grate and I'm afraid I set light to some litter which was there. I was just seeing it was all right when you came in.'

He made the unnecessary explanation with bland charm and even waved a palpably empty pipe at me by way of corroboration. I nodded absently. Whatever he was doing, it had nothing to do with me. I was thinking of Victor.

'You don't know where he's gone, do you?' I said. 'I mean, he'll be in to lunch, won't he?'

'I really don't know.' He looked astounded at my ignorance and faintly disapproving. I realized that Mr Seckker's sister knew to the hour and second when her brother would be in to a meal. 'I've not seen him myself this morning. He was closeted in here with Rorke when I arrived and so I went up to my classroom. Then I saw him go out. Dear me, it's past twelve. I must get back.'

He glanced behind him at the fireplace with misleading casualness and, seeing, no doubt, that all was well, came across the room to me. As he passed I suddenly remembered.

'Oh yes,' I said, 'Mr Rorke. I suppose he'll be all right?'

'All right?' He stopped in his tracks and stared at me with sudden sternness. 'What do you mean by that?'

I told him of my encounter in the stable yard and as he listened I got the impression that he was relieved rather than scandalized.

'Wet, was he?' he said, laughing a little in a dour elderly way. 'Oh yes, he'll be all right, silly fellow. Don't give him another thought, Mrs Lane. Good morning.' Half-way across the hall he glanced back. 'Please don't bother the Headmaster with any message from me. I may or may not drop in tomorrow. The matter I was going to mention to him is of no importance.' Without actually saying so he made me realize that it was a definite request and I said, 'I won't then.'

He still hesitated and finally added, with a diffidence which was quite charming: 'Unless you feel you ought, I don't think I should bother him about Rorke either. He's a silly young juggins, but it's not strictly term time, although he was on school premises ...'

'Of course,' I said. 'I shouldn't dream of mentioning it to him.'

'Ah.' It was a satisfied little sound. He gave me a nod which was almost a bow, and pattered off, letting himself quietly out of the house and closing the door behind him. I started upstairs, the little brindled shadow which was Izzy close at my heels, and smiled at his description of Rorke, who must have been close on the, to me, impossible age of forty if I was any judge at all. The sudden vista of years all to be spent in the aridity of Buchanan House took me by surprise, and to my dismay I felt if not a scream at least a protesting squeak rising up in my throat. I blushed at myself. Things were getting me down farther than I had supposed. I realized this afresh when Izzy's low growl behind me made me start so violently that I almost stepped on him.

'What is it, boy?' I said, and at the same moment I heard from above us the clatter of footsteps on the parquet of the dining-room, and the school housekeeper, Miss Richardson, came bustling out on to the landing.

'Oh, there you are, Mrs Lane,' she said. 'I'm so glad to have caught you. I thought I should have to go without saying goodbye, and I did want to tell you what I've arranged.'

I stared at her. In all my time at the school I don't suppose we had exchanged half a dozen words. In the very beginning Victor had made it clear to me that one of the dangers of my position at the school was that the domestic staff, who were the employees of the governors, might suspect me of intrusion, with the result, of course, that I had avoided any contact with them. I'm afraid I had hardly dared recognize this plump middle-aged woman, with her strings of domestic science diplomas, as an ordinary human being. I had passed her occasionally in the grounds, looking very aloof in her black skirt and twin set, and we had shown our teeth at each other in polite mirthless smiles. Now I scarcely recognized her in a pale grey linen suit with a white flower on her lapel and a smart white straw set pertly on her glossy dark hair. She had a warm voice, I noticed for the first time, and, now that she was in holiday mood, real gaiety in her smile.

'I couldn't find you anywhere this morning, and the Headmaster was engaged, so I couldn't ask when you were going off,' she rattled on. 'I was a bit worried, but I've done what I think will suit you. Williams will be caretaking all through the holiday …'

'That's the porter.'

She looked at me as if I were demented. 'Yes, you know, the man at the lodge. He'll be there all the vacation and he'll have the keys. Mrs Williams is always very anxious to help, and if you should come back at any time you can always send her a card and she'll get the place aired and have a meal for you. But I was really worrying about the next day or so before you go. I've fixed up for Mrs Veal, who is the best of our charwomen, to come in tomorrow morning to see what you need. I've had some cold lunch laid here now, and if you'll just leave everything she'll see to it …'

Her voice trailed away and died before the expression on my face, which I suppose was utterly blank.

'You did *know*, I suppose?' she demanded abruptly.

It was one of those purely feminine questions which seemed to have 'I thought so' lingering somewhere in their depths, and it pulled me together at once.

'If you mean, had I realized that the whole of the staff was going on holiday today, I'm afraid I hadn't,' I said, trying to sound easy and casual, as if minor items of this kind meant nothing to me. 'I was thinking of last vacation.'

'Oh but that was Easter, the short vac. We don't bother to disrupt the working arrangements for three weeks or so. But this is a long holiday, nearly nine weeks.'

'Yes, yes, of course,' I said hurriedly. 'Well, thank you tremendously. I'll look out for Mrs Veal and ...'

'How long do you expect to stay here, Mrs Lane?' She was watching me with black-fringed candid eyes.

'I – I'm not sure at the moment'

She did not seem to hear me but went on as though she had made up her mind to say something and was going through with it at all costs.

'I asked because some weeks ago when I mentioned the holidays to the Headmaster he told me that he would be going off to the Continent almost immediately the term ended, and that you would probably leave at the same time to stay with friends in London. That's why I haven't consulted you before. Do believe me, Mrs Lane, it wasn't until last night, when I realized that you hadn't made any arrangements yet – about travelling, I mean – that I began to worry how you'd get on. This morning I tried to find you, but when I discovered I'd missed you I went ahead and made the best arrangements I could.'

'It was very kind of you,' I said, and meant it.

'Not at all. I feel terrible about it.' She gave up all pretences and was appealing to me for my confidence. 'I wish I'd known you weren't going off somewhere at once. I'd have done anything, I would really. I'd have stayed myself.'

'Don't be silly,' I said cheerfully. 'You go and catch – your train and have a wonderful time. Where are you going?'

'Devon,' she said, and made it sound like a prayer. Then she caught my eye and actually blushed, so that I got a glimpse of fuchsia hedges and bowls of clotted cream and someone waiting for her, no doubt.

She glanced at her watch and fled, but at the bottom of the stairs she looked back.

'You'll have to order some milk,' she called up to me. 'Mrs Veal will get it if you tell her how much you want. Good-bye.'

The door closed behind her and the house became so quiet that even the warm sunlight seemed eerie. I had never known a place to feel quite so empty. I sat down on the top step of the, stairs because I happened to be standing there, and Izzy sat beside me. My first thought was that it wasn't true. 'Men don't behave like that,' I said aloud. But they do to their wives, said a voice in my mind. Don't be silly; you read it every day in the newspapers. Besides, it's so like Victor, isn't it? Just quietly arranging to get his own way without considering anyone else in the world. Victor doesn't get involved in arguments or explanations. He just fixes up to avoid giving any. Sometimes he goes to considerable lengths in this direction, getting married for instance. By all accounts that must have avoided one father and mother of an argument.

I felt myself growing very hot and presently I got up slowly and mounted the stairs to my own rooms. Sitting before my dressing-table, I looked dispassionately at the pale, thin-faced creature in the glass until I awoke a gleam of courage in her eyes. After a while we even laughed at each other.

'Well, he'll be in for lunch in a minute and this is the one argument he isn't going to avoid, my dear,' I said. 'I'd go and get a rolling-pin – if we had a kitchen.'

That was just before one o'clock. By a quarter past three it had become evident that wherever Victor was lunching it wasn't at home. He'd side-stepped again, very neatly, very completely. It was typical.

Izzy and I had some of the cold food which Miss Richardson had so kindly left for us, and afterwards I stacked the two plates and left them on the minute sideboard and tidied the table. There was nowhere to wash up unless one used the bathroom.

By this time I had begun to hate myself and the house even more, so I thought I'd walk it off. Just round the school the fields were dull and highly cultivated but about half a mile farther down the road there was a lane that led to the water meadows which cradled our local river. It would be cool down there and lonely, I thought, a good place to think things out and get myself reorientated. Everyone in Tinworth who was not actually infirm owned a bicycle and I was no exception. I got it out of the shed next to the stable where Izzy had lived so long and put him in the basket. He was too big for it and he made the handlebars wobble, but his legs were rather short for fast running and the main road was very hard for his pads. He was used to this form of transport, so he sat very still, his ears flat, and tried, I was certain, to adjust his weight to the balance. One of the gardeners was sweeping near the back gates and he swung them open for us. I saw his surprise as we appeared and his grin as we passed him. Taking advantage of the pause, he pulled a watch out of his pocket and glanced at it to see how much more he had of the afternoon. It was an insignificant incident. I don't know why I noticed it.

There was very little traffic on the high road and once we entered the lane we did not see a soul. I rode on until the going became too rough, and afterwards left the bike in the hedge and walked on to the stile. Izzy was delighted and showed it in his own sedate way, by taking short meaningless runs through the lush grass, his head ploughing up and down through the green as if he were swimming.

It was Andy who, long before in a London park, had pointed out that Izzy was like a very small old-fashioned railway engine, squat, rusty, and quite incredibly heavy. I smiled at the recollection and dismissed it hastily. I was determined to put Andy right out of my mind. He had loved me and I had jilted him and he had got over it. That was all there was to that story and to think about it now would be to complicate things quite unbearably.

'*I did love you once*' The line from *Hamlet* came back unbidden, the most cruel thing man had ever said to woman, my English mistress had once remarked in a moment of uncharacteristic self-revelation. A whole classful of girls had gaped at her, but she had been right. I knew it now. Andy had said that, almost in as many words, and he'd made it worse by not even meaning to be unkind. I did not blame him. I was just going to forget him, that was all.

I wandered on beside the running water and Izzy puffed and grunted beside me. It was a glorious afternoon, sleepy and golden, and I discovered that I was being careful to think only of immediate things, like the moor hen I disturbed or the lark I tried to see high in the white-flecked blue. It would not do. There was one vital issue I had got to face and the sooner the better if I was going to have it out with Victor. Was it to be divorce, or was I going to sit down under this slow-starvation marriage for the rest of my life?

I lay down on the bank where the turf was short and let my hand dangle in the water, and Izzy came and sat beside me, panting, until he found how to get his nose down to lap. Theoretically the thing was perfectly simple. I had made a hash of getting married and the sensible thing to do was to cut my losses and clear out and get a job. Any civilized young woman of the Western Hemisphere surely knew that by this time. Yet now that I was up against the reality I found there was a remarkable difference between knowing and doing. It may have been just the failure I didn't want to face. Everybody, all my friends, anyone who had ever known me, knew that I was unreasonably terrified of divorce. What Andy had said about me was true. Mother's divorce had coloured my entire outlook from babyhood, and now, although I saw my foolishness, I also saw that one couldn't alter oneself just by knowing one was silly. I still hoped to cling to the crazy idea that somehow I could make it come all right. All the same ... Victor would never alter. That was the conviction I'd been fighting off for weeks. People don't alter. They may with enormous difficulty modify themselves, but they never really change. I'd got myself married to an overbearing selfish man with a masterful personality, and unless I got away from him he'd reduce me to the colourless cipher he needed as a front-of-the-house wife.

But there again ... was it so easy to *get* a divorce? This was England, not one of those countries where a thoroughly unhappy marriage is considered to be, by and large, fair ground for an appeal. If Victor did not help, and I did not think he would for a moment, then I might easily merely provoke a scandal which would ruin his career and leave me tied to him irrevocably for the rest of my life ... or his.

Oh, dear God, I thought, it is difficult, too difficult. I put my head down in the warm grass and shut out everything from my mind but the sound of the gently lapping water. The sun was warm on my back. Izzy waddled over and settled his hard little body against my shoulder. The river sang softly, lipperty-lapperty, lipperty-lapperty....

I woke cold and stiff, and astounded to find it nearly dusk.

Doubtless it was the air, following all the emotional upset, which had put me out. At any rate, I had slept deeply and dreamlessly for heaven knows how long and might have stayed there half the night had not Izzy's patience given out. He prodded my ear gently until I sat up and stared about me. Even if one has nothing in the world to do, one feels guilty at dropping off to sleep unintentionally, and I got up in a fine flurry and set off back to the stile and the bicycle with as much haste as if I had a nurseryful of youngsters to feed. I had no idea what the time was but when we reached the high road one of the cars which passed us had its sidelights on.

I had guessed the back gates of the school would be closed, but the big main ones in front were locked also and I had to rouse Williams in his lodge beside them to get in. He was astonished to see me, and apologetic.

'I thought we was on our own, me and the missis,' he said, his little bright eyes peering at me from out of a mass of wrinkles. 'Thought you'd all gorn. The Guv'nor's out, you know. Leastways, his car ain't in the garridge because I've been to look. 'E's not back.'

There was something in his manner, or else I imagined it, which was infuriatingly knowing. It seemed to epitomize the whole of Tinworth's attitude towards me, a sort of pitying condescension, an inquisitive commiseration. It got under my skin.

'I didn't suppose he would be,' I said, and was shocked by something odd in my own tone. I had tried to sound casual and had changed it at the last moment for authority. Williams seemed interested.

'Shall I leave the gates, then?'

I hesitated and he stood waiting.

'What d'ye think?' he inquired at last, and added 'ma'am' as an afterthought.

'Yes, leave them open,' I said. It won't do any harm. Good night.'

'Good night, m'm,' I heard him muttering as he bent down to fix the gate-stop. 'Harm?' he was saying. 'Harm?'

The house was dark and quiet as a grave. No one had been in. Everything was just as I had left it. I took Izzy upstairs with me. This was too bad of Victor altogether. I assumed he was punishing me for even daring to try to stand up to him on the evening before. The situation was crazy. I realized it now that I'd faced the problem and slept on it.

Meanwhile Izzy had begun to utter that distinctive Scotty mew which is at once the most apologetic and yet the most demanding sound in the world.

'Well,' I said, 'there's the remains of lunch, chum. We'll go into housekeeping tomorrow when we see what the form is.'

Dinner was on the drab side and Izzy enjoyed it more than I did. There was nothing but tepid water out of the bathroom tap to drink, and I discovered that the main boilers from which we were supplied were out and there was no hot water. Finally I had a brain wave and went down to the secretary's room. There I discovered what I expected. Tucked away in a cupboard was a small tin kettle and a half-full packet of tea. There was sugar there and a cup, but no milk, and a gas ring in the fireplace. I made tea.

It was while I was drinking the abominable stuff, and fighting the unreal atmosphere of the empty school buildings crowding in all round me, that it occurred to me that if Victor had been an ordinary human being he would at least have left me a message. If he had it would have been a note. He was a man of notes and the whole school seemed to copy him. At Buchanan House no one ever seemed to use a phone or send a verbal message. If they were going to be late for dinner, or the team had won a match, or a leak had been discovered in a bathroom, someone sat down and wrote someone else a little note about it. There was no sign of an envelope upstairs but it occurred to me that he might have left one for me in his study and I went in there to see. There was nothing on the mantelshelf and I went over to the desk and crossed round behind the big chair. There were no loose papers, no miscellany, and certainly no note propped for me to find. Everything was meticulously tidy, as if its owner had cleared up before he left. The only sign of use was the blotter, well inked over because Victor was careful over small matters like stationery and did not have it changed until he had to.

I glanced at it casually and suddenly stood transfixed, my heart jolting on a long and painful beat.

One of my minor accomplishments is that I can read what is called 'mirror writing' quite easily. I had been the overworked editor of a school magazine which had been produced on one of those home-made jelly duplicators, and I had learned the trick to facilitate corrections. Now, as I stood staring at the blotter, a message in Victor's precise handwriting stood out from the rest with startling vividness.

'Thursday the 27th then, my darling. Until … rest assu .. love you … difficult … know that. Always, V.'

I glanced up from the message to the desk calendar, which was neatly kept to date: 'Thursday, July' and underneath a huge red '27'.

I ought to have been furious, sick, outraged. The conventional streak in me which Andy had pointed out was aware of all the right reactions, but I felt none of them. I felt freed.

I suppose it was the generations of proud law-abiding religious women behind me whose legacies were deep in me, forming my reactions despite any fancy thinking which I might be doing on my own account, who suddenly let up and washed their hands of Victor. I realized I could go. I was absolved. I could depart and not look back … but not untidily. That was the last of the iron rules which must be obeyed. I could go free but I must not take revenge. I must not ruin him and above all I must not foul my own nest. He and I must come to understand one another and the parting must be arranged without fuss.

I took the sheet of blotting paper out of the pad and rolled it carefully into a cylinder.

'Come on,' I said to Izzy, 'we can go from here, old boy. But we must tell him first.'

It was about half after midnight, I think, when I decided to try out the home perm outfit on the side pieces of my hair. I had packed most of my clothes and I had very few other possessions because I'd been living rather as if I were in a hotel. Wherever I was going, I shouldn't have much luggage to bother about. I was not sleepy and I was not worried. At last I knew what I had to tell Victor, and I knew I had to do it the moment he came in. I should not look very imposing with my hair in curlers and he'd probably be scandalized by them, but that didn't matter any more. I had plenty of time and I wanted to get it done.

It was quite a business because of the hot water. Izzy and I trotted up and down several times with our kettle, and the directions on the flimsy folder inside the perm packet were long and complicated. All the same, we conquered, and by the time I'd got to '*Operation* 8: *rinse thoroughly but do not unwind*' the clock on my bedside table said two-fifteen.

I was in the bathroom with my head tied up like a pudding when Izzy began to growl. It was his warning noise, very deep and soft in the back of his throat, and it sent the blood tingling into the nerves of my face and back. I hurried into the bedroom to find him stiff-legged in the middle of the floor, his ears coming off the top of his head, every hair quivering as he faced the open window. Someone was in the courtyard, and since he had not entered presumably it was not Victor. I stood listening and presently I heard an odd splattering sound high up under the window. Izzy growled and started back as a pebble sailed in and rolled on the carpet near him.

I went over at once and put my head out, towel and all.

'What is it?' I demanded.

'Mrs Lane …?' It was Maureen Jackson's voice and I could just see her in the dusk. She was wrapped in something which I took to be an evening cloak. There was another shadow in the darkness behind her. I could hardly make it out at all and I assumed it was her dancing partner. I drew back at once. My towel was slipping and I was coy about the curlers.

'Yes,' I said from just inside the room, 'what on earth is it?'

'Could – could I possibly speak to the Headmaster?' Her voice was most unnatural and it came to me that she was suppressing giggles. This was most unlike her, of course, but then the hour was not exactly usual. I could hear the engine of a sports car throbbing somewhere in the stillness and I decided that they were on their way home from a party where they had got a little high. Perhaps there had been a lot of gossip about us. Perhaps Victor had been seen with someone. Perhaps Maureen had been dared to find out if I knew.

'Is he in?'

Something in the question raised a devil in me that I did not know that I possessed. I made a sudden irritable movement and did the silliest thing I have ever done in my life.

'Yes, of course he is,' I said firmly, 'fast asleep, and I shouldn't dream of waking him. Whatever it is must wait till tomorrow. Good night.'

Then I closed the window.

It was a mad thing to do, criminally idiotic. At the time I felt a vague premonition about it, but I did not dream then just how insane it was going to prove to be, for it was not until the following afternoon that Victor's body was discovered and by then he had been dead between twelve and twenty-four hours, so the police doctor said.

Part Two

The day began quietly enough.

By half past four in the morning I had still had no sleep, although I had been lying on my bed for some time. Izzy was restless too, I noticed, as he lay on the rug before the dressing-table. His ears were pricked forward and he whimpered a little every time the school clock struck the quarter hour.

My wretched curlers were abominably uncomfortable and I was tempted to take them out, but I am one of those people who read instructions very carefully and in this case they were specific that five hours was the drying time. I bore the discomfort grimly. *Il faut souffrir pour être belle*, said the proverb. I didn't know if I was going to look particularly *belle*, but at any rate I thought I'd be a bit better. I had come to hate my role of the forlorn wife, and I was thankful I'd made a start at least to stop looking like one.

At five I got up and made myself another pot of the milkless tea. While I was drinking it dawn broke, and rather guiltily I took another look at the sheet of blotting paper I'd brought upstairs. I wanted to see if I could find out when the revealing message had been written. But all the other fragments were meaningless to me, and there seemed nothing to show how long the paper had been in use. I rolled it up again and put it in the long bottom drawer of the chest which I had emptied when I packed.

By this time I had decided where Victor was. I had made up my mind that he had driven to London to meet someone who had probably gone up there from Tinworth by train. I felt fairly certain he had intended to come home during the night but had changed his mind and stayed. I thought he had not telephoned because he had not wanted to bother to make excuses. He knew that I would put up with it, or had decided that it did not matter if I did not.

The more I thought about it the more obvious all this appeared. The tone of the note had suggested an old love affair, which argued that the woman, whoever she was, probably was one of the local ladies who had caused the scandal last winter. It was because of that scandal that I thought they wouldn't risk spending an evening together nearer than the city, and I guessed he had not kept, me informed because he knew that I would never fly into a panic and start telephoning round the town. He had trained me never to do that. There had been a most unfortunate incident a few weeks after our marriage when Victor had gone over to Tortham College for an evening conference. The meeting had gone on much longer than anyone had expected and he had accepted a bed from one of the house-masters without letting me know. I had got frightened that he might have had an accident with the car and had telephoned the Head's house at one in the morning. My call had caused no end of fuss in that fortress of academic conventionalism, and the savagery and the sarcasm of the reprimand I had received from Victor still brought the colour to my face whenever I remembered it. It had not been very fair, of course, but then that had been one of the lessons which had taught me not to expect ordinary fair behaviour from the man I had married.

I crawled back into my bed and lay there wondering who the woman was. I was ashamed of myself for not feeling more bitter about her. All my upbringing had taught that a good wife ought to know by some sort of magical divination the woman whom her husband prefers, but my intelligence warned me that this was moonshine. Victor had always kept me at arm's length. I did not know him. I did not know his taste, even.

I thought I had only closed my eyes for an instant, but when I opened them again the sun was pouring in through the window, Izzy was barking like a lunatic, and standing at the end of my bed was a little old woman in a bright overall and a shabby black hat which boasted a bunch of tousled but valiant feathers in it. She was watching me with a strange intensity, her eyes very wide open and her thin nose twitching like Izzy's own.

'E's gorn,' she said with dramatic suddenness. ''Is bed ain't slep' in. Did you know?'

I lay looking at her stupidly for a moment while all the facts slowly reassembled themselves in my mind, and I remembered the charwoman Miss Richardson had promised to send me.

'You're Mrs Veal,' I said at last.

'That's right.' Her unnerving gaze never left my face. 'Come to do for yer. 'Aven't slep','ave yer?'

'Not very well,' I admitted, struggling up into a sitting position and wondering what on earth had happened to my head that it should feel as if it had been scalped. 'What's the time? Nine?' I stared at the clock on the bedside table with unfocusing eyes. 'How awful. I'm so sorry.'

'Don't you move.' In Mrs Veal's dramatic tones, which I had not yet learned were habitual with her, the words were a command. 'Stay where you are. You 'aven't slep' a wink, you 'aven't. I saw it as soon as I come in. Lie there until I get you a cupper-tea, and particularly don't look at yerself in the glass. It'll give yer a turn. You look like a pore young corp. Don't you worry about nothing. I've got milk in me bag *and* a small brown loaf. "There won't be nothing there," Miss Richardson said,' she said, 'and so I come prepared.' She paused for breath and gave me another searching stare. 'You *can't* 'ave slep'. I saw my sister's youngest when the undertaker had done with 'er and she looked more alive than you do now, and that's the truth. Tossin' and turnin' all night, that's what you must 'ave been. Lie where you are until I come back.'

She scuttled out as suddenly as she had arrived and I pulled myself wearily out of bed and peered fearfully in the looking glass. The sight was almost reassuring. It was still me. I looked a bit of a mess and my eyes were smudgy and hollow, but I was recognizable. I began to pull out the curlers which had made my head ache, and was gratified to see a gentle but unmistakable wave. I put a comb through it gingerly, but it persisted and there was no sign of the frizzing I had feared. I was still examining my handiwork when the door opened uncermoniously.

'There's no kitchen in this 'ouse.' Sheer astonishment seemed to have robbed Mrs Veal of her histrionic powers. She spoke almost mildly.

'No,' I said, and added almost idiotically, 'I know.'

'*No kitchen!*'

'Well,' I began apologetically, 'you see, in the ordinary way the school …'

'Oh yers, I daresay.' She swept my explanation aside with magnificent contempt. 'The school looks after yer like a mother, I don't doubt, but *no kitchen* … and they call it a gentleman's residence. Well, I never did, I *never* did! I didn't really. I'll go straight to Mrs Williams and see what she can provide and no one shall stop me.'

She was gone again with the speed of a bird, only to put her head in a moment later.

'No master in 'is bed and no kitchen,' she remarked devastatingly. 'Whatever next?'

She went out again and I hurried after her and called to her down the stairs. It had occurred to me that if she was going into the Williamses I ought to make some sort of excuse for Victor's absence, since I'd asked the porter to leave the gate for him.

'It'll only be breakfast for one, Mrs Veal,' I said, 'and I shan't want anything much. The Headmaster rang up late last night. He's been detained in London.'

She paused without looking round. I could see her little figure foreshortened on the stairs below me. Presently she turned and peered up.

'What yer going to do for 'is dinner?'

'What? Oh, I'll think of something. We'll probably go into the town. I don't know when he's coming home, you see. I expect he'll ring again.'

'I see.' She sounded very dubious. 'Don't know when 'e's coming.' She nodded as if it was a lesson she had learned and I suddenly realized that she must have had a word or so with the Williamses already. I went back to my bedroom and began to dress. I felt trapped again, back in the atmosphere of gossip and commiseration. I was very conscious of being a bad liar, too, and I was furious with Victor for putting me in a position when these white lies seemed so necessary.

I was in the little dining-room when Mrs Veal returned. She came steaming up the stairs with a laden tray which she placed proudly on the table before me.

'She done the lot, Mrs Williams did. Wouldn't even look at me brown loaf. Said she was only too pleased,' she announced breathlessly as she prepared to whip off the white napkin with which the offering was covered. 'She's a real good woman, a real good woman, in spite of 'er being under the doctor with 'er legs. Nothink is too much trouble. Is it yer birthday?'

The sudden question bewildered me. 'Birthday?'

'Yes, well, as I said, you never said nothink to me about it, but we wondered if it was yer birthday because of the present, you see.' She removed the covering and displayed a pyramid of stiff white florist's paper amid the breakfast things. 'The doctor brought it,' she rattled on, 'the young one with the eyes. You know. 'E's doing the job while the old gentleman, 'oo is a bit past it, is on 'is 'olidays. He never took an 'oliday before 'e was on the Government, so it shows yer, don't it?'

I laughed. She was doing me good. She was what I needed, a human voice. It occurred to me that if I'd met her before my ignorance of the real and inner life of Tinworth would not be nearly so abysmal. All the same I was shaken by the flowers. It wasn't like Andy to do anything so graceful. I took off the wrappings and smiled. It was a little clump of speckled blue flowers in a small ornamental bowl. I'd seen some like it in the good florist's next the cinema. It was a line they were selling that month and it looked like Andy, charming and unpretentious and somehow solid. The envelope which the florist provided to hold the card was stuck down and I tore it open unsuspecting. The message was scribbled in the handwriting I had once known so very well.

Clearing out today. Fixed it with the local man. All the best, Andy.

I sat staring at it until I became aware that the colour was pouring up my neck and into my face. It was dismay, and yet I had not once permitted myself to hope that our good-byes had not been final. How strange it was, I thought suddenly, that one's body seems to go on living a life of its own, feeling emotions and reacting to them however strictly one makes one's mind behave.

I glanced up to find Mrs Veal watching me with unveiled curiosity. There was nothing of the ghoul about her. She was perfectly friendly and quite clearly on my side, but she liked to know what was going on.

'It suits yer, that bit o' colour in yer face,' she remarked disconcertingly. 'Now you've got it you look better-looking, more like you did when you first come. It's the bit of a curl, I suppose. It's wonderful what it does for yer. That young doctor's goin' away.'

'Oh, is he?' I said in an ineffectual attempt to sound casual.

'So Mrs Williams told me. She's ever so sorry. 'E come round early to take a last look at 'er legs. Nice of 'im, wasn't it? Some wouldn't, that they wouldn't, not today. 'E said 'e was off. Couldn't stick it, 'e said. Known 'im long, 'ave yer?'

It was one of those direct questions which cannot be sidetracked, so I said we were both on the same hospital staff before I was married.

'Oh, I see.' It was obvious that she did, too, the whole story. I could see it in the wisdom of her old grey eyes. 'Oh well,' she said, giving me a friendly little grimace, 'it's just as well, ain't it? I mean people are always ready to talk in a place like this. You mayn't believe it but you'd be surprised. It's not like London. Make up anything, they will, *and* say it. So it's just as well 'e's gorn. Per'aps 'e saw it 'isself. Nice of 'im to send the flowers, wasn't it? I'll put 'em on the side. There, don't they look pretty?'

'Very,' I agreed faintly. 'I – er, I don't know what they are, do you?'

'Nemo-phila,' said the amazing woman calmly. 'They grow a lot of 'em round 'ere, for seed. They mean "*May success crown your wishes*". That's surprised yer, ain't it?'

'It staggers me.'

She laughed. 'I used to work in a card factory when I was a girl. Birthday cards we used to make, very elaborate. We were give the cards, see, with the motters and a pictcher on 'em, and then we 'ad to stick on the right pressed flower. There was lots of 'em. "*Thoughts*

I bring you" – that was pansies, and oh, I don't know what else. Come on, drink yer coffee. So there you are, "*Success crown your wishes*", that's what 'e sent you.' She hesitated, honesty getting the better of her romanticism. 'I don't really suppose 'e knew.'

'Perhaps not.'

'Still it was very nice of 'im. You'll remember 'im gratefully.'

'I shall, very.'

I thought she was going to leave me at last but she still hovered.

'Oh, and there's this,' she said, planking a crumpled piece of paper on the cloth before me. 'Williams give me this to bring over. If the master wasn't 'ere, 'e said, perhaps you'd look after it. It's the receipt for the luggage, see?'

'The …?' I checked my exclamation and took up the paper. It was not easy to decipher. My hand seemed to be shaking so much that I could hardly see it. Mrs Veal explained. Her fund of information seemed to be inexhaustible.

'It's the master's climbing-luggage, the 'eavy stuff that's kep' in the locker room. It's gorn to Switzerland to be ready for 'im. It's sent every year. Williams always sees to it. 'E told Williams to get it off for 'im and Williams did, yesterday.'

'When was Williams told?' For the life of me I could not keep the revealing sharpness out of my voice.

'Oh, I don't know, dear, I mean madam. Sometime in the term, I expec'. Didn't the master tell yer?'

'I expect he forgot.'

'Yers, well, they are forgetful, aren't they, men are. Can't 'elp themselves. So bloomin' conceited they don't know if they're goin' or comin' 'alf the time. Still, it'll be a weight off your mind, won't it, to know it's safely sent? You're goin' with 'im this time, are yer? When you settin' off?'

'Soon. I'm not quite sure, exactly.'

She clicked her tongue against her teeth with tolerant commiseration. 'Keep us on the 'op, don't they, all the time? Well, I'll get on.' She went out at last and left me with the receipt. I folded it carefully and tucked it into the little Chinese vase on the mantelshelf. The whole incident had alarmed me. If Victor had made this arrangement without telling me, what others might he have fixed? For one wild moment it went through my mind he might have just gone off on his trip already, calling in somewhere on the way to see the lady of the note. Perhaps I should get a letter sometime during the day telling me what he'd decided and enclosing a little money for me to carry on with. It seemed incredible, but only because I envisaged it happening to *me*. I had heard of husbands who behaved like that, and what was worse, I knew that if I simply related the fact to some disinterested person – a lawyer for instance – it was by no means certain that he would be sympathetic. How was he to know that it was not merely some phase in a private sex war between us? There would be only my word for it. At that moment I could see, as never before, that the way Victor treated me was my business, and the only person on earth who could do anything about it was myself.

If Victor had behaved like this I'd have to go after him. I went into his room and tried to discover which of his clothes were missing. A more experienced wife would have thought of this before, of course, but once again I was at a disadvantage. Victor's personal affairs had been under control for years before I had appeared on the scene. There was a sort of resident batman, a school valet, who had made it part of his work to look after Victor's clothes and to attend to his mending and laundry, so I had never been permitted to interfere. The man came in every so often, and must now have gone off on holiday with everyone else. I went through the wardrobe and chest, but apart from the fact that I recognized some of the items they might have belonged to a stranger. I simply couldn't tell if a modest holiday outfit had been packed and taken away. The bed was made up with clean sheets and there were no soiled pyjamas about, but on the other hand there seemed a good stock of clean pairs in the drawer. The bathroom was more revealing. His shaving things were there in the toilet cupboard. I realized he might well possess a small travelling outfit, but I had never seen one and I felt mildly comforted. I thought perhaps after all he intended to come back and explain before going abroad. He wasn't going to behave quite so disgustingly. All the same, it was not conclusive evidence, by any means, and after a while I got nervy again and went down to his study.

It was just as I'd last seen it, very bare and shiny. The clean sheet of blotting paper in the folder on the desk made the gleaming expanse of mahogany look even more deserted. I opened the drawers tentatively. They were all very tidy, papers pinned neatly together, letters in spring clips, folders tidily stacked. The school servants were very good, I reflected idly. The polish on every wooden surface was perfect. My finger marks seemed to show wherever I put them. I'd have rubbed them off after me but I hadn't a duster, and I recollected that the place was to be left for a couple of months.

Here again, as in the bedroom, I could tell so little because I knew so little. We never sat in the study and there were very few occasions when I had even entered it. It was Victor's workroom. I had only seen the desk drawers open half a dozen times. I did not go through the papers; I could not bear to. The notion of finding a bundle of incriminating letters from some wretched local girl filled me with such distaste that I was astonished at myself, and I suddenly realized how lucky I was. I realized some women must find themselves in just this same position but with one vital difference. If I had ever loved Victor, then I should have tasted bitterness. As it was, I was hurt and even outraged, and what pride I had was suffering badly, but I was not annihilated. It was my ideals and beliefs and conventions which were crushed, but not the basic me. He had not touched that because it had never belonged to him. And then I thought that if I'd loved him this would never have happened quite like this. I'd have known more about him. We were both to blame. A marriage without love is not marriage. We were playing at it, Victor and I. We were not married at all and it had taken me six months to find out.

I closed the last drawer and stood back. There was only one thing missing that I remembered seeing there before and that was a revolver. It was a big army thing in a service holster. It had lain in the back of the middle drawer and I had seen it there one day in the winter when I had taken Victor some typing he had asked me to do for him. He had opened the drawer to get a clip for the sheets and I had seen the gun and commented on it. He told me that he kept it as a souvenir of the war, and that he had a licence for it, and I said that with so many children about it was dangerous and that he ought to keep it in the safe. Now that it had gone I assumed that he had agreed with me, and I was glad to have had some little influence over him, however small.

I looked round the room again but there was nothing left about, not even a newspaper. The only thing in the least untidy was the charred sheet in the empty grate, a single oblong, quite large. I only noticed it idly and I had no time to consider it or the odd little incident which had put it there, for just then the telephone bell sounded from the deserted secretary's room just across the hall. I caught my breath. This was it. Now I should hear some sort of explanation and I knew I must take myself in hand and be as firm and ruthless as he.

But when I took up the receiver it was not Victor but a much slower, deeper voice which greeted me. I must have been in hypersensitive mood that morning, for although it was the first time that ever I heard it, yet it made me vaguely uneasy from the start. I can only say it sounded friendly but sly, like an uncle asking trick questions.

'Would that be Buchanan House? I wonder if I could speak to the Headmaster, Mr Lane. It's the police here as a matter of fact. Superintendent South. Just put me through to him, will you?'

'I'm sorry,' I said, 'he's out.'

'Oh. And when are you expecting him back?'

'I'm afraid I don't know.'

'I see.' The avuncular voice sounded dubious. 'Would that be Mrs Lane by any chance?'

'Yes. Can I help you?'

'Well, I don't know, Mrs Lane. It's a little difficult. It's an enquiry from the Metropolitan Police, Northern Division, about a John O'Farrell Rorke.'

'Oh dear,' I said involuntarily.

'Pardon?'

'Nothing. What's happened to him?'

'Well, he seems to have been involved in an accident and quite a nasty one. He's in the Watling Street Hospital with multiple injuries, but he seems to have been inebriated at the time and the driver of the bus which ran him down has got a story which has got to be confirmed. Meanwhile, the police want details of any relatives he may have. He's unconscious and the only address they have is the school's. They got that from a couple of envelopes in his pocket.'

'I'm terribly sorry, and I don't see how I can help,' I began. 'I don't know anything about Mr Rorke's home life, but I'll tell my husband to ring you the moment he comes in. Meanwhile, I wonder if you'd like to ring his secretary? She might know something.'

There was silence for a moment and then he said, 'Would that be Miss Maureen Jackson?'

'Yes. She knows ...'

He cut me short. 'As a matter of fact, Mrs Lane, I've been on to her already. I know her quite well, d'you see? She and her family are old friends of mine. I thought of her at once and I rang her because I wasn't sure if the Headmaster had gone off on his holiday or not, and I thought it would save time.' He laughed apologetically, but making it quite clear to me that he was as parochial and gossipy as anyone else in the town. He added shamelessly. 'We have to save time, you know, Mrs Lane. Maureen, that is Miss Jackson – she's in bed with a chill, by the way – told me that Mr Lane was at home last night so I thought I'd catch him.'

I hesitated. I nearly told him that I hadn't seen Victor for twenty-four hours and that I'd lied to Maureen because she had irritated me. It would have been an embarrassing confession but I have an ingrained respect for the police and I am fairly certain I would have done it if I hadn't realized that he was on neighbourly terms with the Jacksons and guessed the sort of chatter which must inevitably have followed. As it was, I simply said good-bye.

'I'll tell him to ring you as soon as he comes in,' I finished.

He was not satisfied. 'Do you know where he's gone, Mrs Lane? I'd like to get hold of him.'

'No, I'm afraid I don't.'

'Did he take his car?'

'Yes.'

'And he didn't leave any message, didn't say anything at all? Just drove away?'

'No.' It was beginning to sound awful and I groped round for something to say which would at least convey that we were more or less on speaking terms. The Superintendent forestalled me.

'Hell be in for his lunch anyway, won't he?'

'I don't know. I mean, the school is shut. We're not eating here. I think he will be back this morning, but I – I …' I made a great effort to struggle out of the morass of words and succeeded. 'I know,' I said suddenly, 'I know who is sure to be able to help you. Do you know Mr Seckker?'

'Now that's an idea, Mrs Lane.' To my relief the Superintendent gave up worrying about Victor at once. He sounded approving. 'Mr Seckker's a friend of Mr Rorke's, is he?'

'I think so, in a way.'

There was a laugh at the other end of the wire. 'You're going to say that Mr Seckker is a friend of every lame duck.' The voice had lost its slyness and sounded merely hearty. 'You're right there. So he is. I'll get on to him immediately. But, Mrs Lane, do tell your husband the moment he comes in, because I think there may be a bit of trouble about this case – or not trouble, exactly, but publicity, and a thing like that never does a school any good. A word from your husband now might save a lot of bother later on. See what I mean?'

'I do,' I assured him. 'Thank you very much.'

'Not at all. We're all very proud of the school in Tinworth, so it's in everybody's interest to keep everything clean and sweet. So if you do happen to remember where your husband's gone this morning, and you can reach him on the telephone, have a try, see? Good morning.'

'Good morning,' I said huskily, and hung up.

I made a note on a pad for Victor and left the sheet propped up on the hall table where he could not fail to see it. Then I went slowly upstairs.

I told Mrs Veal that Mr Rorke had been run over. There seemed no harm in telling her and it kept her from chattering about Victor or, what was worse still, Andy. She had put the bowl of flowers in the middle of the dining-room table, I saw, and was prepared to mention it as soon as I appeared. My news sidetracked her.

'Run over? In hospital?' She echoed my words with genuine pity. 'What a shame! What a shame after all 'e's done to keep 'imself you-know-what after all this time. Never once, never once not in two terms 'as 'e been – well, we-won't-mention-it. I was only saying so to Mr Williams. "It's a miracle," I said, "and 'e ought to 'ave a medal for it." It's not easy, no it's not easy, that it isn't, to keep yerself you-know-what once you've let it get 'old of you like 'e did. And now runned over as well. I never!'

She made herself perfectly plain for all her ladylike censorship and I understood why Mr Rorke had not struck me as the drinker his reputation had suggested. His sobriety since I had met him had been the result of effort. I had not realized that.

'I am afraid the end of term was too much for him,' I murmured.

She considered me with serious eyes and nodded her head like a Chinese mandarin.

'The night before last, that was when it started again. Pore chap! As I said to Williams, you would 'ave thought 'e'd 'ave waited until 'e got off school premises, I said, but no, 'e couldn't. Down the town 'e went and come back when the pubs closed, swearing, Williams says – well, 'e couldn't tell me what 'e said and I'm sure I didn't want to 'ear.'

'It's a great pity,' I said. 'I had not realized it was a habit with him.'

'It used not to be,' she assured me earnestly. 'Not for years it wasn't. And then last year it seemed to come over 'im and it was quite bad. Then there was the noise at the end of the winter term and we all thought 'e'd pulled 'isself together.'

'Noise?' I inquired, fascinated.

She dropped her eyes modestly. 'Some persons say "row",' she explained primly, 'but it's not a very nice expression. 'E did something and the 'Eadmaster 'eard of it and oh my! we all thought 'e'd 'ave to leave, we did really. Then it all blowed over and the next term – that was the term you come – 'e was as good as gold and sober as a judge. Did 'im good.'

I felt I ought not to gossip but she seemed to hold the key to the school and to Tinworth. No one else had been half so informative. In fact she was the only person who had treated me like a woman. Everyone else had seemed to think I was a new boy.

'What did he do?' I inquired guiltily.

'I'm not dead certain.' She lowered her voice conspiratorially. 'But we understood at the time that 'e said something to one of the boys – I'm not sure 'e didn't write it, which would 'ave been worse – something in the swearing line, it was. The boy was a bit soft and told 'is parents, and the parents were a bit soft and told the 'Eadmaster. That's what we 'eard. There *was* a to-do! The 'Ead, well, 'e can use 'is tongue, can't 'e? Sarcastic! Vinegar's milk when 'e gets goin', vinegar's milk, I say.'

She glanced at me anxiously. 'Not that I ought to say such a thing to you, dear – I mean madam. I must get on. Still, I'm sorry that Mr Rorke's runned over, I am indeed. People are never the same again after that 'appens, sober or – well, we won't mention it. No, they're *not*.'

She began to sweep with great vigour, and since there was nothing I could do I took Izzy and we went round the school grounds, battered and deserted in the morning sun. I saw no one at all No one was at work. No one came up the drive. No tradesmen. No visitor. No boy.

I sat down on one of the well-worn seats on which generations of children had carved their names, and waited, watching the gates, but there was no sign of Victor. Finally I saw Mrs Veal wobble off down the path on a bone-shaking bicycle. She waved to me and shouted that she'd 'see me termorrer' and then she was gone and I was quite alone. I thought of Rorke and wished there was something I could have done for him. He seemed to be an unhappy sort of person, probably most unsuited to be a schoolmaster, and yet someone had said that he taught brilliantly. Possibly it had been Victor; I couldn't remember. At any rate, I was glad that Mr Seckker would be his rescuer on behalf of the school. I felt pretty certain that if one was in some sort of scrape it would be nicer to be rescued by Mr Seckker than by Victor.

My thoughts returned to Victor and I rehearsed what I had decided I must say to him. I could imagine his opening sarcasms as he began to reply, but I had made up my mind that I must wear all that down. I must stand up to it and defeat it and get my point into his head. Andy was always creeping back into my mind but I pushed him out resolutely. As Mrs Veal had put it so devastatingly, it was just as well he'd gone, and perhaps he'd seen it himself!

At last I went back to the house, dressed myself for the street with as much care as possible, and, taking Izzy on the lead, went down the town. Izzy loathed the lead but he was a fighter, and I seldom dared to take him into a crowd where every second woman had a dog with her. However, today I did not feel like parting with him even for a moment.

The Flower Club lecture was at a quarter after two in the Public Library's smaller room, and I thought I'd go. It seemed to me that I'd found out a great deal about Tinworth in the last twenty-four hours, and I wanted to see all these people who had seemed so unaccountably alien to me during the few months I had known them, in the light of all this new information. It was a chance I did not imagine I should have again. Everyone would be there. The Flower Club was Tinworth's latest craze. It was amusing, it was elegant, and it was cheap.

As in most British provincial towns, even the well-to-do ladies of Tinworth managed their lives on a very rigid budget, and local crafts and crazes were apt to fade very quickly if the materials required cost even a little actual money spent. Flowers had the enormous advantage of being practically free. Everybody grew flowers; the seed fields round the town were full of them and the garden bloomed like the Sunday hats of long ago. So the art of floral decoration flourished, and the cult took on a seriousness which was almost Japanese. In that year the Flower Club was definitely the thing to join, so I should have plenty of opportunity of seeing everyone. As I walked down the road I reflected that I must also eat. This idiotic business of my being taken so utterly by surprise by the sudden closing down of the school commissariat had shaken me more than I cared to admit. I am not incapable. I was quite able to cater and care for myself and a family, and I was eager to do it. To be caught out like this suddenly, without even a saucepan or a stove to put it on and no way of telling what, if anything, was required of me, put me in wrong. I did not like to rush out and buy some temporary equipment which I should not need for long, because I had very little money. This was another irritation. I was used to earning a reasonable living, but I had no inheritance and after six months my savings were dwindling rapidly.

I bought myself a cheap lunch at the Olde Worlde Teashoppe in the High Street and managed to smuggle half of it to Izzy, hidden behind me on the olde worlde settle. We dawdled over it as long as we decently could and then went over to the Library.

The staircase was cool and quiet after the sun-baked streets and I assumed I was the first to arrive, but as I crossed the landing I saw that the doors of the lecture room were open and heard the sibilant mutter of voices inside. I picked up Izzy and, carrying him under my arm, walked in.

As I appeared on the threshold there was sudden and absolute silence.

The big shabby room was dim as a church and nearly as cool, with the same smell of dust and paper faint in the air. The rows of cane chairs stretching up towards the platform made a vast flimsy barrier between me and the four women who stood together in the aisle before the front row. For a full minute they stood quite still, a picture of arrested movement, their bodies still bent towards each other as if they had been whispering. But every head was turned, every face blank, every eye watching me. It only lasted a short time but it was long enough to tell me that they had been discussing me.

I did not care in the least. At least I felt sure once again that I knew a great deal more about my own business than anyone else did, and that was a very good feeling.

I knew all four women slightly. There was the inevitable Mrs Raye, looking at least half ashamed of herself; Mrs Roundell, the pretty, pleasant wife of the Town Clerk; Miss Bonwitt, a slightly vague spinster who was chiefly remarkable for her wonderful garden out on the hill above the golf course; and Mrs Amy Petty.

Amy Petty was rather better known to me than the others. She was Maureen Jackson's widowed elder sister, for one thing, and I had met her calling at the school several times. She had the Jackson family's direct manner, their money, and their clannishness, but her face was like a mean little hen's set atop a long flat figure clad in very good but very ugly country clothes.

I had often thought that for some reason she disliked me, but in the normal way she was polite enough. Today she astonished me by letting her eyes flicker away from me without a gleam of recognition, while her mouth shut in a firm hard button. It was a brief reaction, and by the time I had found my way round the chairs towards her she was pleasant, yet there was something new and strange about her which I did not understand. The idea seemed ridiculous, but it did go through my mind that she was behaving as if she were afraid of me.

There was something strange about them all. Even Mrs Raye did not seem sure of herself. It struck me as odd at the time because Tinworth ladies were so often caught gossiping by the subjects of their scandal that it was hardly considered a social contretemps any longer. The conversation began jerkily, with me the only person quite at ease.

Mrs Raye said it was good of me to come. Miss Bonwitt agreed with her rather too quickly. Mrs Roundell hoped the lecturer wasn't going to make flower arrangement too scientific, and Amy Petty asked me bluntly if I knew when I was going on my holiday. I was prepared for that one by this time and I said the day was not actually fixed but I expected to be off by the end of the week. Hester Raye came back into form at that point and slid her arm through mine.

'My dear,' she said, her words tumbling over one another in her usual rush, 'the Chief Constable and I were wondering if you and your husband could come to dinner with us tomorrow night? I do know it's terribly short notice and I am so sorry, but we've been terribly rushed lately and I do want to fit you in.'

I opened my mouth, but she forestalled me.

'Don't say no until you've heard me. We've got some quite interesting people coming – the Wedgwoods, the Rippers, that girl Sally French, and – oh, by the way, did you know that that nice young doctor of yours had gone? Left the town, my dear. Fixed it up with young Pettigrew, wrote Dr Browning, and simply left. I believe it was fearfully sudden, he made up his mind last night. Dick Pettigrew told me.' Her eyes peered brightly into mine. 'Perhaps you knew about it?'

'I – I wasn't surprised. I mean it doesn't astonish me.' It was not a good effort on my part but then she had flustered me, as she always did with her well-meaning blunderbuss tactics.

'You'd known him before, had you, Mrs Lane? I thought he was a complete stranger.' This came from little Mrs Roundell, trying to be nice in her fluttering ingenuous way. 'We all liked him so much. He attended Mother last week and she adored him. Said he was sweet.'

'And now he's gone.' Hester Raye grimaced. 'Just our luck in Tinworth. Well now, Mrs Lane, what about tomorrow? Could you pin Victor down for a quarter to eight or eight o'clock? Do come.' She was still holding my arm and now she shook it slightly and came out with one of her typical pronouncements. 'My Reggie is dying to see you both. I told him all about meeting you yesterday and he was terribly intrigued. He's been worried about you too, you know, just as we all have.'

How dared she say it! She took my breath away, although she had long since ceased to amaze me. I could not believe that the old Chief Constable, who was a very decent but not particularly sensitive man, could have grieved much on my account, but I could easily guess what she had told him.

It was on the tip of my tongue to say that I did not imagine that Victor and I would ever be going out to dinner together again, but that after all was a thing that Victor had a right to know before anybody else and so I merely stalled.

'It's very kind of you,' I said, 'but I really think you'll have to count us out. I don't think I dare fix up anything definite at the moment.'

'Why not?' This was Amy Petty. She spoke too sharply and too brashly for even the known Jackson family manner to excuse her. Everybody turned and stared at her. She looked very odd, her small eyes defiant and bright spots of colour on her high cheekbones. She said no more but stood her ground, waiting for me to reply. In the end I had to say something.

'I'm not at all sure what Victor has fixed,' I explained. 'He's in London at the moment and I'm not quite sure when he'll be back.'

It seemed an ordinary social pronouncement to me but its effect was extraordinary. There was dead silence. Amy Petty remained looking at me while everybody else glanced awkwardly away.

'He was home last night. You told my sister so.' The words were forced out of Amy. She was being more impolite than even Tinworth permitted and she realized it, but she appeared to be incapable of controlling herself. I felt almost sorry for her.

'Why yes,' I said glibly, more, I think, with the idea of putting her at ease than for any other reason, 'so I did. I thought I'd heard him come in, you see, but he was detained in London and couldn't get back. He telephoned this morning.'

There was a little sigh from them all. Mrs Roundell alone smiled contentedly, as though to say that she had been right after all, and I was just going to pass on down the row to find myself a seat when Miss Bonwitt, who until now had been perfectly silent, said quietly: 'I am so glad. It was his car, you see. There is just one place in my garden where one can look down through the trees and see it in that corner by the cottage wall.' She had one of those high-pitched apologetic voices which seemed to make every pronouncement sound like a spirit message, inconclusive but faintly ominous.

I swung round on her, startled into frankness. 'Cottage?' I demanded.

'Yes, your cottage. Mr Lane's little cottage,' she continued placidly. 'I daresay you feel it's quite remote out there on the edge of the golf course. I know if it were mine, I should. But actually, as I say, there is one point in my garden where one can look round the shoulder of the hill and see down through the leaves right into the corner where Mr Lane parks his car. I can't see any other part of the cottage, just that one wall at the back. I happened to notice the car there yesterday and naturally I thought nothing of it, but when I went to the same place this morning to see if I'd dropped one of my gardening gloves I saw the car was still in the same place.'

I stood staring at her, my face drawn and frozen. The cottage! I thought. Oh, how *could* Victor do such a thing so near, so dangerously near? How *could* he subject himself and me to this humiliation?

'Go and look for him, Mrs Lane.' Once again Amy Petty spoke explosively, as if she could not keep the words back.

'Oh no,' I protested far too violently, 'no, of course not. I mean to say, I think Miss Bonwitt must have caught sight of the car on the only two occasions when it happened to be there. I know Victor was calling at the cottage to – to take some things on his way to town, and I expect he called there on the way back. He keeps his golf clubs there, of course. He's probably home by now.'

Miss Bonwitt shook her wispy grey head at me and I noticed for the first time that her eyes were hooded, with webby lids, and were not just dull as I had always thought.

'Oh no,' she said in a quiet singsong, 'it wasn't like that, Mrs Lane, it wasn't like that at all. I first noticed the car about four o'clock yesterday afternoon when I was tying up my chrysanthemums, and when I went in about seven it was still there. This morning I got up very early because there is a lot to do in the garden, and it is so cool and pleasant in the dawn. I was out about five and, as I say, I went up to the chrysanthemums to see if I had dropped one of my gloves. The car was still there with the hood still down and the rug half hanging out as I'd seen it before. I did wonder, because you know we had a very sharp shower during the night.'

'Victor must have forgotten it,' I murmured, and even to my own ears I sounded idiotic.

'I hope so,' murmured Miss Bonwitt, 'I hope so indeed. But since the car was still there, and still in exactly the same condition when I set out for the lecture three quarters of an hour ago, I did wonder if Mr Lane could have been taken ill up there alone. I was just mentioning it to the others when you came in … Mrs Lane.'

She made it sound frightful. Although her voice was placid and there were no undertones in it, yet she made it perfectly clear to everybody that she had watched that car all through the hours during which there was light enough to see it.

Hester Raye attempted to come to my rescue in a pleasant heavy way. She had her faults and was often rude, but she had the remnants of a decent upbringing and Amy Petty's performance had shocked her.

'But if Mrs Lane says Victor telephoned this morning there's some other explanation for the car,' she said cheerfully. 'Quite probably someone gave him a lift to London from the golf club so he hid his own car. It sounds as if it was hidden if it was in such a funny place, behind the cottage, I mean, and not in front.'

'Yes,' said Miss Bonwitt quietly, 'no one could have seen it from the road. That's why I wondered.'

She was silent for a long time and I felt myself shudder. It was a rather extraordinary and unlikely thing for Victor to do. I could believe he might be sufficiently inconsiderate to entertain someone at the cottage for an hour or so, even, since he seemed to have made an effort to conceal the car, all the evening, but I couldn't think that he'd stay there all *day*, especially without looking at his car. He was fussy about things like that. I had not noticed that there had been a shower, but Victor would have made sure, particularly if he had left the hood down.

'I suppose he did telephone, Mrs Lane?' continued Miss Bonwitt after a long pause, and she raised her wrinkled lids and gave me a surprisingly intelligent stare. 'Himself, I mean?' She was offering me an easy way out and I hesitated. It occurred to me that she knew rather a lot and had probably seen things before when she was tying up flowers at seven at night or pottering about in the dawn. I did not know what to say. It was rather peculiar, rather alarming.

'Who sent the message, my dear?' Hester Raye's practical mind was troubled. 'Who spoke on the telephone?'

'It came from his club,' I said. It was the only lie I could think of and I hated it and myself and wished to goodness I'd stuck to the truth in the first place. If Victor *had* been taken ill, broken an ankle or something, as they suggested, I had put up some fine behaviour!

Little Mrs Roundell laughed and clapped her hands. 'How mysterious!' she said. 'Or didn't you get it right? I often don't. I hate telephones. Percival says I'm mentally defective when it comes to messages. People gabble and the thing goes plop-plop-squeak, and you get cut off …'

'Go out there and see, Mrs Lane. I'll drive you.' Amy Petty made it a command and when I glanced at her I saw that there was a queer sick look in her small eyes.

Hester Raye objected. 'Not *now*,' she said with characteristic blindness to everything but her own convenience. 'Not before the lecture. The hall is filling up, thank God, but there aren't nearly enough people here yet. My lecturer will be here any minute. Stay. You must stay for the talk.'

'But if he has been taken *ill*,' said Miss Bonwitt with gentle firmness, 'and I think he has, you know – the car has never been there so long bef … I mean I think she ought to make sure, Mrs Raye, I do indeed. I think Mrs Lane really ought to make sure.'

Amy Petty's big thin hand closed over my shoulder blade as if she were arresting me, and Izzy, feeling me jump, growled at her from my arms.

'Go and see.'

'I would,' announced Mrs Roundell with sudden decision. 'I think I would. Telephones are the limit, and if he's there in pain or something, well, you'd never forgive yourself, would you? Just go and make sure and then tear back. I'll bag some seats for you near the door. Then you can just slip in.'

'I'll never forgive you two if you clear off now,' Mrs Raye began, but turned away with a cry of welcome as a stout woman with her arms full of mixed flowers, followed by a pale girl staggering under a tray of vases, came sweeping down the hall towards us.

Amy Petty turned me bodily towards the nearest exit. 'I'll drive you,' she repeated woodenly.

I went out into the side street which runs down past the back door of the Library with her, but as I reached the pavement I hesitated.

'Don't trouble,' I said. 'I'll go back and get a bicycle. You go to the lecture.'

'No. I'll come with you. My brother will drive us.'

I stared at her. I knew she had eight or nine brothers, in fact Tinworth appeared to be populated with Jackson menfolk, but I hardly expected to find one standing about in the street waiting to do taxi work.

'Good heavens, no!' I exclaimed so loudly that a woman passing turned to look at us. I recognized her as the younger of the two sisters who kept the Teashoppe. I smiled at her awkwardly. 'You certainly won't,' I added to Amy. 'It's probably all nonsense. I'll go home and see if Victor's back and if he isn't I'll cycle over to the cottage and investigate.'

'No. We'll drive you.' The Jacksons seemed to be obstinate as well as outspoken. 'Come along.'

I went with her, her determination adding to my growing alarm. I was through with Victor and in the moments when I permitted

156

myself to think about him I rather hated him, but I didn't like the idea of him lying helpless on a stone floor with a broken leg, him or anybody else. After Miss Bonwitt's tale about the car I knew I'd got to go to the cottage.

As we came over the road I realized why Amy had mentioned her brother. Jim Jackson owned the leather shop on the corner and kept his car in the open yard at its side. He came out of his office at once when she called him and listened to her explanation with tremendous interest. As I observed his slightly foxy face, pink under his sandy hair, my misgivings returned.

'I *can't* give you all this trouble,' I said. 'Let me take a taxicab.'

His eyes were bright and knowing and, under his secret amusement, kindly, I thought.

'Oh, it's no trouble,' he said, and if he had added, 'It'll give her something to talk about for weeks,' he could not have made himself more clear. 'You sit in the back with her,' he went on, looking at his sister.

There was nothing for it. They had decided to take me and take me they did. If I'd not been so worried and embarrassed I should have found them comic. To all intents and purposes I was kidnapped. Jim refused point-blank to call at the school.

'It's not worth it,' he explained, treading on the accelerator as we passed the gates. 'It's only a mile and half to the cottage. If he's not there we'll call coming back, unless you want me to run you to London.'

This last remark appeared to strike him as inordinately funny and he kept grinning to himself over it all the way to the golf course. I could see his face reflected in the high polish of the dashboard. I sat in a corner of the car with Amy very close to me and Izzy crouching on my knee. I did not want Victor to be injured, but I found that I was praying that we should find anything in the world rather than an unexplained and inexplicable visitor.

The cottage lay on the farther side of the golf course, at the end of a long overgrown lane tucked into a grove of lime trees. I had not seen it since my last visit in the early spring, when the trees had been bare. It was one of those very primitive lathand-plaster hovels which looked like something out of a fairy tale but turn out to be about as comfortable as a heap of rubble. When I came near I saw that a pink rose in full bloom had climbed all over the discoloured front, obliterating one window and even dislodging some of the tiles on the crazy roof. Ragged grass and untended flowers grew up almost to the eaves, and any passer-by must have thought it derelict.

As Jim Jackson put his foot on the brake I leant forward and felt suddenly sick. The front door stood wide open. Amy Petty got out before I did, scrambling over me in her haste, but she did not cross the moss-grown path. She hesitated and looked back and waited for me. Jim, too, seemed in no hurry. He remained at the wheel, leaning back and watching me still with the same silly grin on his face. I let Izzy out on to the path and climbed after him, my knees weak.

'Victor!' I shouted, 'Vic-tor!'

I think we all held our breaths. There was something quite horrible about the open door, a dark rectangle in the flowery wall.

No one answered. There was no sound at all save the hum of the bees in the limes and much twittering in the branches. I could see where the car had been driven round to the back of the house. The tall grass was beaten down in a line which ran past the open door to the derelict water butt in the corner. I followed it without speaking and Amy Petty came with me. We found the car. It had been driven into the bushes and was as completely hidden as one would have thought possible had one not known that the minute triangle of colour far away up the hill was a corner of Miss Bonwitt's garden. The car was quite damp inside and lay just as she had described it, the hood down and the rug hanging carelessly over the door. I hurried back with Amy at my heels and stepped into the cottage.

It was dark inside and cool. My feet sounded sharply on the brick floor. I was in the one reasonable room the place contained, a pleasant square place with a ceiling of white-washed beams and a few pieces of old furniture scattered round the walls. There was a couch covered with a faded cotton thread, an armchair with a crumpled cushion in it, a gate-legged, table and a rug. On the whitened chimney-piece was an empty glass. A newspaper lay on the floor and Victor's bag of clubs leaned against a chest in the corner.

Amy Petty pushed past me and pounced on something lying in

the armchair. I looked over her shoulder as she leant forward and I saw what it was, a half-filled packet of cigarettes.

I called again, startled by the tremor in my voice.

'Victor! Victor! Vic-tor!'

Once more everything was silent. Not a breath, not a sigh, replied to me.

There was only one inner door, which led, as far as I recollected, to a back kitchen which looked and smelled like a dungeon. This door also stood open and I was advancing upon it when one of the most unnerving and horrible sounds I have ever heard in my life cut through the sleepy quiet of the afternoon. It was a long-drawn-out quavering howl which sent me starting back, while Amy made a noise in her throat. Immediately afterwards I knew what it was, Izzy of course. He had pottered on, investigating on his own account unheeded by either of us.

I rushed into the kitchen, which was minute and quite derelict, plaster falling off its walls and a trail of yellow-looking bindweed creeping in through a crevice under the old brick copper. I heard him howl again but I could not see Izzy.

It was a moment or so later when there was a movement in the darkest corner of all and a cupboard door which was swinging on a loose hinge opened wider as the little dog came backing out, his tail down and his ears flattened. He gave me one long meaning look and then, sitting back on his haunches, threw up his head so that the full sack of his hairy throat was showing and began to howl in earnest. Scotties are not noisy dogs, but when the occasion does arise they can hold their own with any breed on earth.

The noise was like an air-raid siren, horrible with the quaver of fear. Amid the wailing I heard from afar off the door of the Jacksons' car slam as Jim sprang out and the clatter as he blundered into the house behind us. Amy clutched me with a shaking hand.

'Look,' she commanded. 'Go on, look.'

As I pulled the cupboard door open Izzy stopped howling and began to bark, snapping at my dress and dancing about like a lunatic. It made me careful, which was fortunate because there was practically no floor to the deep recess and I could have stepped into the yawning hole at my feet.

It took me some seconds to make out what it was. It was the old iron pump with its corroded bucket which I first saw, I think, and then I looked down and the whole thing became frighteningly clear. The cupboard was not a cupboard but a door put over an alcove to hide the pump. It was a construction which is fairly usual in very old cottages. The iron pump handle came through the wood at the side so that one could use it while standing in the kitchen. The well was under the pump, its head level with the floor directly under the place where the bucket would hang. When it had been put in upwards of a hundred years before the cover had been made of elm three inches thick. The years of dripping water had won, however, and now the crazy lid, rotten as tinder wood, had disintegrated. A hinge tongue, sharp with years of rust, stuck out over the dark hole and attached to it was a six-inch sliver of newly rent wood.

I strained my eyes to see down into the darkness, and damp air, chill and revolting, reached my nostrils. Mercifully I was standing in my own light so I could see nothing, but it was not difficult to imagine what might be floating in the dark bottom of that narrow pit. I felt a scream coming up in my throat and pressed my hands over my mouth to silence it, just as Jim pulled me out of the way.

The thing I remember best of the next ten minutes was the character displayed by the Jacksons. They were sound people, thoroughly country and thoroughly crude, but once they had got their own way, and once there was something obvious to be done wherein their motives could not be questioned, I found them willing, and in a domineering fashion good to me. Jim insisted on pushing us into the outer room while he went to the car for a torch. When he returned with it, it proved to be a typical Jackson possession, expensive and highly efficient. It was quite two feet long and threw a beam like a searchlight. He took it through into the kitchen while I sat in the chair and held Izzy. Amy stood with her back to the chimney, her face white as the lime-washed wall but with a queer satisfied expression in the curl of her tight lips.

We could only have waited for three or four minutes before Jim's high-pitched East Coast voice sounded from the inner room.

'Amy, come in here, girl, will you?'

She went hurrying in and I could hear them whispering for a bit before she returned with Jim following her, his face nearly as white as her own but his eyes bright with a shamed excitement.

Amy paused before me, her lips trying out phrases silently without uttering one of them. At last she gave up any attempt at finesse.

'He's in there, Mrs Lane.'

I showed no astonishment. I am not half-witted and it had been perfectly obvious to me from the first moment I set eyes on the broken trap door that something of the sort must have occurred. I was stunned by the shock and I remember that the two silver bangles on my wrist were rattling together with a sound like fairy bicycle bells. But I was no longer astonished. That first reaction was over.

'How – how awful,' I said huskily.

Amy Petty looked at me for a long time and then she opened her bag and took out a clean handkerchief which she gave me gravely. I don't know why, but the precaution struck me as funny and to my horror an explosive snort escaped me. To cover it I said I'd rather have a cigarette. She gave me one as if she was a hospital nurse inserting a thermometer, and her brother lit it for me with a great trembling hand which had curling yellow hairs and tiny beads of sweat standing out on it. He was so relieved that I was taking it quietly that he made the mistake of treating me as a disinterested spectator.

'There isn't above a foot of water in there!' he burst out. 'I can see just what happened. Mr Lane went to get himself a drop of water for the kettle, stepped on the little old door, which was as rotten as piecrust, and down he went, stunning himself most likely. He's lying in there, his head right under. I'd know him anywhere.'

I tried to stand up. My whole world and all its problems had taken a complete somersault and I felt as if I had nothing to hold on to.

Amy forestalled me. 'He went to get a drop of water,' she repeated thoughtfully. 'That's about it. We'll have to get him out. You go down to the clubhouse, Jim, for help. Just tell them quietly that there's been an accident. We don't want a whole lot of them coming up here. Tell – now I wonder who you'd better tell? Ring up Maureen.'

I heard her as if I were listening to a play and suddenly my common sense reasserted itself.

'That's no good at all,' I said. 'You'll have to fetch someone in authority. You'll have to get a doctor and –'

'The police!' Amy exclaimed as if she had had an original idea. 'That's it, Jim, ring up Uncle Fred South. He'll be at the Chief Constable's office as it's Friday.'

I was not surprised to hear her call the Superintendent 'Uncle', and I remember reflecting with that part of my mind which was still working normally that quite probably he was their uncle. It would be positively queer if anyone totally unrelated to the Jacksons had any sort of responsible job in the town.

They argued with country thoroughness on the exact form of procedure suitable to the occasion, while I stood listening to them in a stunned sort of way and wondering why Victor should try to get himself a drop of water for the kettle, and where the kettle was now, and what he had intended to do with it when he had it full. There was no fire in the house. I also wondered why he should have stepped into the cupboard at all when the pump handle was outside.

There was no answer to any of these questions and I made the mistake of thinking that they did not matter. I was absorbed by the one staggering fact: Victor was dead. I found I was desperately sorry for him but not in the least for myself. However awful this accident was, it still meant I was free, free to be myself and free to earn my living, free to live.

With Jim's departure, Amy became more of a menace. I found that I couldn't sit still in the room with her and I began to potter about, tidying up absently. It seemed that she felt the same way because she joined me and we used the worn cushion cover as a duster. How we could have been so criminally stupid I do not know, except that we both accepted it as a fact that Victor had trodden on the trap door by mistake, and we were both tidy women to whom dust in that neglected room was an affront.

Amy found the carton. It was on the shelf behind the curtain near the couch. She took it down with both hands and, as I met her eyes, set it on the table. I recognized it at once, as would anyone who shopped in Tinworth. Bowers, the delicatessen people in West Street, put them up in dozens for people who wanted picnic luncheons. The cardboard box was covered with a willow-pattern design and tied with a scarlet cord. In comparison with everything

162

else in the room it was very clean and new-looking. Without saying a word, Amy pulled the string and turned back the lid. Inside there were two packets of sandwiches in cellophane, two plain cakes and two cream ones, two cardboard plates, two drinking cups, and two apples. Everything was quite fresh. We stood on opposite sides of the table looking down at this forlorn meal, each waiting for the other to speak. After what seemed an interminable pause she took the initiative. When it came her blunt remark epitomized Tinworth, its interest, its perception, and its inescapable common sense.

'This'll cause *talk*,' she said.

'Yes,' I agreed sadly, but not now with any bitterness. 'Poor Victor.'

Her small eyes opened wide at that. 'That's a funny attitude to take,' she remarked disapprovingly. 'No one thought you knew what he was. Well, there's no need to make more trouble than there is. I'll do this.'

While I watched she took out one cup and one plate, crushed them into the smallest possible wedge, and stuffed it into her leather handbag.

'That can go out of the window when Jim drives me home,' she explained coolly. 'Then I'll take the box and put it in Mr Lane's car. Any man can take some food for himself if he's going to golf. You couldn't eat one of the apples, could you?'

'No,' I said, 'I couldn't.'

All the same, she removed an apple before retying the string. Two looks a lot for one person,' she explained. I'll take a bite out of this and break it up in the grass. You never know what that Miss Bonwitt might rake round and find.'

She went out on that line, taking the carton with her and leaving me alone in the cottage. I was astounded by her prompt handling of the embarrassing incident, and even admiring. I had not realized that she had it in her to do anything so charitable for anybody's reputation. I was grateful too. I was going to look pretty idiotic anyway after my crazy story of the telephone call. If there was concrete evidence of scandal as well, there *would* be an outburst of twittering.

Jim came back at last with the secretary of the club, two local members, and a rope. The police were on their way out, he said, and meanwhile he'd had orders from 'Uncle' Fred South to drive Amy and me home at once so that she could put me to bed with tea and a hot bottle. It sounded a miraculous suggestion and I blessed the man, whoever he might be, for his kindness. However, it soon became rather obvious that neither Jim nor his sister had any intention of leaving the scene. Excitement of any kind was rare in Tinworth. Yet 'Uncle' appeared to have considerable authority and they were in a great pother about it until one of the club members, a pleasant youngster who had brought his own car, offered to drive me to the school and turn me over to Mrs Williams.

I never went anywhere so willingly. Izzy and I curled up under a rug at the back of the car and shivered together. Shock makes one cold. I had learnt that in my A.R.P. days, but I'd never realized it before. My hands were icy, and to make things really horrible I had begun to imagine I could smell again the damp, chill reek which had come up from the well. I knew this was hysteria and I had got myself on a very tight rein, but when the boy drew up at the school gates I begged him not to bother to disturb Williams and swore through chattering teeth that I'd call him myself. He drove off gratefully and I fled down the path to the Headmaster's Lodging. I could not stand any more just then. I wanted to be alone more than anything in the world.

The hall struck cold when I opened the door and the first thing I saw was my own note to Victor, telling him to telephone the Superintendent about Rorke, propped up on the hall table. It might have been a hundred years since I had put it there, and it brought home the awful thing that had happened to Victor more vividly than anything else could have done. I snatched up the paper and crumpled it into a ball. I was glad of Izzy. Without him the house, empty and surrounded by empty buildings, would have been fearful. But he kept close to me, very much aware of all that was happening and very much on my side.

I went straight up to my bedroom. To run up and downstairs with boiling water seemed too difficult, so I thought I'd do without the tea and the bottle. I kicked off my shoes and pulled off my suit and only then remembered that all my things were packed. I found the right suitcase at last and got out my thickest dressing-gown and some slippers. I gave Izzy some water and stripped the blankets off the bed. I though if I could roll myself in them and curl up in a sort of bundle I might possibly get warm again. I also thought I might take a couple of the sedative sleeping-pills which Dorothy had given me last holidays when she spent a week-end with me while Victor was away. I did not remember packing these and I looked into the empty chest to see if the tiny phial could have slipped under the paper with which the drawers were lined.

The first thing I found was the roll of blotting-paper which I had taken from Victor's desk, left there ready for me to show him as soon as he came in. I took it out and tore it up. I tore it into little square pieces and let them float down in a shower into the wastepaper basket. Poor Victor! At least we had both been spared one beastly half-hour, and if Amy Petty of all people could protect his reputation so at least could I.

Then I went back to my search for the sleeping-pills, but I could not find them anywhere and as I was growing colder and colder I got on to the bed and tried to doze. It was hopeless. My head began to throb violently and I could not stop shivering. Also, of course, I couldn't stop thinking. Finally I got up and went down to the dining-room and lit the gas fire. Izzy came and sat on the rug with me and the heat slowly soaked into our bones.

I suppose it was about an hour later when the detective came. He made such a noise hammering at the door that I was quite angry with him when at last I got down to the hall to answer the knock. I had thought it must be Williams and the sight of the sturdy fresh-faced young man in the clumsy blue suit took me by surprise.

'Hullo,' I said, 'what is it?'

'It's the police, madam.' He was breathless, as if he had been running. 'I am a detective officer. Will you allow me to enter?'

Now even in England policemen do not talk quite like this unless they are very young or very new to the job. I decided he was both. He had taken a slanting glance at my old flannel dressing-gown which covered me most decorously from chin to toe, and a deeper scarlet had stained his cheeks. I thought I should probably make him most comfortable by being as formal as he.

'Of course,' I said. 'I've been sitting by the fire in my room

165

upstairs – my *dining*-room. Would you like to come up there?'

He thought he would and clumped after me up the stairs, treading as cautiously as if he thought the parquet were glass. Once in the dining-room, he sat down on the extreme edge of a hard chair and I took the low one by the fire.

'Well?' I inquired at last.

He cleared his throat. 'My orders were to stay with you, madam.'

'Stay with me?'

'Yes, madam. I understood that a Mrs Williams from the lodge gates would be available to sit with us, and I called on her as I came in. But she, I understand, has been took bad and her husband is seeing to her. They have sent for a Mrs Veal. Meanwhile I must ask you to stay where you are and await the Superintendent.'

He finished with a gasp and grew redder than ever.

I was puzzled and uneasy. It seemed to me very extraordinary that the Superintendent had not telephoned.

'Why does he want to see me?'

The full pink lips closed in a line. 'That, madam, I cannot say.'

'I see,' I murmured, and there was a long silence during which Izzy made the most thorough examination of the visitor's boots which any sleuth alive could have achieved.

The pause went on and on and finally I just had to say something or burst. I said, 'Have you been a detective long?'

'Two weeks.' His face was beetroot red. 'When we've done two years in the uniformed police we're allowed to volunteer for the plain-clothes branch. I volunteered.'

Because anything was better than the awful breathy silence, I went on asking him about himself, and since, presumably, he had had no orders to prevent it he went on answering me. I learned that he was about twenty-two, was ambitious, was going to get married – nearly married, he said he was – and that he liked dogs but kept pigeons. Gradually I wore down his excessive formality and he hitched himself a little further back in his chair.

He was telling me how lucky he was to have been chosen for the exalted brotherhod of the County C.I.D. when he forgot his caution altogether.

'It's a privilege to serve under "Uncle", madam. You wouldn't believe. When he sent me out here today I was as proud as if I'd got the Police Medal.'

I gaped at him. 'Good heavens,' I said, 'the Superintendent can't be your uncle too?'

That made him laugh and we were buddies. 'I didn't ought to have said that,' he confessed. 'It slipped out. That's the sort of thing you have to be so careful about. One slip and you've got a black mark against you. It's a nickname the Superintendent's got. He's always been known by it, ever since he was first in the force. Everybody calls him by it to themselves. You can't help it. You'll find you will.'

'He sounds pleasant.'

'Pleasant?' My visitor's laughter was derisive. 'Not half! He's pleasant all right. He's wonderful.' He shook his head admiringly. 'You think he's your father and mother rolled into one and then – crash! He's seen right through you and bit your head off.'

I made no comment. There seemed little to say. The two-week detective was not looking at me. He was smiling with the fatuous delight of hero-worship.

'He thinks of everything, Uncle does,' he murmured. 'Look at today. The second they see the bullet wound he turns to me. "Root," he says, "this ain't accident, it's murder. You nip down to 'is wife, don't let her out of your sight until I come" ... oh, lor'!'

His dismay was as comic as anything I had ever seen in my life, but I had heard his words and every drop of blood in my body felt as if it had congealed. We sat staring at one another.

'You'll have to explain,' I said at last.

'I daren't, I daren't, m'm. They'll send me back to the uniformed branch and –'

They'll sack you altogether if you don't use your head,' I said brutally. 'Come on, out with it. Do you realize you're talking about *my husband*? You can trust me not to give you away if you're not supposed to talk, but you certainly can't leave it like this.'

He licked his lips. Poor young man! He'd never make a policeman.

'I don't know much more, m'm,' he muttered. 'I went and told you about the lot, I'm afraid. That's all there was. We thought we were going to an accident but when we got there Sergeant Rivers – that's my sergeant – got down the well and tied a rope on the chap who was drowned. We heard him holler something as if he was surprised, and then we all pulled.' He considered me helplessly. This'll just about finish me, this will,' he mumbled wretchedly. 'Diane, that's my young lady, said I'd never be any good at this lark, and it looks as if she's ruddy well right.'

'What happened when you pulled?'

The body came up. That was when Uncle stepped forward. "'Ullo 'ullo 'ullo," he says, and shouts down to the sergeant, "Got a gun down there, Charlie? Have a look for one, will you, now you're there," and he turns to me and tells me what I've just told you. If you tell …'

I did not hear any more.

Murder.

Victor murdered, shot presumably, although it sounded a spot diagnosis unless Detective Root was trying to spare me gruesome details. After the first paralysed moment I decided it was nonsense. It was too incredible. It simply couldn't have happened. Victor, of all people. Who would want to kill Victor?

I think it was that final question which brought the position home to me. I think it was only when I asked it of myself that the elementary and obvious answer occurred to me. *I* was the person with real cause to hate him.

I totted up the motives as Tinworth knew or guessed them and added the new personality which Mrs Raye had invented for me and had already discussed with her husband, the Chief Constable. And finally there was my own behaviour during the past thirty-six hours! Steadily, and with the reientlessness of a machine, my mind played the record back. There was my conversation with Mrs Raye, my lie to Maureen. I'd actually told her that Victor was in the house! My lie to Mrs Veal. My lie, heaven help me, even to the Superintendent. And then there was my bicycle ride. Who could swear where that had taken me? There was my reluctance when the Flower Club ladies wanted me to go to the cottage. There was my behaviour when I got there, the dusting and the tampering with the luncheon carton. As I sat remembering, it seemed as if every tiny thing I had done during the whole time could be misconstrued.

I felt beads of sweat coming out on my hairline and I stole a fearful glance at the detective, but he was lost in his own misery and sat there glumly, staring at his feet. On and on the dreadful catalogue of circumstantial evidence piled up in my mind until I was almost frantic. I found I was searching for replies to imaginary cross-questioning, explaining, twisting, trying to wriggle out of the net which I had woven for myself.

An hour passed and then another, but there was no sign of the Superintendent. Nobody telephoned. The detective sat on, moody and silent, afraid to open his mouth.

At dusk Mrs Veal arrived in a great state. She had not got the Williams message until she had come in from 'the pic'chers' and 'could never forgive herself' for the delay. Fortunately for me, she diagnosed my condition as shock and not terror, and she bundled me into bed and made tea and brought hot-water bottles. She let Izzy out for a run and promised to feed him, and she did not try to talk to me. I think she sized up the unfortunate Detective Root and decided that for information he was the better bet.

At first he wanted to sit in the room with me but she was so scandalized and so scathing that once more he failed in his duty and was prevailed upon to sit on the stairs outside. For a long time I could hear the drone of her questions and the wariness of his monosyllabic replies.

I drank the tea and lay looking at my suitcases. I could not tell whether it would be worse to unpack them again very quickly, or to say that I had thought that Victor and I were going on holiday at once. Either was impractical because I'd packed everything I owned, so I lay there and just thought.

The Superintendent arrived about midnight. His appearance was quiet and sudden, like an amiable demon's in a children's play. He made no sound at all. One moment I was dozing with my eyes closed against the bright light, and the next, when I opened them, there he was smiling at me from the middle of the room. As soon as I set eyes on him I knew who he was and why he had got his nickname. He was plump and grey-haired and amusingly ugly, with a face which could have been designed by Disney. His eyebrows were tufts over bright little eyes which danced and twinkled and seemed ever stretched to their widest. His old tweed clothes were a little too tight for him, so that he looked disarmingly shabby, and his step was the lightest and most buoyant I have ever seen. The moment I saw him I felt assured.

He waited for the effect to sink in and then he said, 'Awake?'

'Yes. Yes, I haven't slept.' I scrambled into a sitting position. 'I know who you are. I've been waiting for you. What have you found out?'

He spun round and flicked on every remaining light, and, in continuation of the same movement, took up a chair and sat down astride it so that he was looking at me from over its back.

'Everything,' he replied, and his movements had been so swift that there did not seem to have been a pause between question and answer. 'How much do *you* know?'

I remembered the unhappy Detective Root, at this moment trembling on the stairs no doubt.

'I know that my husband was found in the well.'

His brows shot up, but his eyes still twinkled, intelligent, worldly, bright with secret entertainment.

'But you found him, didn't you?'

'Mr Jackson found him. I looked first, but I hadn't a torch.'

'Nor you had. A very nasty thing to happen to a young girl. A dreadful experience. I'm not going to ask you if you were fond of him because you won't want to be asked anything like that yet. It's too soon. It'll only upset you.'

He paused, but I did not speak and he nodded as though with satisfaction.

'Do you want to know what happened to him?'

'Yes,' I said. 'Yes of course I do.'

'He was shot.' He pulled out the information like a rabbit from a hat and held it up for comment.

'Shot ...' I echoed. The light was full in my eyes and I blinked as I spoke.

'With his own gun.'

This was another rabbit from the hat and this one did astound me.

'With ...? Are you saying he shot himself?'

He smiled broadly. It was the first time I had seen him do that, but I was to find out that he did it all the time. He smiled if he was condoling with the bereaved, or giving evidence in court. It was said to have cost him a career in the Metropolitan C.I.D. and to be the reason why he was still a provincial.

'I'm not saying anything.'

'But he can't have!' I protested.

'Why not?'

'Because he wouldn't. He wasn't that sort of person.'

'No,' he agreed, and made a gesture with his hands as if he was throwing away some little trifle he had picked up and now decided was useless. 'No, and he wasn't an acrobat either, so he didn't shoot himself through the back of the head whilst falling down a well. That's right.'

'Then someone else shot him?'

He nodded, holding me with those bright dancing eyes.

'Who?' I demanded. 'Do you know?'

He nodded again, still with the same expression. For the first time I began to feel afraid of him. There was something sinister in that knowing twinkle with its undercurrent of irrepressible gaiety. Almost I expected him to invite me to guess who. By that time I had begun to notice that he was forcing me to do all the talking. Detective Root had said something about him. What was it? 'You think he's your father and mother and then – crash! he's bitten your head off.'

I grew very still. Perhaps he did suspect me and was trying to make me give myself away. My lips were very dry and I licked them.

He noted the fact openly, with another nod of satisfaction.

'What can I tell you?' I murmured at last.

'Nothing.' He got up and moved about the room, still keeping his eyes on me. It was an odd performance and I could not think what it was in aid of until I realized that he was simply seeking the position in which he could best see my face. 'Nothing,' he repeated. 'Nothing now. I'm going to leave you to sleep. That old woman can stay the night and she can make you some hot grog. All this tea, very lowering. Doesn't get you anywhere. I shall leave my poor little boy with the great thick boots and the great thick head here too. He can chase away visitors and you can sleep. Good night.'

I was amazed and utterly relieved. 'Good night,' I said breathlessly.

He walked to the door, paused with his hand on the knob as if he'd suddenly recollected something, and walked back into the room to the exact spot on the carpet which he had just left.

'We pulled him in,' he remarked, still beaming. 'I thought you'd like to know. He was very gentlemanly about it. Came at once without any bother. Hopped on the train with the sergeant and they were down here by supper-time.'

I hadn't the faintest idea what he was talking about and I gaped at him like an idiot.

'Who?'

'The young feller we want.' The country voice shook with suppressed exuberance and his gaze never once left my face. 'The young man you slipped your husband's gun to. The lad you curled your hair for. The doctor fellow who couldn't bear to see you so unhappy. I hear he sent you some flowers this morning to tell you it was safely done ... little blue flowers meaning "success". Pretty idea, really. I like that. But I'm not condoning it, mind. He's been a very bad boy and he'll have to pay for it. There's no getting round that.'

Part Three

The Superintendent's voice died away but the words hung terrifyingly in the quiet room. For a long time I could not even believe that I had heard them, or that they meant what I thought. I sat up in bed, looking at him woodenly and feeling that the world had come abruptly to an end.

'Well?' he inquired at last.

I just sat and shook my head at him, too appalled at first even to protest. He was watching my face eagerly and my silence seemed to puzzle him.

'Go on,' he insisted. 'Admit it. It's true, isn't it?'

'No.' I got the word out at last and, having done so, did not seem able to stop saying it. 'No, no, no.' I knew I was shouting and could not keep quiet. His expression changed immediately and his voice rose with authority.

'Look out, that's not the way. That's not the way. Pull yourself together.'

'I'm sorry,' I muttered, 'but you were *too* wrong.'

His chin shot up and his eyes were narrow. 'What exactly do you mean by that? Take your time. Explain yourself. I'm here to listen.'

I did my best but things seemed to be happening to me. For one thing, I suddenly became so tired that I could hardly speak at all. I heard myself ploughing on hopelessly.

'It's not only rubbish, it's wicked rubbish,' I was saying wearily. 'You could ruin his career with your silly mistakes. You've got it utterly wrong.'

At that point I realized I was making it sound as though it wasn't Andy because it was me, but I was too exhausted to explain. My head fell forward and I straightened up with an effort and made myself look at him.

He was eyeing me very curiously and I could see him hesitating in the middle of the room. He looked ridiculous, like a captive balloon swaying there on the balls of his feet. It went through my mind that he was trying to choose between two entirely different courses of action and at last he came to a decision and pointed a long finger at me.

'This has upset you a thousand times more than the death of your husband. Why?'

I remember making a gesture of helplessness as my eyes widened and my vision began to blur.

'Well,' I said brokenly, 'it's come on top of it.'

The point got home to him. I felt the impact of his comprehension as clearly as if it had been a physical contact. He stepped back, made a startled cluck of a sound and immediately, like a conjuring trick, his personality changed back to the avuncular gnome again.

'Now I'll tell you what,' he said. 'We'll both have a spot of steak-and-kidney pudding. You haven't had any dinner, that's what's wrong with you. I haven't either. We shall be getting ourselves upset. Let's have a bite and talk later.'

The extraordinary thing was that he actually had some steak-and-kidney pudding, in fact he had a whole meal, enough for a family, packed up in an old-fashioned open basket covered with a cloth. It was down with the police car, being kept hot on the radiator, and he had it brought up into our dining-room. I put on my dressing-gown again and had some with him, and Detective Root waited on us, with Mrs Veal hovering and whispering in the passage outside. Izzy was brought in and he had some as well.

Uncle Fred South explained this latter-day miracle with a nonchalance which, I was to learn, was all part of his legendary personality. His wife did not like him to miss his meals, he said, and now that he was so high up in the police hierarchy that he could afford

to be unconventional he got her to send his dinner out to him whenever he had to stay late at the office. He mentioned cheerfully that
at the moment his office was downstairs. He smiled at me
confidingly.

'She *likes* doing it,' he said.

It was a peculiar pudding of a hard old-fashioned kind and it
had dried fruit and heaven knows what else in it, besides meat, but
I think it saved my life. The pause snapped the tension and my feet
touched ground again. It also gave me time to think. I could see that
our only hope, Andy's and mine, was for me to tell the truth, the
whole truth and nothing but the truth, and to be double quick
about it, but my fear was that even so it wasn't going to be good
enough. In my efforts to save the appearances of my 'ordinary'
marriage I had made some colossal blunders, and by making them
I had involved one of the few people I had to care about in the
world. I decided to let the Superintendent talk first and we had our
meal almost in silence.

He was eating some very strong green cheese, which he had
pressed me to share but had seemed relieved when I refused, when
he looked up suddenly and asked me if I knew Izzy was deaf. I said
I did not think so.

'He is. A little.' The round man nodded at me. He was glowing
again, the meaningful twinkle which I had grown to fear reappear-
ing in his eyes. 'It's not much, probably only a bit of wax. We'll take
him down to Mr Cooper the vet and get his ears syringed sometime.' As usual, he made me feel that there was some hidden signif-
icance behind this statement which he expected me to follow and
share, and his next remark was equally bewildering. 'Have you ever
been to the zoo, Mrs Lane?'

'The – the zoo?'

'That's right. In London. They've got a beehive there in a glass
case. You can stand and see everything in it, the bees all moving and
working and eating and talking and quarrelling.' He paused again,
and again the alarming twinkle invited me to understand and be as
entertained as he was. When I continued to look at him blankly, he
laughed. 'I always go and look at it,' he said. 'It reminds me of
home. Just like Tinworth.'

At last I saw what he was talking about and it was like suddenly

175

understanding a new and frighteningly economical language. I saw that he was telling me that I had not a hope of hiding anything from him, and that the gossipy interest of Tinworth in everything and everybody had ensured that every move I had made and every word I had spoken had gone back to him with the speed of light. *I* was in a glass case, that's what he was saying. I also thought I understood what he meant about Izzy. The dog had not barked when I had thought we were alone with Detective Root.

'How long have you and your people been in the house?' I demanded.

His twinkle grew approving as if I were a pupil who was coming along nicely.

'Hours and hours,' he said cheerfully. 'You gave us a lot of work with that piece of blotting-paper from your husband's desk. It's not complete yet. What do you think we are – jigsaw puzzle experts? What was on it?'

I looked down. 'Part of a letter Victor had written to some woman, arranging to meet her yesterday.'

He was not in the least surprised. 'Did it say where?'

'No.'

'Did you read it with a looking-glass?'

'No, I can read that kind of writing.'

'Can you? That's useful. Done a bit of printing – at school, I suppose. When did you tear it up?'

'This afternoon, when I came in.'

'Ah.' I'd told him something he didn't know at last. 'When you knew he was dead, eh? That's why it was upstairs. What were you saving it for? Divorce evidence?'

'I don't know much about divorce evidence,' I said. 'I was going to show it to him as soon as he came in.'

'In that case why did you move it?'

'Because I didn't know when he was coming in. I didn't want it to get tidied up or inked over, but I wasn't going to sit by it.'

He grunted, not too pleased. 'It's a good story.'

'It's not a story, it's true.'

'All right,' he said testily, 'I'm not questioning you.'

'But you are.'

'Now look' – he pointed his table knife at me – 'I am doing no such thing and don't you forget it. You and I are having a quiet preliminary chat. Once I want to start questioning you I've got to caution you, and once I caution you I've got to charge you, and once I charge you I've got to bring you up before a magistrate pretty *toute suite*. That's the law of the land. You don't want that, do you?'

'No.'

'And you want to find out who shot your husband, don't you?'

'Of course.'

'Well then, don't be so silly. Let's go on chatting away about it and see where we get to. Did you enjoy your bike ride yesterday afternoon?'

I leant forward impulsively. 'I've been thinking about that. The gardener saw me go and Williams saw me come back, but I shall never be able to prove where I went.'

'Why not?'

'Because I only went to the river.'

He settled back in his chair with a cigarette, loosening his belt very discreetly, convinced, I am certain, that he was unobserved.

'Tell us about it,' he suggested. 'We've got all night.'

There was very little to tell, but I made it as circumstantial as I could. It did not sound very convincing even to me, and when I came to the end I said so.

'I hardly expect you to believe this,' I finished lamely.

The knowing gleam returned to his eyes. 'I don't believe you could invent anything worse as an alibi,' he admitted cheerfully. 'So you just went peacefully to sleep under a willow, did you? And very nice too.'

'I didn't see any willows that I remember,' I said uncertainly.

'No,' he agreed, 'you wouldn't There aren't any there. Funny thing, it's the one stretch of bank where they won't grow. Well, that doesn't get us anywhere, does it? Suppose we get back to the Headmaster, Mrs Lane. When did you see him last?'

'On Wednesday night.'

He looked up at that but did not ask the obvious question about Thursday morning. Instead he said casually, 'I don't suppose you can remember what his last actual words to you were?'

I remembered them very well, but I hesitated. As well as being distasteful in the extreme, the prospect looked horribly dangerous. He was waiting, however, and I took the plunge. I remember feeling that my only hope was to shut off every part of my mind except the actual bit I should need to recollect, and go on steadily regardless of everything except the exact truth.

'We had been talking about the holidays,' I began. 'Victor said, "My dear child, I cannot put it any more plainly to you. I will discuss the matter later. Now I am very tired and there is still a great deal of school business to be done. If you will excuse me I will go to bed. Good night."'

I raised my eyes to find Uncle Fred South regarding me fishily. His mouth had fallen open a little.

'Quarrelling?'

'Not exactly.'

'I see.' It was quite clear that he did nothing of the kind. 'Did he always talk to you like that?'

I felt myself growing red again. 'He talked to everybody like that.'

'I know he did. But … were you alone?'

'Yes, we were in here.'

'I see,' he said again, still in the same unconvinced way. 'Was there anything special about the holiday?'

There was nothing to do but to tell him and to make it as factual as the bicycle ride. I found myself talking very fast to get it over.

'Yes, there was. At least, I thought so. I had not seen much of Victor during the term, although we both lived here. The school took up all his time. I asked him about the vacation several times but he never had a moment to discuss it. On Wednesday, when the school was actually closing, the matter seemed to me to be rather urgent, so I waited for him when he came up from his late-night session in his study and I asked him again. He told me he thought he should have to go on his usual climbing expedition after all, and asked me if I couldn't go to stay with friends.'

I stopped, but Uncle Fred South was quietly firm.

'Go on,' he said. 'I knew him, you know. I've known him for years, much longer than you have. Just tell me what happened.'

'Well,' I said, 'I told him I did not want to do that, and that we had been married for six months and seemed to be still virtual strangers. I said I thought we ought to go away together. He said I was talking like a novelette and that he was very tired and would see me in the morning. I attempted to insist, because I wanted the thing settled, and he then said what I've just told you. That's all.'

'But he didn't see you in the morning?'

'No. When I came down at the usual time he had already break-fasted, and when I'd had mine he was with Mr Rorke in his study. I went down the town to get away from it all and when I came back he had gone. I never saw him again.'

The Superintendent stubbed out his cigarette. His eyes had lost their twinkle but not their knowingness.

'And when you went down the town you met your old sweetheart and told him all your troubles and how you were neglected, and that your husband was unfaithful as well ...'

'No.' I was too earnest even to be angry with him. 'No, I didn't even know then that Victor had even been faintly interested in any woman.'

He sat back, throwing up his hands. 'Oh, come, Mrs Lane,' he said, 'think again.'

I stuck to my guns. 'I did not,' I insisted. 'I can understand now that the whole of this beastly town must think me demented for not knowing as much as everybody else did about Victor, but they've all known him longer than I have, and besides, there is one great dif-ference between us.'

'What's that?'

'They *wanted* to know something unpleasant about him. I didn't, naturally. I'd married him.'

He regarded me with a new respect. 'You're not quite the gentle little mug – hrmmph! party you look, are you? When did you find out?'

'Mrs Raye told me, or conveyed it, rather, when she drove me home from the High Street after I'd said good-bye to Andy. Later on I saw the blotting-paper.'

'Oho!' said Uncle Fred South with sudden triumph. 'Oho! That explains quite a bit.'

'What? The blotting-paper?'

'No, no. Mrs Raye spilled the beans, did she? She didn't mention that, my lady didn't. Well, well, so she's got a conscience after all. Perhaps I'd better give you this lot.'

He felt in his coat pocket and pulled out a collection of envelopes.

'These kept coming for you all the evening,' he explained blandly. 'We had to take 'em in at the lodge or you'd have come downstairs and found us at work. We notified the exchange to divert all telephone calls to the station for the same reason. You read these and you'll find out something about this beastly town, as you call it, that you didn't know before.'

'What's that?' I inquired warily.

'That it's only uncharitable in word,' he said with unexpected seriousness. 'It's all right when it comes to deeds, sound as a bell.'

I did not answer him. I had opened the first of the letters and its contents had caught me unawares.

Dear Mrs Lane,

I thought I must just write to you and let you know that we are here. *If there's absolutely anything that Percival or I can do, from walking the dog to running you to London, do please let us know.*

Ever yours sincerely,
Betty Roundell

There were so many of them, all in the same strain, from Hester Raye's '*Dear Elizabeth, Don't be frightened. It will be* ALL RIGHT. *Love from Hester* to dear Miss Seckker's three pages in a fine gothic hand:

My dear Mrs Lane,

My brother has had to go to London to visit poor Mr Rorke, who has been taken to hospital, or he would be at your side. I have been to the lodge gates myself but have not yet been able to gain admittance. Pray believe me, my dear girl, when I say that I am thinking of you all the time and sending you my heartfelt sympathy. I hope that you will come here as soon as it is permitted. We have three cats but they are good and your little dog will be more than welcome....

I looked up at the Superintendent, who was watching my shaking hands.

'You've had these steamed open,' I accused him.

His eyes were at their small widest and the twinkle was bland with meaning. He nodded shamelessly and said, 'I never.'

'They're very kind,' I murmured huskily.

'More than kind, downright interfering,' he observed. 'You know why we've had to sit up all night? The Chief, Colonel Raye, has sent to London for his own solicitor to represent you. He's a terrible big bug, name of Sir Montague Grenville. The Colonel didn't think you ought to be in the hands of a local man. Thought it might not be fair. He'll be down first thing in the morning and then I don't suppose I'll be able to say howd'you-do to you without him sitting there listening. That's why I had to get such a move on. Still, if Mrs Raye felt guilty about what she hinted to you, that explains that. Very human, people are, especially women.'

I had no time to comment on this extraordinary and in some ways outrageous statement, for just then a detective I had never seen before came into the room and there was a muttered conference. Uncle Fred South put on a pair of spectacles and eyed me over the top of them.

'I've got a transcript here of the items from the blotting-paper. I see the one you mean.' He nodded a dismissal to the detective, who went out, leaving us alone again. It was quiet in the room and, despite the fire, cold. Uncle Fred South had undergone one of his changes. Now that he was off guard for a minute or so I could see him as he was without the mannerisms, a single-minded, kindly but utterly inexorable machine for finding out the wrongdoer and bringing him to justice. He was not satisfied with me. I could smell it rather than see it. I knew I had shaken and puzzled him, but as yet he was unconvinced.

'You see, Mrs Lane,' he said suddenly, just as if he had been following my thought and was answering it, 'someone shot your husband between one o'clock and four o'clock yesterday afternoon. Someone holding Mr Lane's own gun forced him back through the door of the kitchen, across the floor towards the cupboard door, which was probably standing open. Whether your husband stepped in there with some idea of shutting the door on himself as a protection, or whether he just went blindly where he could to get away from the gun, we do not know, but at any rate the rotten floor gave way under him and more than likely he stepped back involuntarily, turning his head towards this new danger. At that moment someone fired. The bullet entered the back of the neck and ploughed its way up into the skull, the body plunged down into the water, and someone threw the gun in after him.'

He made it all so horribly vivid that I shrank back into the chair. I had an instinct to cover my eyes but I controlled it and kept staring at him.

'I didn't,' I said.

'I never suggested that you did,' he reminded me gently. 'I don't even think you were there. But I want you to realize one thing. The deed has been done. Someone shot him in cold blood while he was running away. There was no fight, so there's no question of self-defence. Understand?'

'Yes, I understand, but to suggest that Andy –'

'Wait.' He held up a hand to stop me. 'Wait. Don't say anything until I've finished. Just give your mind to what I'm telling you. There's the killing, that's the first thing. Then there's your behaviour. You've told lies to everybody about your husband's whereabouts. You've attempted to destroy evidence. You've packed your bags. And on the night after your husband died you sat up beautifying yourself for the first time since your marriage. Also, you were one of the few people who could have got possession of your husband's gun.'

'Anybody in the whole school could have got possession of that gun if Victor left it where it was when I saw it last term,' I protested.

He shook his head at me. 'I told you to wait till the end. Now I want you to think of Dr Andrew Durtham's behaviour. He comes to a town where the girl he loves is unhappily married to another man. He knows she is there, mind. He takes a locum's job there, deliberately. He meets her "accidentally" in the street and they take a long drive together round and round the town, talking their heads off. The very same day he drives out to the golf club, where he is made an honorary member. He lunches there with the doctor who has sponsored him. One of the other members who is lunching there also is your husband. In the bar afterwards the two men are introduced and stay chatting for a few minutes. The deceased was in good spirits. Dr Durtham was noticed to be downcast,'

'Victor lunched at the club?' I burst out, but again he silenced me.

'Quiet. After a while the deceased says good-bye and drives off in his car, only a few hundred yards as we know now, to his own cottage, where he secretes the vehicle. Meanwhile Dr Durtham, who is noticeably preoccupied, refuses a round of golf but goes off alone, ostensibly to walk round the course, which he has never seen before. He is out till nearly half past five, returns to the clubhouse, picks up his car, and drives back to Tinworth, where he makes arrangements to leave the town, the job, and everything immediately. In the morning he buys a bowl of blue flowers alleged to mean "success" and delivers them at the school lodge, where he calls to see a last patient. Now what have you got to say?'

'Andy didn't shoot Victor.'

'How do you know?'

'There was no reason why he should. Andy came here to tell me what he thought of me for jilting him, not to make love to me.'

'I've only got your word for that.'

'Have you? Haven't you asked Andy?'

'It's the story you arranged between you, is it?'

'Oh, nonsense!' I was suddenly and recklessly angry with him. 'This is absurd. I don't know why Andy went to the golf course, but I don't see where else a stranger to Tinworth would go on a half-day, do you? How would he find the cottage anyway, and if he did, why would he kill Victor? He certainly isn't in love with me any more.'

'Are you sure?'

'Of course I'm sure.' The words were pouring out of my mouth and I was saying things I did not know I knew. 'Andy came down here to get me out of his system. When he saw me I'd changed and he probably wondered what he'd been making all the fuss about. This must have upset him and so I suppose he thought he'd clear out and get away from it all. I expect he thought I must be in love with Victor or I'd never put up with him.'

'And were you, Mrs Lane?'

'No,' I said slowly, and the words were a revelation to me too, 'no, I was just out of love with love. I was trying to make do without it.'

He cocked a bright eye at me. 'And then you suddenly saw the light and …'

'No. Superintendent, you're behaving as though Andy and I and Victor were alone in the world. What about all the other people? To begin with, what about the girl?'

Uncle Fred South was leaning over the table, his clown's face grave and the twinkle absent from his circular eyes.

'The girl?' he began. 'You're still harping on that message on the blotter, are you? That's not very conclusive evidence, you know. How d'you know it referred to this month even?'

'But he expected someone,' I insisted. 'In fact, since he had lunch at the club-house it must have been she who brought the picnic box, not realizing he would have eaten, you see.'

'The picnic box!' He bounced half out of his chair at that. 'I knew there was something funny about that great parcel of food in the car. You did that! You moved it! What other evidence have you been monkeying about with, eh? You and your crazy face-saving which doesn't fool anybody. Out with it!'

'I'm sorry,' I said, 'I thought Mrs Petty would have told you about that – she seems to have mentioned everything else.'

He stiffened like a dog at a rat-hole. 'Amy Petty? Was she in that?'

I told him exactly what had happened over the box and he took me back again and again until the entire incident had been reconstructed in the most minute detail.

'Huh!' he said at last. 'So Amy destroyed the extra cup and plate, did she? And why did you suppose she did that?'

'To save scandal. We didn't dream he'd been murdered.'

A crow of laughter with no mirth in it whatever escaped him and his round eyes were wary for a change.

'How long have you known Amy? Six months, eh? I've known her thirty years. She married a lad I loved like a son and I always reckon he died to get away from her. Caught pneumonia and died just to get a bit of peace.' He was genuinely moved, I saw to my astonishment. Forgetting himself entirely, he leant across the table and wagged a finger at me. 'I said to him on his death-bed, "George," I said, "make the effort, old son, Hang on, hang on." He smiled at me and said, "What's the use, Pop? I'm tired of her and her darned family." Then he died. That's Amy.'

He smiled at me with surprising bitterness, remembered who I was and where we were, and pulled himself up abruptly.

'I ought not to have said all that,' he said seriously. That's what's wrong with knowing a town inside out. The people become too real to you. But Amy's a Jackson and to a Jackson no one matters two-penn'orth of cold coffee but another Jackson. Amy was saving scandal all right.'

A great light broke over me and at last I saw what ought to have been obvious to me from the very beginning, but which had been completely mysterious because I did not want to know of its existence.

'Maureen,' I said aloud. 'Maureen. The scandal last winter was about Victor and Maureen?'

Uncle Fred South nodded casually. That this might be news to me did not seem to occur to him.

'The family was just banding together to make him marry her,' he went on, 'when along he comes with a brand-new wife who was much more his style, much prettier, much more polite, and without a family behind her. They were always a bit slow, the Jacksons, slow off the mark. They can't help it. It's the country in them.' He grinned. 'They'd have got rid of him, banded together, and forced him to quit the town if it hadn't been for Maureen. She was angry, but she couldn't do without him seemingly. Well, well, we'll see if Maureen bought that picnic box. Maisie Bowers is a sharp kid. She'll remember if she served her.'

I was crouching over the table with my head between my clenched hands. Many things which before had been mysterious were now devastatingly clear. But not the main problem. This development seemed to make that more dark than ever. Amy Petty had forced me to make the discovery of Victor's death. As I looked back that seemed so very obvious that I was amazed I had not spotted it at the time. I remembered her pallid smile of triumph when Jim had gone to find the torch, and understood it at last.

'But in that case why did she come round here with someone asking for Victor?' I said aloud. 'If Maureen shot him, why …?'

'She didn't shoot him.' Uncle Fred South spoke as flatly as if had had inside information from some heavenly headquarters.

'Well then, if a Jackson shot …?'

'No Jackson ever shot anybody.' Again he made the statement sound irrefutable fact. 'They'll band together and beggar a man and drive him to suicide or out of his mind. They'll have their revenge on him if they consider he's crossed them and they'll never let up if they take it to the third or fourth generation, but they'd never shoot anybody, or poison them or bang them on the head like you or I might.'

'Why not?'

'Because they're very just, upright people and the backbone of this here nation,' he said primly. 'Did you say Maureen wasn't alone when she came round here in the night? Who was with her? Was it Amy?'

'It could have been she.' As soon as he made the suggestion I felt sure he was right. 'Whoever it was stayed in the shadow and I assumed it was a man. Maureen was very upset. I thought she was giggling.'

He moved his head up and down very decidedly once or twice.

'It was Amy,' he said. 'That's about it. Maureen would go to Amy and they'd discuss what to do. Finally Maureen would get her way and they'd come round to make sure.'

'Sure of what?' I demanded, completely foxed by him and his lightning reconstructions.

'Sure he wasn't down the well,' said Uncle Fred South calmly, 'the well with the broken trap door. That's what Maureen found when she went in to meet him yesterday afternoon with her picnic box. That wasn't Tinworth's idea of a lunch, young lady, that was tea, or a cocktail snack to be washed down from a flask. Depend upon it, that's what happened. Perhaps she waited around for a bit and then got to exploring, but when she saw the broken trap, well, it's my bet she wasn't in the place two seconds after that.'

'But he might have been in there alive.'

'Not a hope. Maureen would know that, and she'd be off like a streak so that no one tried to connect her with any trouble. Once she was safe, then she'd start thinking. Amy is the one she would tell. Yes, come to think of it, Amy is obvious.'

'How can you possibly know all this?' I demanded 'You're jumping to conclusions, just like you were about me and Andy.'

He acknowledged the thrust with a bow of his close-cropped head and for a second the twinkle returned to his eyes.

'I know the Jacksons like my wife knows the ingredients she puts in her cooking,' he said. 'Show her anything that comes out of the oven and she'll tell you every item that's in it, and what was done to them before they were put in there. Perhaps I don't know you and the doctor quite so well, but I'm learning. What sort of footing are you two on? Tell me that and I could tell you things about yourselves that neither of you know.'

'But I've told you,' I began helplessly.

He beamed at me with unexpected friendliness. 'You've been very frank, more than Amy has, the vixen. I've a good mind to go and get that madam out of her bed. Fancy her thinking she could put one over on me after all these years!' He got up and stretched himself. 'Would you be afraid to stay here alone tonight?'

'No,' I said. 'I've got Izzy and it's almost morning.'

He seemed still undecided. 'The old woman had to go home but she'll be back very early. I'd leave one of my boys with you but I need 'em all.'

'It's perfectly all right,' I said firmly. 'I'd like to be alone.'

He pounced on that. 'There's no point in you prowling round the house looking for more evidence to destroy. We've been over it with a toothcomb. What we've missed doesn't exist.'

'I don't want to look for anything. I've told you the truth. All I want to do is to go to bed.'

He appeared to come to a sudden decision. 'All right. All right. Hurry upstairs and pop under the blanket. You can lock your door if you like. Take the dog. He's a nice little chap, likes me.'

He bent to scratch Izzy's ears and laughed when the little animal flattened them and shied away from him. I gathered the dog up in my arms and stumbled upstairs, too tired to be anything but thankful to get away. My room was very tidy and I knew at once that it had been searched. All my suitcases had been opened. I was sure of it because they were fastened so neatly, the straps pulled so tight.

I got into bed, put Izzy on the end of it, and lay down. Then I turned off the light.

Downstairs there was considerable movement. The police, who had arrived as silent as ghosts, were leaving like the boys at end of term. Although I was at the top of the house I could hear their boots on the parquet and twice the door slammed. My window was wide open and I heard them leave one after the other. I heard the Superintendent's voice in the courtyard and another which I was pretty certain was Detective Root's. Outside the sky was brightening rapidly and from far away over the fields the unearthly cry which is cockcrow echoed in the quiet air. I heard the police cars drive off and the sound of their engines fading away down Tortham Road. Then everything was silent.

I was too exhausted even to sleep and I was horribly afraid. While I had been listening to the Superintendent talking about the Jacksons I had fooled myself into thinking that I had convinced him, and that everything was going to be all right, but the moment I was alone the full frightfulness of the situation returned and I remembered his summing up word for word, as if I were hearing it over again. Someone had killed Victor in cold blood. I had lied again and again concerning his whereabouts. Andy had been wandering about in the vicinity of the murder at the time when it had been committed.

I lay there letting the thoughts turn over and over in my mind until the whole story became distorted and out of touch with reality. It was the crime itself which became so utterly monstrous. I thought of a dozen unlikely explanations for it. Once, even, I wondered if Andy could conceivably have got into some extraordinary set of circumstances in which he had somehow fired the shot. Yet in that unreal, half-light world of terror I knew that was absurd. It was far easier to imagine that in a fit of amnesia I had done it myself. The problem remained.

Meanwhile the sky grew slowly brighter and the early morning sounds began to multiply in the world outside. I don't know how long it was before I first heard the car. The noise was very faint at first, a far-off petrol engine, not very new, pounding towards me through the dawn. It got louder and louder and I could hear it roaring up the road.

The squeal of brakes as it stopped took me by surprise, it sounded so close. Then a door slammed loudly and in the clear silent air I heard feet on the gravel in the drive. They came closer and closer until with a sharp, swift tattoo they found the stones of the courtyard. Someone was striding quickly and noisily into the school with as much assurance as if it belonged to him. Izzy sat up, his ears pricked, but he did not bark and I wriggled up on the pillows, my heart thudding so noisily I could hardly hear anything else. Under my window the footsteps paused and there was a moment of complete quiet until, quite suddenly, there came a tremendous banging at the front door, sharp, hard knocking as though from a man in a rage.

Izzy began to bark at last and I leapt out on to the floor just as the the very last voice in the world which I had expected came up to me, loud and unmistakable.

'Liz!' Andy was shouting at the top of his voice. 'Liz, where are you? What are you doing in this darned morgue alone? Liz!'

I put my head out of the window. My eyes were smarting but I was half laughing too, I was so glad to hear him.

'Andy, be quiet. You'll wake the neighbourhood. Here I am.'

'Well then, for heaven's sake,' he exclaimed, turning a relieved face up to me in the faint light, 'come down and let me in. What do they want to do, turn you into a raving lunatic?'

'I'm all right,' I assured him. 'Wait a minute.'

I raced down the stairs through the silent house, with Izzy flip-flopping behind me, got the door open, drew Andy in and took him up to the dining-room. It was warm in there and the cloth was still on the table, although the remains of the meal had been cleared. I opened a window to air the place and I recall that my hands were so unsteady I could hardly find the catch.

Andy was silent, which was unusual in him, and when he helped me with the window I was aware of the suppressed anxiety that possessed him.

'It was madness to leave you up here alone,' he said. 'I can't understand them.'

I'm all right now I know you are,' I admitted frankly. 'I thought they'd arrested you.'

'Arrested me?' His dark hair appeared to bristle as he turned towards me, lean and rakish, his skin drawn tight with weariness. 'Did they tell you that?'

'Not exactly. They conveyed it.'

He grunted. 'They think they're being clever, don't they? I've been invited to talk, that's all so far. But they can't pin anything on me. How can they? I'd only met the man for five minutes.'

I was not convinced. 'You don't understand,' I began, 'they've got it all worked out. They think I rode out to the golf course on a bicycle, gave you Victor's gun, and –'

He was standing close beside me and at that moment, without any preamble whatever, he turned and put his arms round me and kissed me very hard. I don't remember any surprise, only an intense relief. It was as if a load I did not know I was carrying had slid off my shoulders forever. I kissed him back and put my hands behind his head to hold him to me.

We stood quiet for a long time. At last he said earnestly, 'I love you, Liz. I'm crazy about you. I must be or I shouldn't be here now. It's gone on for a long time, too, or I shouldn't have come to Tinworth in the first place. You love me just as desperately, you know that, don't you?'

'Yes,' I said, still in the same strange liberated mood. 'I realized it tonight when I was talking to the Superintendent.'

He sighed. 'I was pretty clear about myself Thursday, when we were in the car,' he admitted gloomily. 'However mad it seemed at the time, we ought to have just kept on driving. I haven't been very intelligent.'

I stepped back from him and walked down the room because I could not bear to be close to him any longer, and as soon as he was out of reach I felt I could not bear that either. I sat down at the table and he stood staring at me wistfully.

'What are you thinking?' he inquired at last.

I opened my mouth to reply, changed my mind, and shrugged my shoulders. I could not bring myself to say it, but there was a dead body between us. We'd got to find out about Victor. He was watching me closely, and presently he grinned at me wryly with rather heartbreaking fondness.

'You're not so much conventional as civilized, aren't you, Liz?' he said, and settled himself on the arm of the chair by the fireplace.

I put my elbows on the table and rested my head in my hands while the nightmare settled over me again.

'I didn't know those blue flowers meant "success", did you?' I demanded inconsequentially.

'No, and I'm not at all sure of it now,' he observed promptly. 'I challenged that when they produced it. It was only some tale of a char's. The copper didn't seem too sold on it himself. That was one of the things which made me feel that they had very little evidence against anybody. A perfectly idiotic story.' He glanced at me with abrupt directness. They told me you had done the shooting.'

'Did you believe it?'

He appeared utterly scandalized. That was the best thing about Andy, he was the sanest thing on earth.

'Hardly,' he said stiffly. 'I assured them they could cross that idea off their list to start with. I said that the last time I'd seen you you were determined to keep your marriage going if it suffocated you. That's what made me so depressed.'

'Did you say that in so many words?'

He nodded and grimaced at me. 'That wasn't very clever. After that they started worrying about my movements. I'd met Victor Lane at the club bar.'

'But only for five minutes,' I put in hastily.

He slid down into the chair and leaned back, his hands behind his wiry black head.

'Long enough to take a dislike to him,' he said distinctly. 'I was prejudiced, no doubt, but I did hate his guts. He wasn't our sort at all, Liz. That sort of sneery smart conceit always means a shallow chap. Oh well, that's over. Anyway, after I'd met him and loathed him I didn't feel like being sociable, so I went off for a walk. I got into a lane I found beside the course and after a while I sat down on the bank and tried to sort out what I'd better do. It was obvious that I couldn't avoid you if I stayed in the town, but on the other hand I thought it might prejudice me with the profession if I threw up the job and cleared out. I thought I might get a reputation for instability at the outset of my career. So all that had to be weighed up. There was quite a lot to be considered one way and another, and it took me the whole afternoon before I came to a decision.'

I watched him helplessly. 'You thought you'd go.'

'Yes,' he agreed briskly, 'yes. It seemed the lesser of two evils. I knew I'd make love to you if ever I saw you again so I walked back to the club, picked up the car, and drove into town to fix up about leaving. Not much of an alibi, as it happens, because I've got no witnesses and I seem to have been only a quarter of a mile from the cottage all the time.'

'Did you hear the shot?'

He frowned. 'They asked me that. The trouble is I don't know. I was so preoccupied. As I was walking along just before I sat down I did think I heard something in the distance, but I'd only just left the clubhouse then and Lane went off only a few minutes before I did. If that *was* the shot, he must have been potted almost as soon as he stepped in the cottage, which doesn't seem feasible.'

I sat staring at him in undisguised dismay. 'Didn't you see anybody at all? Didn't anyone pass you?' As an alibi it was worse than mine.

'No one of any use,' he said. 'One car went by, but it was blinding. I don't think the driver could have noticed me. I fancy it was a Morris Eight, but I didn't notice the colour or the number. They're going to broadcast for the driver, but I can't imagine there's any hope of him turning up or being any use if he does. The only other living soul who passed down the road while I was there is now in hospital, unconscious, and is not expected to recover. He's one of the masters here, by the way.'

'Mr Rorke?'

'That's the man.' He seemed surprised. 'You've heard about

him, have you? He came down the lane while I was sitting there and he eyed me, but we didn't speak. I'd never seen him before and he was in a fine old state. I thought he was a tramp. When I described him, the police recognized him at once. He'd been to the club and they'd slung him out.'

'I saw him start from the school,' I remarked. 'He'd been trying to sober up under a shower, that's why he was so wet. What was he doing in the lane?'

Andy shrugged his shoulders. 'The police say he was taking a short cut to the London Road. A lorry driver has reported giving him a lift as far as the northern suburbs. After that the poor beast seems to have had an argument with a double-decker bus, so he won't be able to help much. Not that it matters.'

I sat up at that 'But it does matter,' I objected. 'I don't think you understand. Uncle Fred South –'

'Who's that? Old turnip-face, the Superintendent?'

'Call him what you like,' I insisted, 'but he's no fool. You imagine he's let you out to come up here because he hadn't any evidence to hold you. Well, my bet is that he did it on purpose. He's slippery, he's –'

'My dear girl, he wasn't there,' he interjected. 'For the final three hours or so I was interviewed by a mere Inspector and a brace of helmetless bobbies. The Inspector read a report which came in to him and let it out quite casually that you were up here alone. When I insisted that in that case I was coming up myself he tried to object. I called his bluff by pointing out that he must charge me if he was going to hold me, and after a bit he gave way. I wasn't followed here, Liz. The road was perfectly clear.'

I was not satisfied. 'It's the gun,' I said, 'that's what they're worrying about. It's because they can't connect you with Victor's gun that they haven't arrested you. They think I must have given it to you somehow.'

He thought that one over and I saw I'd got the point home.

'I knew where it was kept, you see,' I added. 'They found my fingerprints on the drawer, I expect.'

'But that's ridiculous,' he protested. 'What does that prove? I knew where the gun was kept for that matter.'

'*You* did?'

'Of course I did. In the top middle drawer of his desk. Everybody knew it. It was one of the first things I ever heard about Victor Lane when I first came to the town. "A colourful personality," so I was told. "Kept a loaded revolver in the top middle drawer of his desk. So dashing and original." I thought it sounded dangerous. Well, it's proved so, hasn't it?'

'But, Andy,' I exclaimed, horror-stricken, 'you didn't tell the police this, did you?'

'No,' he admitted seriously. 'Being cautious by nature, I forbore. But I assure you it was common knowledge. Provincial people like whispering things like that. It makes home sound like the movies. When did you look in the drawer? Yesterday?'

'Yes,' I said slowly, trying to remember about a thing which was as remote as if it had happened ten years before. 'I went into the study once the day before, when I first got in from the ride with you, but I didn't go up to the desk. I was looking for Victor, but the only person there was Bickky Seckker.'

'Who's that?'

I told him and he listened with interest. 'What was he doing there alone?'

'He wasn't near the desk,' I assured him, smiling at the idea of the gentle Mr Seckker being in any way concerned with the theft of a revolver. 'He was at the fireplace on the other side of the room, burning something, I think.'

Andy was puzzled. 'Destroying the documents, as in a spy play?' he inquired politely.

'No, only burning a sheet of paper. I think he said he'd been trying to light his pipe with it.'

'Extraordinary.' Andy spoke without excitement. 'An odd place, though. No place for you and me, Liz. To fit in with Tinworth we'd have to have been born here. We'll have to get out of it, and out of the country, just as soon as we can. I love you. I love you, darling, more than anything in the world.'

I leant across the table, my hand outstretched. 'It's good to hear you say it, my dear.'

As Andy stumbled to his feet to come towards me the door

behind me opened. I felt the draught on my neck and turned just in time to see a familiar clown's face looming in out of the shadow of the staircase. Uncle Fred South stepped lightly into the room and closed the door behind him.

'Perhaps I ought to have knocked,' he said, and his country voice was broader and slyer than ever.

Andy turned on him savagely, his face dark with blood and his eyes furious.

'Do you always walk into people's houses unannounced, Superintendent? The ordinary laws of the country don't affect the police down here, I suppose?'

Uncle was unabashed. 'I haven't walked in because I ain't been out, Doctor,' he said pleasantly, favouring me with an alarming battery of confidential twinkles. 'I changed my mind. I thought I wouldn't leave Mrs Lane in this great set of buildings all alone, so I went to the study, which we've made our headquarters, and sat there writing my report. Then, I don't know how it was, I must have fallen asleep in the chair.' He smiled at me, his face glowing with good temper. 'I reckon it was that pudding that did it,' he said.

He did not expect to be believed, but it was impossible to be angry with him. He was so cheerful about it all.

'I came up for some of my equipment,' he went on placidly. 'I always carry it about with me because I don't like to see a constable scribbling in the corner whilst I'm conducting an interview. It doesn't seem friendly. This equipment is not official. I bought it meself. Out of the proceeds of the last Police Concert, as a matter of fact. I left it up here by mistake.'

Andy and I stood staring at him, mystified but with growing apprehension. As we watched he dived under the white-draped table and came up with a box which looked like a portable radio set. A flex which had been attached to the candle lamp which we used at the evening meal hung limply from its side. The Superintendent put it gently on the table.

'Well, I never did!' he said calmly. 'My little old tape recorder's been on all the time.'

There was a long and dreadful pause. We all three stood looking at the little machine, its turntables moving silently on the open top.

Andy sprang towards it and just as quickly a broad body inserted itself between him and the moving tape.

'Wait a minute, son,' said Uncle Fred South. He edged himself round until he stood facing us, but still shielding the wicked little machine. 'Now look here, you two,' he began, his round-eyed glance flickering from one to the other of us in shrewd appraisal, 'I'm more than twice as old as either of you and that gives me the right to speak, policeman or not. What I want to tell you is this. I'm not against you and I'm not for you. In this business I've got just about as much heart as this table I'm sitting on, but I'm just as sound as it and just as useful as it too.' He was speaking with tremendous sincerity and managed to be strangely impressive. I know we both stepped back. 'If you've killed a man between you I'll turn you in,' he went on. 'I shan't hang you, because that ain't my business, but I'll hand you over to the law and the lawyers and I'll read about you in the papers and never give you another thought. But if you're innocent I'll get you out of this here business so fast you won't know you've ever been in it, and we shan't have a pack of London legal-eagles upsetting all our summer holidays and keeping us all standing about until Christmas.'

He paused and, after giving me a steady, not unfriendly stare, concentrated on Andy, whose dark face was unrevealing.

'Now, I told this young woman in this very room not so long ago that if I once knew the footing you two were on I'd tell you things about yourselves you didn't even know,' he announced. 'That is why I fitted up this here little arrangement and set it going as soon as I heard your car come up the Tortham Road. I'd sent word to my Inspector to let you go, and I figured out that you'd come straight up here if you heard that Mrs Lane had been left in the school alone. There's nothing against you in that. In your position I'd have done the same. Now I could have had a fellow listening and taking everything down in shorthand, and that would have been in order. But I didn't do that because there's a great deal of difference between the spoken word and what's been taken down by a chap with a pencil, and I didn't just want to catch you out. I wanted the truth, and by gee I'm going to get it. Will you sit quiet while I play this through to the three of us? That's the honest way. If there's a bit I don't understand, then we'll take it back and listen again.'

There was silence for awhile. My mouth was dry and I felt sick with fear, not because I was guilty but because I couldn't remember anything we'd said and because he was going to find out that Andy and I were in love after all. I glanced at Andy, but he was watching the Superintendent, an odd, defiant expression on his face. Without looking at me he thrust an arm round my shoulders so that we stood together.

'All right,' he said.

The old man sighed. 'That's more like it,' he said. 'Sit down. It'll make you shy, you know. Still, we can't help that. Now listen.'

The dreadful performance began. I had not dreamed that ordinary conversation went so slowly. It was terrible. Every word seemed to have twice its normal meaning, and the pauses to go on forever. Andy's voice I knew. It sounded exactly as it always did, very much alive and deeper in tone than most men's. But who the breathy young woman with the squeak in her voice was I could not believe until I heard her saying the things I'd said. Andy and I sat side by side at the table and stared down at our hands clenched on the cloth. But Uncle Fred South just watched the machine, his eyes half closed and his shining knobbly face quite expressionless.

It went on and on. The whole picture was there but it was magnified. We sounded as if we were overacting, and when I heard Andy admitting once again that he had known where Victor kept his gun my heart turned slowly over and I could scarcely breathe. I stole a glance at the Superintendent after that, but he had not moved.

Yet the really damaging passage took me by surprise. It seemed to spring out of its context and to obliterate every other line. It was Andy's voice, calm and matter-of-fact yet full of determination.

'*We'll have to get out of it, and out of the country, just as soon as we can. I love you. darling, more than anything in the world,*'

I did not hear my reply. I was looking hopelessly at Uncle Fred South and he was sitting up, a wide broad smile which yet had something grim in it spreading over his face. The recording went on; the Superintendent's own voice and the sound of Andy's protest as he heard it were all faithfully reproduced. We did not move.

At last the Superintendent leaned forward and switched off the recorder and there was a long silence.

I spoke first. I could not bear the suspense any longer, and the grim smile on the shrewd yet comical face of the old man seemed to fill the world

'Well?' I said huskily 'Now you know the – the footing we're on, what can you tell us about ourselves that we don't know?'

He rose to his feet and sniffed. Something had happened to him. His whole attitude towards us had changed. He looked tired and somehow more ordinary and when his eyes met mine there was no knowing twinkle in them. Andy sat stiffly at the table, his dark face sullen and quiet.

'Have you found out anything you did not know, Superintendent?'

Uncle Fred South cocked an eye at him. 'Yes,' he said distinctly, 'I've got my man, and I'd have had him before and we'd all have had a night's rest if this young woman had thought to open her mouth earlier.'

I stared. The ground was opening beneath my feet.

'It's not true –' I was beginning when he turned on me.

'Now pay attention,' he said. 'The police don't give witnesses explanations. Silent and mysterious, that's the line the police take in an inquiry, and then it's all a nice surprise for everybody when the evidence comes out in court. But because you've been very helpful, and because it won't make a mite of difference anyway in this particular case, I'll tell you. I'll be as good as my word. I'll tell you something you didn't know about yourselves. You didn't know you could tell who killed Victor Lane. Does that surprise you?

I put my hand in Andy's and looked at the Superintendent.

'How did I tell you?'

He shook his head at me wearily. 'You told your young man, you didn't tell me,' he said calmly. 'You told me who burned the sheet of paper in the fireplace in the study. That was the important thing.'

My universe performed a dizzy somersault.

'Mr Seckker!' I exclaimed incredulously. 'I don't believe it.'

'I don't ask you to.' He sat down again and leant across the table. 'I could lose my pension gossiping like this,' he murmured, lowering his voice to elude, no doubt, the long ears of Tinworth strained to hear. 'That bit of paper was the first thing we found. It was charred but intact and we got a nice pic from it very quickly. It turned out to be a little document that this whole town has heard about, on and off, for the past year or more. It was the Pitcher boy's examination paper.'

We looked at him blankly and he laughed. 'You two seem to be the only people in this place who don't know what goes on,' he said. 'You're "foreigners", that's your trouble. The Pitcher boy is a nice little boy who comes from a very strait-laced home. He had the misfortune to turn in a very silly bit of work for his end-of-term exam last winter and –'

'Oh!' I exclaimed as Mrs Veal's story came back to me. 'And Mr Rorke wrote something on it.'

'That's it, that's it.' The knowing gleam had returned to the round eyes and Uncle Fred South was himself again, encouraging me as a promising pupil. 'Mr Rorke was a bit elated, shall we say, at the time when he corrected it and he wrote a few terse Anglo-Saxon words at the bottom of the sheet and sent it back to the boy. The boy sent it to his pa, who had no more sense than to send it to the Headmaster, and the Headmaster ...' He broke off and his twinkle vanished and he looked at me with unusual kindliness. 'Mr Lane's dead, isn't he, poor fellow?' he said. 'So we musn't judge him. But he could be hard, and, saving your presence, Mrs Lane, he could be dirty in business and no mistake. He held that bit of paper over the man Rorke. He'd only got to show it, you see, and the man would never get another job in a good school.'

Andy drew a long breath. He looked utterly astounded.

'But did everybody know this?' he demanded.

'Oh yes, Doctor.' Uncle Fred South appeared equally surprised that anyone should query that point. 'Rorke made no secret of it to his few friends, and in Tinworth if you've told one you've told all. Lane said he'd destroy the paper if Rorke went on the water wagon. Rorke did. It must have cost him something, but he had strength, that man. Then at the end of this term he went to Mr Lane and asked him for his release and a reference and for the paper to be destroyed. Lane refused but said he'd think it over. That was on the

Wednesday. Rorke came down the town and told one or two people about it. I'd heard it myself before the night was out.' He cleared his throat and leaned back in his chair. 'We don't have a lot to talk about, Doctor, so we talk about each other. That's human nature.'

'But' – Andy thrust his long hands through his wiry black hair – 'if you knew all this why didn't you suspect Rorke in the first place?'

'We did. I made sure of it.' The Superintendent's eyes were round as shillings. 'Naturally, as soon as I heard that Rorke was the last person to see Lane alive I made sure of it. But as soon as I got into the study, what did I find? Why, the document destroyed. If the body had been there beside it, well, it would have been simple. But it wasn't there. Lane was known to have been at the golf club for lunch. When he left Rorke he was alive. We worked it out that he'd destroyed the document in front of Rorke when they were both there together, so we didn't expect the young man to go after him and kill him once he'd got what he wanted. It wouldn't have been reasonable, would it?'

He was silent for a moment. 'Now, of course, I can see it all,' he went on. 'Lane refused Rorke and went off to the golf course. Rorke took the Headmaster's gun and followed him.' He nodded at Andy. 'You were quite right when you said someone must have waited for Mr Lane in the cottage and shot him as soon as he appeared. That's what Rorke did. Then he hitchhiked to London and – well, poor fellow, it's saved us a lot of trouble. He can't last. His back's broken.'

'Bickky Seckker,' I began slowly and the Superintendent caught me up.

'Bickky Seckker hasn't been questioned. No one saw any point in asking *him* anything. But I bet I know what *he* did. I've known him for years. It's just what he would do. I bet he was up in his classroom waiting to see what happened at Rorke's interview with Lane. I'll be bound he saw the Headmaster drive off and Rorke come reeling out just after him, and I bet he went down to the study to see if things had been settled. He found the exam paper hadn't been destroyed, and it so shocked him that he took matters into his own hands, burned it there and then, and was caught redhanded when

Mrs Lane appeared. That's about it.'

'But how would he know where it was?' I demanded, fascinated by this pyrotechnic display in the art of deduction. 'If Rorke didn't know, how would Bickky?'

Uncle Fred South laughed outright. 'Bickky has been in this school for more years than I've been in Tinworth,' he said. 'Depend on it, there ain't much he doesn't know.'

He moved towards the door, a plump and even joyous figure on his light feet.

'Doctor,' he said, holding out his hand to Andy, 'you made a very intelligent remark on that there machine of mine. You said that you young people ought to get out of Tinworth right away, and afterwards out of the country. Good luck to you. But later on, in a year or so maybe more, come back and see us all.' He grinned. 'You'll find you'll know a lot more about us then, and we're remarkably nice people once you get to know us. A little bit inquisitive perhaps, but, think of the time it saves. Good night to you both. If there's anything I can ever do for you, you know where to find me.'

When the door had closed behind him, Andy turned to me.

A NOTE ON THE AUTHOR

www.bloomsbury.com/MargeryAllingham

Margery Louise Allingham was born in Ealing, London in
1904 to a very literary family; her parents were both writers, and
her aunt ran a magazine, so it was natural that Margery too would
begin writing at an early age. She wrote steadily through her school
days, first in Colchester and later as a boarder at the Perse School
for Girls in Cambridge, where she wrote, produced, and performed
in a costume play. After her return to London in 1920 she enrolled
at the Regent Street Polytechnic, where she studied drama and
speech training in a successful attempt to overcome a childhood
stammer. There she met Phillip Youngman Carter, who would
become her husband and collaborator, designing the jackets for
many of her future books.

The Allingham family retained a house on Mersea Island, a few
miles from Layer Breton, and it was here that Margery found the
material for her first novel, the adventure story *Blackkerchief Dick*
(1923), which was published when she was just nineteen. She went
on to pen multiple novels, some of which dealt with occult themes

and some with mystery, as well as writing plays and stories – her first detective story, *The White Cottage Mystery,* was serialized in the *Daily Express* in 1927.

Allingham died at the age of 62, and her final novel, *A Cargo of Eagles,* was finished by her husband at her request and published posthumously in 1968.

JOIN THE MARGERY ALLINGHAM COMMUNITY

Margery Allingham loved to build relationships with her readers and as the Director of the Margery Allingham Estate I am continuing to do just that on her behalf by building an Allingham community. Fans of Margery Allingham are passionate about her work and I intend to keep that passion alive by communicating all news Margery Allingham.

If you are new to Allingham, we'd love to introduce her to you. If you are a long established fan, we'd love to be in contact.

If you sign up to the Margery Allingham mailing list we will occasionally send you updates on new editions and other news relating to her.

You will get all of this for free along with:

1. An unpublished Margery Allingham short story – previously unseen and exclusive to the Margery Allingham society.
2. Exclusive Margery Allingham photos and 'day in the life' content from her life and times.

Did you know there was a society for Margery Allingham? We can give you the details of how to join.

You can get all of this by signing up at www.bloomsbury.com/margeryallingham

We look forward to hearing from you.
Best wishes,
Camilla Shestopal